'Louise makes you care about her characters, deeply so and way too much, until they stop being characters and become real people. So when they inevitably get hurt in one way or another, you're hurting along with them … Fabulous, amazing, glorious Louise, you have done it again!' From Belgium With Love

'This story is full of twists and turns that definitely took me by surprise, right up to the end. Louise Beech brilliantly ramps up the tension and maintains an unsettling atmosphere throughout the book … A dark story about secrets and the things people will do for love, this would make an excellent film' Portobello Book Blog

'There aren't the words in English to describe how great, how fabulous, how mind-blowing this book is. This isn't the book of 2019. This is the book of the decade. I feel changed' Mrs Loves to Read

'The writing is beautiful … Although *Call Me Star Girl* is a very original story, Beech explores themes that are universal to us all. Her take on families, relationships, motherhood and even death allow the reader to look at the world in a new light' Portable Magic

'With a brilliantly crafted story that uses different character perspectives and goes back and forth in time, the story unfolds with twists and turns that had me wondering who had done what to who and when!' GoodReads

'The plot, thick and chilling, echoes in my head … Louise Beech, queen of literary fiction, has turned psychological thriller magician in the blink of an eye … If you haven't experienced Louise Beech's phenomenal storytelling, grab *Call Me Star Girl*' Chocolate 'n' Waffles

'The writing is pure class and honestly it will stay on your mind. Every single chapter gives you something else to consider. At the heart of this is a complex, layered and absolutely resonant mother-daughter relationship that will touch your reading soul … Absolutely highly recommended. Not a single beautiful word wasted' Liz Loves Books

'If Beech is writing it, I'm in. It's as simple as that. I'd probably read her shopping list. I'd definitely read her diary. She just has the most sublime turn of phrase, and I don't think I'll ever tire of it … loving how Beech slotted every last piece into place as she tied things up' The Motherload Book Club

ABOUT THE AUTHOR

Louise Beech is an exceptional literary talent, whose debut novel *How To Be Brave* was a *Guardian* Readers' Choice for 2015. The sequel, *The Mountain in My Shoe* was shortlisted for Not the Booker Prize. *Maria in the Moon* was compared to *Eleanor Oliphant Is Completely Fine* and the early work of Maggie O'Farrell, and was widely reviewed. Her last, *The Lion Tamer Who Lost*, commanded stunning reviews, and hit number one on the ebook chart. Her short fiction has won the Glass Woman Prize, the Eric Hoffer Award for Prose, and the Aesthetica Creative Works competition, as well as shortlisting for the Bridport Prize twice. Louise lives on the outskirts of Hull.

Follow Louise on Twitter *@LouiseWriter* and visit her website: *louisebeech.co.uk*.

Call Me Star Girl

Louise Beech

ORENDA BOOKS

Orenda Books
16 Carson Road
West Dulwich
London SE21 8HU
www.orendabooks.co.uk

First published in the United Kingdom in 2019 by Orenda Books

A catalogue record for this book is available from the British Library.

ISBN 978-1-912374-63-2
eISBN 978-1-912374-64-9

Typeset in Garamond by MacGuru Ltd

Printed and bound by CPI Group (UK) Ltd, Croydon CR0 4YY

For sales and distribution, please contact *info@orendabooks.co.uk*

This book is dedicated to Granny Kath.
When I got pregnant at nineteen you cried because you wanted me to 'go places'. It took years and years to 'go someplace' and get a book deal, but I finally did it.

ALSO

Tyler Benjamin Washbrook-Reynolds
12th August 2017–29th August 2017
A Star Boy now.

'Look up at the stars, not down at your feet.'

Stephen Hawking

'It's good to have darkness, because when the
light comes, it's that much better.'

Abel Tesfaye (The Weeknd), about his album _Starboy_

1

STELLA

THEN

Before they found the girl in the alley, I found a book in the foyer at work.

The girl would be found dead, her neck bloody, her body covered with a red coat, and with no obvious clues as to who had left her that way. The book was brand new, unopened, wrapped in brown paper, and had a single clue as to who had left it there.

A note inside the first page:

Stella, this will tell you everything.

After I had picked up the package, unwrapped it carefully and read those words, I looked around the silent radio station, nervous. I'd been about to leave after my show; about to turn off the last light. The nights can be lonely there with just you and the music, and an audience you can't see. Between songs and commercials, every sound seems to echo along the empty corridors. Every shadow flickers under the cheap fluorescent lights. I don't scare easily – if anything I love the isolation, the thrill of doing things no one can see – but the book being on that foyer table, where it hadn't been an hour ago, unnerved me.

Because no one had been in the building since the start of my show.

I looked at the front cover, all smoke greys and silvers; intriguing. The man's face – half in shadow, half in light – was an interesting one. The eye that was visible was intense – its eyebrow arched, villain-like; and the damp hair was slicked back. The title said *Harland: The Man, The Movie, The Madness.*

It was Harland Grey. I vaguely remembered the name from news stories. A murderer. Hadn't he killed a girl on camera, in a movie? Yes. When she disappeared, no one even realised the last scene she filmed had been her death, at the hands of Grey in a cameo as her killer.

I read the blurb, standing alone in the foyer, but it told me little more than I already knew.

What did it mean? Who the hell had left it there?

Why?

Stella, this will tell you everything.

Presenters often receive weird things in the post, but someone had been in the building and delivered this by hand. Tonight. How had they got in? I hadn't heard the door slam. You need a code to enter the building. Maybe it was just one of the other presenters messing around? But why would they?

The lights buzzed and flickered. I held my breath. Exhaled when they settled. I would not be spooked by a trickster.

Stella, this will tell you everything.

How did they know what I wanted to know?

What was *everything*?

I opened the main door, book held tight to my hammering chest. The carpark was empty, a weed-logged expanse edged with dying trees. It's always quiet at this hour of the night. I waited, not sure what I expected to happen – maybe some stranger loitering, hunched over and menacing. They would not scare me.

'I'm not afraid,' I said aloud.

Who was I trying to convince?

I set off for home. I usually walk, enjoying the night air after a stuffy studio. I'm not sure why – though now it seems profound – but I paused at the alley that separates the allotment from the Fortune Bingo hall. Bramble bushes tangle there like sweet barbed wire. It's a long but narrow cut-through that kids ride their bikes too fast along and drunks stagger down when the pub shuts. I rarely walk down there, even though it would make my journey home quicker. The place disturbs me, so I always hurry past, take the long way around, without glancing into the shadows.

I did that night too.

But I looked back. Just once, the strange book pressed against my chest.

It was two weeks before they found the girl there.

Two weeks before I started getting the phone calls.

I didn't know any of that then. If I had, I might have walked a little faster.

2

STELLA

NOW

People listen to music in their cars, in kitchens, in bed, in the bath, at work, and it takes them somewhere else. A familiar tune might return them to the day they first heard it; to a lover who thrilled them beyond words, to a reunion; to a night when their whole life changed.

I play these songs for people; you could say I play their lives. But tonight is the last time I ever will. It's my final Stella McKeever Show. I began by telling listeners what they could expect for the next three hours. I didn't tell them I was leaving though.

Instead I said, 'Tonight I want to hear your secrets.'

I felt devilish. I felt like having some fun, mixing things up. I imagine that what I said came as a surprise to my listeners. It did to me. My late-night audience usually get a variety of hits from all decades, dull requests and tame discussion.

'That's the theme tonight,' I said, and then I listed all the ways they could contact me. 'Don't be shy. I'll keep it anonymous. But I'd love to talk about all the things we don't usually mention...'

Now I'm fifteen minutes into the show and I'm restless. No one has been in touch yet. Rihanna's voice fills the studio. I push my wheeled chair away from the desk, shove the microphone towards the mixer and close my eyes.

My sandwiches have curled already and smell warm; the unappetising odour joins the dusty hum of heat from the equipment. The coffee I bought half an hour ago is so cold its aroma has died.

I'm alone in the WLCR (We Love Community Radio) building. It's just me until Stephen Sainty arrives before midnight to read the news. I run repeats from his noon bulletin on the hour. Social media means information gets old fast. Community radio can't compete with up-to-the-minute tweets, though it's rare our mostly older listeners object to the reheated news. Maybe they like the safety of information that only changes twice a day.

Sometimes I lock the studio door. Most female presenters do on late shifts. They do it to feel safe. I turn the key to put up an impenetrable barrier between the world and me. Gilly Morgan, who does the 3am insomniac slot, said that at least if a killer somehow got in the building he couldn't get in here because the door is so thick. And by the time he'd figured out a way in, she'd have called the police, her boyfriend, *and* her mum. Maeve Lynch, the Irish beauty who presents the Late-Night Love Affair between 1 and 3am, said she'd just call the police.

I'd call my boyfriend, Tom.

But tonight, I've left the studio door open. What's supposed to happen will happen. I'm not afraid. If I say it enough, it will be true. I know the girls would say I'm reckless, that there's a killer out there. They'd say, 'Think of that poor girl in the alley.' I am; I *have*. It's hard not to when I hear the news every hour, her name every evening. But I've always believed that if something's going to happen it will, lock or no lock.

Someone has been waiting for me after work. For weeks now. Since I found the Harland Grey book but before the girl in the alley was killed. It's not every night. Usually a Tuesday and a Friday, when I finish just after one. He – it could be a she, I suppose, but it looks like a man – is waiting near the tree in the carpark, hood pulled over head. He pretends to be on his phone, and never looks at me.

The first time, I went back into the building, locked the door and called Tom to come and walk me home. Since then I've shouted, 'I see you there! I've got a key that could cut you up a treat!' Once I cried, 'Did you get in here, leave me a book?' But he disappeared.

I'm sure I've sensed someone following me home a few times. When I turn there's no one there. I sometimes think I hear a voice, but strangely it's soft and not very male-sounding. *Stella*, it says. *What are you trying to escape from*? Then I refuse to walk faster, to let anyone scare me, even though my feet are itching to run, thrilled that I might be chased.

I shiver.

The cool draught from the open door reminds me of Tom's breath when he puts an ice cube in his mouth and blows on my skin. I close my eyes, imagine it softly clinking against his teeth, his low curse at the chill, my whispery *yes*. I run a hand over my neck as though it is his. How easily he wanders into my thoughts. How fast my body responds.

I open my eyes and check emails to distract myself. My heart mimics the drumbeat of the song that's playing. My hand waits; it knows instinctively where to go when the song dies. I think I'd be able to do my show in the dark. I'd be able to play the reheated news on the hour.

I remember the headlines the night my show first started. A new factory meant hundreds of jobs. Football fans celebrated a big win. Nightclub shut after massive blaze. Police questioned teacher about missing schoolboy. And there were no new leads on the dead girl. It's been three weeks since they found her in that alley, and still mostly speculation.

I check my phone for messages.

Nothing.

Then I play 'A Whiter Shade of Pale' for Buddy because it's Friday. Buddy is a sixty-two-year-old man who rings every week and requests the song for his wife, Elma. She died six years ago. During one call, he told me they slow-danced for the first time to this song; that he held her so tightly she coughed for five minutes after. They were married thirty-five years.

How do people manage it? What's their secret? Do they still tear one another's clothes off?

I slide the microphone fader up and tell the world this one's for Buddy and his beloved wife. Then I stare at the wall. It's pale green, chipped where old posters were once tacked, with faded, picture-shaped squares. On a board are photos of Christmas nights out, our trips to the races, interviews with Z-list local celebrities and politicians. I've looked at them so many times that our smiles look tired.

I stand, stretch, my socked feet sinking into the carpet. Radio studios need low noise levels and a high standard of acoustic isolation, so the carpet is fat, the walls thick and the ceiling corked. We're small, can't afford the best, but we make do; we improvise. A tiny window allows light in during the day, something I rarely see on my shift.

Instead, I've only the stars.

Suddenly, the phone illuminates the studio with supernatural sparks. They don't ring aloud here; they flash blue like tiny immobile police cars. This is in case a listener calls while a presenter is talking live. They ring so infrequently now, once or twice during my three-hour show, that I wonder why anyone bothers muting them at all.

I sit back down and answer the phone. It's a woman called Chloe. I know her; not in a relationship sense of knowing, but because I spoke to her twice this month and once the previous month. Each time she couldn't sleep and wanted 'that song about Van Gogh'. I have six minutes to speak with her before the record and following batch of commercials finish and I must talk to our listeners again.

Tonight she says, 'I keep thinking about the girl they found in the alley.'

I wonder if she's going to request a song for her.

'I suppose people get nervous when things like that happen so close to where they live,' I say.

'Maybe.' Chloe pauses. 'Makes you scared to go out alone. It was three weeks ago, wasn't it, but you still wonder if the killer will strike again. Is he biding his time? I carry an alarm with me now and always let my husband know where I'm going.'

'Understandable,' I say.

'They said in the paper that it was personal. How did they know that? Because of stuff we don't know? And surely murder is always personal? Even a serial killer has feelings about what he does.'

'Maybe.'

'I don't know why your newsreader, that Stephen Thingy, reports the details so coldly,' she snaps suddenly. 'He sounds like he's just talking about the weather or what's coming up later.'

As well as reading the news, Stephen Sainty runs the station, and he does it closely, often messaging during our shows to tell us what is or isn't working.

'I don't think it's that he doesn't care,' I say. 'He reads things like that every day. In large doses tragedy is mundane.' I suppose I sound cold too, but the things we say are not always what we feel. The mouth doesn't always follow the heart. 'If he gets too upset he won't be able to do his job. He won't be able to be objective and give us the news fairly.'

'I suppose.' She doesn't sound convinced.

'Did you want me to tell him?'

'What?'

'That his tone is cold.'

'Oh, no, don't do that. I was only thinking aloud.'

'"Vincent"?' I ask her.

'Sorry?'

'The song. About Van Gogh. Should I play it?'

'Yes, please,' she says. 'Tonight, play it for the poor girl in the alley. Say you're playing it for Vicky, because no one says her name like that. They either say her full name or call her *the girl*.'

'And how about your secret?' I ask.

She pauses.

'Weren't you listening earlier?'

She hangs up. I line up her song for later.

I'm not a big talker. Friends ask why I work in radio, and I tell them it's about listening a lot of the time; listening for the beats, to the tunes, to the in-betweens, with the people, in the dark. Listening to the backing vocals in a song to find clues in those blended words. Listening to and counting the chorus repeats, timing the end of one song and the start of another. Talking on the radio isn't the same as chatting with friends, family or a boyfriend. Even though I'm entertaining listeners, I'm talking to myself.

Tonight, I imagine locking the studio door and saying aloud all the things that never normally leave my mouth. *Tell them, Stella.* These words come to me and I'm not even sure they're mine. I frown. Then I picture shocking our sleepy audience, inciting a barrage of complaints, then someone unplugging the power because I won't stop. I feel anxious, as if I just might do that. I've been anxious for weeks.

So much has happened.

And it's my last show; they can't sack me.

There's too much time during the songs to think. I slide the microphone fader up and tell listeners they can expect the weather sponsored by Graham's Haemorrhoid Cream in five minutes, followed by a classic from The Beatles, then 'Vincent', and that Maeve Lynch will be here later with some songs for all the lovers out there. And in the meantime, if they have anything at all they want to reveal, they can call the usual number.

'Come on,' I say, 'you can tell me anything. You don't have to give me your name. And just to be fair, I'll share something no one knows about me every half hour.' I pause. 'How about this?' I pause again. 'Tonight's my final show.' I wait to feel sad about it, but it doesn't happen. 'Yes, my very last one; so how about calling in and making it extra special...'

Then I play the music.

I nibble on my warm sandwich but can't finish it. I should make fresh coffee; there's time, but I never drink it all. I'll make a pot before Maeve arrives for the Late-Night Love Affair. I often wonder why love songs are given precedence in a late-night slot. Is romance only for the hard of sleeping, the owls? What if someone is frisky at breakfast? Sentimental at lunch?

I think of Tom again.

He's never far from my thoughts, like he's standing behind an open door in my head, ready to leap on me every time I close my eyes. Once, when neither of us could sleep, he asked what I was doing in 1991. I reminded him that I was hardly born, that for some of the year I resided in my mother's womb, lying crossways, according to her grumble about my stretching her in all the wrong places. Tom lit a cigarette as we talked, and I took a long drag and asked what he was doing in 1991. Why was he interested in that year, since he'd only been two then?

He didn't answer that question; instead he said he preferred the years with odd endings, like 2007 and 2017. 'Those seem to be the years that have meant the most,' he said. 'When I left home and came here and started university. When I met you.'

I thought about it. 'Maybe,' I said. 'My mum left in 2003. I met her again this year – 2017. A month before I met you.'

'Odd years, odd stuff,' he said. '*Good* odd.'

I can listen to Tom talk forever; it means I don't have to. It means I can lean back, and all my thoughts go to sleep. I'm at peace. If he ever bored me, I don't know what I'd do. I'm not tired of him yet, but he does scare me sometimes. Is that the thrill of being with him? But how much fear is too much?

The radio never used to bore me. Every shift was different. The commercials were repetitive, like a heartbeat between songs, and they sustained the show. But the music varied; the beats changed. Recently it's begun to feel samey. Like I've run out of words. People have been saying that radio is dying for years, but it's only the *way* that people listen that has changed. Thanks to apps and streaming we're actually *more* accessible.

Accessible: the thought of that depresses me. I like difficult to reach. Challenging.

The music ends, and I talk about what's happening on the local roads, about the schedule for tomorrow, and say the next song will be 'Love Yourself' by Justin Bieber because no one has asked for it. I could talk about the murdered girl. I could say her name, unlike the tweeters, where she's *#thegirlinthealley*. It's late enough for dark musings, just as it's late enough for romance.

No one has responded to my open invitation yet, but I know one person will. Because he has called every Friday for the last three weeks, and one random Tuesday.

To tell me he knows who killed Victoria Valbon.

That's her name.

He might call and tell me *everything* tonight. His name. How he knows. And who he thinks it was.

For now, I play music I hardly hear because I keep thinking about Tom; about when we first talked about playing dead.

3

STELLA

THEN

My mum once told me I began wrong.

When I was eleven, she lit a cigarette with a jewelled lighter and said I grew transverse in her womb, an elbow nudging her cervix as though to escape early. She said that, when my feet emerged before my head, covered in mucus and blood, she knew I'd be an awkward girl.

When I was twelve she left me with the woman next door. The only thing I had to remember her by was an antique, cut-glass perfume bottle with a star-shaped stopper, and enough perfume inside to let me smell her now and again. She was floral, sweet, *gone*.

When I was twenty-six she came back.

Eight months ago, we met again.

She was waiting at her window for me, as though she'd been standing there for the last fourteen years, and I simply hadn't known. Where her hair had lost some of its colour, her eyes remained bright; they flashed blue, like the phones at the studio. The way they always had when I was small. I felt that if I went away for another fourteen years and came back, she would still be standing there, still waiting, and that I'd feel again the buzz of our reunion.

I've tried to retain that high since we first met again. I've tried to let it carry me. Tried to let it thaw my heart. Replace her perfume.

I did still sometimes carry my mum's antique bottle with me after we'd met again. I used to unplug the star-shaped stopper when I was alone and let the floral scent fill the air. I wanted to keep her sweet like it was. I wanted to flush away the many questions she hadn't – and still hasn't – answered. Ones I haven't asked because I don't want to ruin anything.

'Oh, you still have it,' she said, when she saw it in my bag during our reunion. 'All this time, I wondered if you'd keep it.'

She held it in front of her face, the thick glass decorating her cheeks with flecks of rainbow. Her eyes dimmed with an emotion I couldn't decipher – because I didn't know her well enough.

'I thought I'd never see it again.' She looked at me, perhaps realising she had lost much more than the bottle the day she left. 'You looked after it all this time?'

'Have it,' I whispered.

'Oh, no, *you* should keep it.'

I shook my head and said she should take it back.

'No, it's yours.' She touched the intricate stopper.

I shook my head again, more insistent. I had carried it around with me all through school. Some kids had laughed when they found it, threatened to pour it away. I could hear them still, their voices shrill. I was prepared to surrender it now though, now she was back.

'I want *you* to keep it,' she said again. 'Because...'

'What?'

'Nothing,' she said softly.

We both looked at the bottle.

'Anyway, in a way I don't need it ... *You*'re my star girl now.'

'Am I?'

She had never given me an affectionate name when I was a child. Never called me sweetheart or angel. I wanted to cling to this new name, to bask in her attention. And I also wanted to smash the bottle on the floor.

I laughed instead. 'Sounds like one of those novels that has "girl" or "wife" or "sister" in the title,' I said. 'We just need a killer twist and a cliffhanger ending, and we could have a bestseller called *Star Girl*.'

'I didn't even realise,' my mum said after a moment.

'Realise what?'

'*That*'s what your name means: star. I read it in some magazine a few months ago. I didn't know that when I picked it after you were born.'

I knew this already. But I didn't ruin her words by saying so. I let her talk. I let her in. I try every day now to remember all we said to each other at that reunion. Then I'll be prepared if she leaves me again.

Floral, sweet, *gone*.

4

STELLA

WITH TOM

Tom brought up playing dead three weeks ago, the day they found Victoria Valbon in the alley.

The news of her death broke at lunchtime. I was in the garden with the laundry, wondering why the yellow washing line bounced too high for my fingers. Damp clothes hung heavily over my arm – Tom's underwear, my blouse, our sheets. Hot vapours filled the air, like steam from post-shower-sex bodies. There was something erotic about washing Tom's clothes, even after ten weeks of living together. Even now I bury my face in his T-shirt when he's not there, inhale the scent of work and car and sleep and man.

When I was ten, I told my mum I'd never wash a man's socks; I was adamant I'd be subservient to no one. She said if I loved someone, one day I'd do anything for them. No, I insisted. *No, I won't*. But I've learned with Tom that if he'll wash mine, I'll do anything he asks.

I jumped again to reach the washing line, like a child trying to catch a butterfly. It was like the world had dropped, leaving the line beyond my touch. I loved its distance; the challenge. Finally, I got a chair. Our clothes flapped on the line like those flag markers at a CSI crime scene.

Stephen Sainty's familiar voice drifted from the kitchen.

Despite what my caller, Chloe, said, I find his tone rich and warm; he delivers misery with beauty. He looks nothing like his voice; most of our presenters don't. I can't count the times a listener has come to the studio and said with disappointment that Stephen isn't what they expected. He sounds like a large furry bear, but he looks like a bulge-eyed frog, his spindly arms as white as new sheets, his hair loose stitching. His voice filled the garden. I always play the radio at home. Antisocial shifts mean daytimes alone. I like my own company, but I need background noise to drown my thoughts.

Stephen said a young woman had been found in a local alley. His voice didn't waver as he said *looks like a savage murder* and *unidentified* and *motive not clear*. I felt sick when I thought of there being relatives; a family without their girl, not yet knowing they didn't have her anymore. That gets me every time. It was what every newsreader said on every station and all the TV shows for the rest of the day – *a family are going to be utterly bereft*.

I know all about families without their girl.

I've been that girl.

I went inside, holding the peg bag. On the radio, *brutal* and *police are baffled* and *mindless* continued. I ran to the sink and threw up green stuff that swirled into the plughole like venom. At least she wouldn't have to have to pay bills or worry now. She would never be sick.

I waited for more vomit. A knock on the door interrupted my pause. I wiped my mouth and went to answer it. It was our builder wanting payment for some recent roof repairs; he admitted that some tiles had fallen on the washing line and snapped it, so he'd retightened it. Wild ginger hair sprang from a weathered face covered in red freckles.

'Ah, *that*'s why.' I was disappointed at the mundane explanation for my elevated washing line.

'Why what?'

'I can't reach to hang out my clothes.'

He shrugged. There was egg in his ginger beard. I handed him three hundred pounds in twenties. He scribbled a receipt on a headed notepad covered in soil and gave it to me with fat fingers.

'What am I supposed to do?' I asked. 'Get a chair every time I needed to hang laundry?'

He put my money in his back pocket and said, 'A local girl died, I just heard it in the van – and you're worried about a length of bloody washing line?'

'You don't *know* me,' I snapped, and shut the door.

I leaned on it and closed my eyes. He was right. I always worry more about the small stuff, about too-high washing lines, about broken toasters, and getting to appointments late. Life's greater tragedies – bereavement, childhood abandonment, loss – seem to make my body produce endorphins that blunt its response. Blunt might be the wrong verb. Cushion. Disguise. Protect.

But I always throw up.

I walked around the house, looking, as I had so many times, at our things. Tom is messy; I'm tidy. But we compromise. He leaves the chopping board wildly diagonal, covered in jam and crumbs, a knuckle's distance from the worktop edge. I prefer it further back so the crumbs don't fall on the floor – unattainability intrigues me, but I like my inanimate objects within easy reach. Tom and I meet halfway: the chopping board sits a fisted hand's distance from the edge. But I wash it and put it back straight, while he leaves it crumby. It's our game. Each of us is briefly right when the chopping board goes our way. Neither of us complains at the other; we each just quietly put it our own way.

It's the same in all the rooms.

The blood-red sofa in the living room sags where we sit, Tom always on the left, me on the right with my head in his lap. If he's not here, the four grey cushions sit in a row like prisoners queuing to be executed. If he's home, they're on the floor. I love his mess. That he can sit without worrying about disarrayed soft furnishings or wonky picture frames.

It might rub off on me, eventually.

Tom would be home soon; he'd taken a rare afternoon off. I couldn't wait. I hadn't yet lost the thrill of his return. Hadn't yet let him see me looking untidy or undesirable.

We've known each other seven months. 'Known each other' is an odd set of words. Do people know each other after seven months? After seven years? Seven decades? I hope not; that they might makes me want to sell up and go and live on an island. I don't *want* to know Tom. I want there always to be something still to learn.

But I realise one day I'll know everything, just as he will know everything about me.

Will we cope with it?

When we moved in together I had a special key made for each of us. One of the maintenance men at work was making them, mostly to sell as gifts for people turning twenty-one, but they weren't selling very well. People had complained they were too sharp, like the edges hadn't been finished properly. Someone even told me they had slashed their finger open on one. But I felt sorry for him, so I bought two. They're not the kind of key that opens a door, but a larger version in sterling silver. I had our two initials engraved into them: S and T.

Tom hardly spoke when I gave him his unusual gift. He studied it quietly, his eyes appraising the silver with great seriousness.

'Thank you,' he said softly. 'I love it.'

He attached it to his keyring with all the other keys.

'I love *you*,' he said. 'I know we've only been together nearly four months, but ours isn't just any four months. Ours is the kind of four months that people write books about.'

The phone rang, disturbing my reverie. I should have known it was my mum. Even though we'd only recently met again, I still felt I knew her; maybe because all the things we'd done separately in between somehow fused us, smoothed out the flaws, allowed space for acceptance. This didn't mean it was easy – it still doesn't, even now.

After we got together again she somehow seemed to know when I was thinking of her. I'd look at a picture of us on the computer and she'd text me; or I'd wonder if I should ring *her* for a change; and then she'd call. This time though I'd been thinking of Tom.

'I hope you don't mind,' she said, like she always does, eternally apologising for being here again after so long away.

'Why would I mind?' I switched the kettle on and straightened the chopping board.

'I'm never sure you'll be there,' she said.

'I am.' *I'm not the one who left*, I can't help but think.

'I'm going to the shops in a bit. Do you want anything?'

She asks this every time we speak. It touches me deeply because I secretly long for her to take care of me; and it annoys me thoroughly because she should have asked this when I was a kid. Even if I don't need anything, I tell her that I do. I let her take care of me, so she won't feel so bad for not having done so since I was twelve. I can't handle that I might cause her any sadness; it's hard enough dealing with your own.

'Get me some eggs if you like,' I said. 'I broke mine.'

'A dozen?' she asked.

'Whatever you think.' A pause then, which I quickly tried to fill. 'I'm at work tonight. I leave at nine.'

'Oh, I'll listen,' she said, excited as ever about my being 'famous'.

The radio was how she found me again. She moved back to the area at the beginning of the year. She said she hoped to see me again, some-where, somehow. And then, one night, she turned on the radio to try to help her sleep.

'There you were,' she told me when we met. 'I knew it was you, even before you said your name. Even after all this time. I was dead proud because you sounded so elegant. So confident. And I knew I was wrong – about what I said when you were small. You aren't awkward or wilful; you're strong. You came feet first, so you'd be able to stand on them without me.'

'Great,' I said, that afternoon when Victoria Valbon had died.

'Great.' Realising she'd mimicked me, she added, 'Um, okay. I'll give you the eggs when I see you later this week.' She paused. 'I could drop them at yours?'

She has never been to my house. Even though we had been seeing each other again for seven months, I'd never invited her over.

'It's okay,' I said quickly. 'I'll get them off you. Tell you what, I'll pop by in a bit. Yes?'

'Yes. Did you hear the news? Isn't it terrible about that poor girl. The one they found in that alley.'

'I know,' I said softly.

'I wonder who she is.'

'They probably won't announce it until her family are found.'

'No. That's understandable. Well, I should go.'

She hung up.

I wondered for a moment if all relationships could do with a period of separation. They say sex is better after estrangement, too. Tom and I discovered it, of course. Sex. That's what *he* said anyway when we first moved in, even though he had a fiancé before we met. I guess every generation of experimental twenty-somethings thinks they discover it; each couple smiles and thinks it was theirs first. But I can't imagine anyone else ever had a boyfriend suggest something called 'playing dead' and didn't tell him to go to hell.

It was later that day, when Tom had been home for an hour and we'd been in bed a while. His black hair was damp from the shower and his jeans were only part fastened, as though he'd changed his mind halfway. He said, 'What would it be like if we played a game where you were dead?'

I was thinking that I'd have to get up soon and get ready for work. We'd come upstairs early for sex, and now I had to leave. That's the only downside to evening work; when others are switching off I must turn on. Tom's hours are unsociable, too; as a hospital porter, he works all hours, but at least he gets to do days occasionally.

'What do you mean?' I asked.

My heart stilled. A game of being dead? We had played many games, ones far sexier than the one with the chopping board. Games of domination with scarves as our handcuffs. Games of pretend where I dressed as a school teacher.

But playing *dead*?

It felt wrong with a girl just found dead in the alley.

When I was seven I almost drowned. I don't remember being scared until afterwards, when I scrambled up the slimy river's edge and was on the shore, dripping toxic liquid into my shit-brown shoes. My mum had reprimanded me for being reckless and began the practicalities of drying a stubborn child who has just escaped death and is trembling with exertion and exhilaration.

I wondered if playing some game of being dead with Tom would prompt the same feelings.

He was watching for my response. He always does when he sets me a challenge. No matter how I feel, I have to play. I love him.

'It could be me, I suppose,' he said, as though he hadn't considered it.

'You what?'

'Me who ... played dead.'

'Dead?' I frowned, still not understanding.

He sat on the bed, mistaking my frown for reluctance, for being afraid and wanting out before we'd begun. 'I read it in that weird book of yours.'

I followed his gaze to the Harland Grey book on the bedside table. I'd had it two weeks now. I'd shown Tom the curious note inside the cover – whispered the words *Stella, this will tell you everything* to him – and asked if he had left it at the radio station, even though the handwriting was nothing like his. He had shaken his head, suggested maybe I had a stalker.

I didn't have much time to read, but I was a few chapters into it then, hoping for clues as to why it had been left for me. Grey had strangled twenty-one-year-old Rebecca March on camera. The moment – in close-up – had featured in the film *In Her Eyes* and was almost released in the UK. Then he was caught and imprisoned.

I still had no idea why anyone would leave me such a book.

Or what the note meant.

And now, with a girl having been found in an alley dead, I wasn't sure I would read any more. It was downright creepy to have received it just two weeks before this shocking murder.

'*You've* been reading it?' I asked Tom.

'You seemed so caught up in it – I had to look myself.'

I ran my fingers over his dark, stubbled chin as though to sharpen my senses. 'Are you *sure* you didn't leave it there just so you could suggest weird stuff to me?' I said evenly, though my heart fluttered inside my chest. 'And do I need to worry about what you're doing with those dead bodies at work?'

Tom smiled, shook his head. 'You know what I love about you, Stella? How brave I can be with you.'

He looked vulnerable then. Sad even. I sometimes think he's more afraid of his light than his darkness – that he has to keep up the bravado of being adventurous when really he would like to be tender with me.

'I'd *never* hurt you,' he said, 'but that scene in the book made me think that you being totally out of it during sex would be hot. I don't know if it's even a *thing*. But when I think of you ... lying there, as helpless as anyone can be...' He squeezed my arm. 'I'm not even saying we should try it, I'm just saying it excites me.'

I didn't say anything. I loved the thought of exciting him. Keeping him that way. Keeping him. It surpassed any fear of a game called playing dead.

'*How* do you think we could play it?' Tom asked.

He wanted me to answer, so I didn't. This was how I took over the game.

'Shall I make us something to eat?' I suggested.

I hoped he would go on talking. I love Tom's voice. He can say the ugliest thing and it sounds like something from the Bible or a great poem. When he said *play dead* it was like he had suggested we eat some exotic food. His mouth follows his heart more than anyone I know.

'Now I know you're interested,' said Tom.

'And how do you know that?'

'Because you're changing the subject.'

'No,' I said, getting up. 'I have to go to work soon and I'm hungry.'

We ate together and listened to the radio and talked about the roof tiles. The reheated news came on at eight and Tom said very softly that the family of the girl in the alley must surely be wondering where she was now, twenty-four hours later.

'Maybe they've been told about the murder now.' The words caught in my throat. 'That was just a repeat of the news at noon.'

'Maybe.' He paused. I waited. Watched him. 'I'd *know*,' he said.

'Know what?' I asked.

'Know if something had happened to you.'

'You didn't know when that weirdo was hanging about near the radio and I had to call you to walk me home.'

'That just looked like some kid in a hoodie,' he laughed. 'You could probably take him.'

'And what would you do if someone *had* killed me in an alley?' I asked softly.

'Kill *them*,' Tom said, without pause.

He held my gaze. His eyes misted. He got up and stood behind me and held me to him until I could barely breathe. I loved it. The intensity of his need. The feeling that he would never, *ever* abandon me.

Neither of us talked about playing dead again that evening.

Then I went to work and played people's lives.

5

ELIZABETH

THEN

I was hurting when I had Stella. Not just the way all labouring mothers hurt. Not just because of the contractions and the tearing and stretching. I hurt in my heart. I was angry that I was doing it alone. That the man I loved wasn't at my side, holding my hand, telling me to breathe slowly and promising me it would all be okay. Even if I'd told him I was pregnant, he wouldn't have been at the birth. He wasn't father material.

I wasn't really mother material either.

And then Stella arrived, all wrong.

The scans had told me she was lying transverse in my womb, but the midwife said I was young, and that I could still deliver normally. Breech deliveries were tricky but possible, she said. Stella's feet emerged first, so that the worst pain came at the end of her expulsion, not at the beginning, like for most mothers. I screamed as her head completed the journey.

I screamed at the unfairness of it.

Then the midwife put her in my arms and told me she was a girl. I said I already knew. I hadn't found out her sex, I'd just known. All along. Just as I knew she would change my life. Disrupt it, inconvenience it, bless it. She was a fighter; little red fists pushed open the blanket. She screamed the way I had giving birth to her.

One of my first feelings was disappointment: she was covered in mucus and blood, nothing like the clean, pink babies in films and soap operas.

I called her Stella. I had no names ready. But the next day, in the visitors' waiting room, a black-and-white movie called *Stella Dallas* was on the TV. And that was that.

I took Stella home. Part of me wanted to leave her at the hospital. I was sure they would take better care of her than I could. I was young. Alone. This wasn't what I'd expected my life to be. Only a year ago I'd been nineteen, cutting hair by day and partying at night, with the pick of the men. I'd only wanted one though. I only wanted *him*. The one who changed everything. The one I could never see again. Stella's father.

None of my friends came to see me in those early, lonely weeks. They loved me when I was up for clubbing every night, when I styled their hair into glamorous waves before we went out. When I shared the phone numbers of the all men I knew. Once I had a screaming kid, no babysitter and no money, they disappeared. My only companion was frumpy Sandra from next door. She was a retired foster mum who made time to call around when she'd made pies, who fussed over Stella, who could quieten my screechy daughter with just a whisper.

Fuck them, I thought, when my friends didn't ring.

I washed bottles, changed nappies and tried to smile at my newborn. Tried to meet her never-ending demands. Tried to hide my frustration and sadness. I decided there and then that the best thing I could teach Stella was to be self-sufficient. I could hardly do it by example, but I'd do it the hard way.

As soon as she was a toddler and didn't need night feeds, I found a part-time hairdressing job, got frumpy Sandra to babysit for nothing, and started going out once more. Alone. To bars. I was stunning. My figure had sprung back, my hair was golden from days in the garden with Stella, and I wore the same skin-tight dresses I had before my pregnancy, with a slash of my favourite fire-engine-red lipstick.

Men flocked around me again. The simmering resentment at being alone dissolved. I could live on this. It would get me through motherhood. The warmth of this attention helped me get up in a morning to a noisy child who asked questions all day. It helped me do all the things that bored me: the cooking, the washing, the story-reading.

But it didn't erase the face of the only man I had ever loved.

Stella's father.

Who she would never know.

I would not share his attention with anyone, not even our child.

She first asked me who he was when she was five and the kids at school had been talking about their daddies. Wanted to know why she didn't have one. We all have them, I said. Some just don't stick around. Some don't need to know they have a child. Some aren't good men, I thought, even if you love them so much that nothing tastes right and sleep evades you, and sometimes, just for a moment, you think your heart has stopped.

Stella asked again when she was seven. And then eight. Each time, I said that she had a dad; he just was the kind that was better out of her life.

I was that kind of mother too. But here I was anyway. Trying to be something that didn't come naturally to me. Trying to love a needy child when all I craved was the oblivion of nights with men who showered me with compliments, affection, and gifts.

New man Dave bought me perfume.

He said I never wore any. Asked me why. I said I couldn't afford it. I didn't tell him about my favourite scent, hidden away in the drawer. The beautiful cut-glass bottle with a star-shaped stopper that I opened every now and again, just to smell. I wore Dave's cheap, sickly eau de toilette until I got rid of him for being dull. After that I demanded perfume from every man I dated. Most of the fragrances lasted longer than they did. I hoped that each would drown out the smell of my star perfume, wash away the memories that bottle held.

Stella's childhood flew by. It was a blur of late nights and late mornings, when I'd wake to find that Stella had made her own breakfast and taken herself to school. The haze was punctuated with occasional shared moments, when I'd style Stella's hair, paint her nails, give her advice. Frumpy Sandra was a blessing, taking her in when I worked late at the hairdressing salon, and always remembering a treat on her birthday. She sometimes went to Stella's parents' evenings when I didn't and helped pay for school trips when I couldn't.

Sometimes I felt I hardly knew Stella at all. I'd look into her intense eyes and wonder what went on in her head. Other times I wanted to squash her to me and apologise for all my flaws. But mostly I got by on the wave of love men gave me at night, letting that carry me through the dirty dishes and school reports and head lice and ironing.

Sometimes she looked like him. It wasn't so much her appearance as something she did. A way she'd move. A turn of the head. And my heart would contract.

I loved Stella.

I *did*.

I just loved her father more.

6

STELLA

NOW

Sometimes, when I'm in the WLCR studio alone, and I'm off air, I undo my shirt to the waist.

We're not required to wear a uniform, but I like to dress for my show just as I might for any other job. I have five blouses in various pastel shades. Tonight, I selected pink. No particular reason, other than it was the closest to hand. When I lean back in the chair and unfasten my buttons, slowly, one after the other, it's not because it's warm in here – though it can be, with all the equipment – but because it feels bad.

There's a chance I might be caught in this state of semi-undress.

It makes me smile.

I know Stephen Sainty won't be here until eleven-thirty, and Maeve won't be in for the Late-Night Love Affair until just before twelve, but there's still a chance of being seen by someone. Cleaners turn up at random times, maintenance men come, and presenters sometimes arrive early for their shifts. I imagine them seeing me before I can cover up. There's something about shocking people that I love.

But that need is missing tonight. Even though I've left the studio door open. I don't *care* if Stephen arrives early and bursts in, gasping at the sight of my bare chest.

I suddenly want to go home and cry.

Five years of the show and I'm tired. It's partly why I handed in my notice. But, unless he was listening earlier when I shared this information, Tom doesn't know. He's at home, so he may have tuned in. I think he'll be surprised, which is always good. He has surprised me a lot recently, so maybe it's my turn.

When the Beatles song ends, I slide up the fader and say, 'That was "Hey Jude", and you're listening to WLCR with me, Stella McKeever, from now until one. After that, the lovely Maeve Lynch will be here to play some classic love songs, so get ready to snuggle up with your special someone. Let's get some weather first and then I'd love to hear your secrets. Come on, don't be shy. I can feel you all out there, itching to share. Email your thoughts to WLCR.co.uk, tweet us or give us a call on the usual number.'

Why hasn't anyone called in yet?

I was hoping for a memorable final show. How much do I have to share before listeners will, too? How much should I say?

I link to the weather and fasten my blouse. I stand, stretch until my bones click, and go to the tiny window that permits a view of a sliver of night sky, her stars random, and her moon absent. I have no idea what I'm going to do when I leave here, but I *can't* stay. I try hard not to be my mum, but at times I feel her pulsing inside me – her restlessness, her resistance to routine, her hunger for new things.

Something moves outside.

I freeze.

I stand on my tiptoes to see more through the thin strip of window.

Was it just a shadow flickering? The black trees waving against the dark-blue sky? Or was it the man who's been waiting for me after work? The person who left the book? Did I just imagine it?

I wait. I watch.

Nothing. No more movement. It *must* have been my imagination.

Stella.

Who said that?

Is it the wind in the trees?

Stella, Stella, Stella.

Yes, just the wind.

I look up at the stars and remember the perfume stopper glinting at me all those years ago on my bedside table. I remember going to my window then, feeling that the sky was my refuge. Now all those efforts to sustain the bubble I've lived in, to ignore my hurts, are coming undone.

The room lights up electric blue: the phone. I decide that if that weirdo is loitering outside after work tonight, I'm going to confront him. I return to the mixer desk. I've lined up a song to follow the weather, so I have three minutes to talk to this caller.

'Stella McKeever,' I say.

'I'm sorry you're leaving, lass.' She sounds elderly, her voice as frail as thin china. I bet she's got secrets. 'I'll miss your show. I always listen while I'm getting ready for bed. My Derrick likes to watch those benefit-fraud shows, but I'd rather listen to you. Your voice is like syrup.'

'Thank you,' I say.

'Why are you going? Are you having a little 'un?'

'Oh, no. I'm...'

What can I tell her? That I'm tired, after she's told me I'm part of her bedtime routine and have a syrupy voice?

'I'm leaving the area,' I lie.

'What a shame.' She sniffs heartily. 'Please tell me they won't get some young, screechy thing to do your show.'

'I think Maeve Lynch will cover until they get someone.'

'Oh good. She's nice. I love her Irish accent.'

I smile. 'Would you care to share a secret?'

'Ooh, not sure I should.' She pauses, then adds, guardedly, 'I think my neighbour Jean listens. Mind you, I know some things about *her*...'

'Do tell,' I smile.

'I couldn't possibly.'

'I won't name her.'

'You're a minx!'

'You have no idea,' I laugh.

'Well ... Jean, she used to take in chaps when her husband was at sea. They'd come around the back when it was dark, and she'd get them to leave at three in the morning.' Her voice has lost its frailty. 'She wasn't picky either. Young, old ... sometimes two at a time. I only know because I'm an insomniac. I was often at the sink, no lights on, just drinking tea, you know? This was some years ago now. Don't think she knows I saw.'

The song is coming to an end; I must hang up. 'Thank you for calling,' I say, 'have a lovely evening.'

To the listeners I say, 'It's just after ten-thirty, you're listening to WLCR, and I'm Stella McKeever. Ah, secrets. I know one about ... well, you *know* I can't say the name. About a lady – a naughty neighbour – who let's just say was a naughty wife too. While the cat was away, the mouse certainly played. Are you such a naughty wife? Do you have one? Share all – you know you want to.'

As I play the next song, my phone vibrates in my pocket. It's a message from Stephen Sainty. He tells me to be careful about what I share on air, and how I word it. I want to remind him that I've done this for five years; I *know*. Is he scared of how I'll be on my last night? He says he'll be here in an hour. I suddenly wonder if there will be a gift. A card signed by all the presenters. Will I be upset if not?

No.

I'm used to goodbyes without a word.

Sometimes I think of just leaving, the way my mum did. Would I ever do that to Tom? Could I do that to her now she's found me again? Most mornings recently I feel sick when I wake up. I feel like everything is coming close; that my past and my future are going to collide.

The song finishes. Silence is unforgivable here. There must never be gaps between tunes, between a presenter's last word and the news. I go straight into the adverts and play the number-one song.

The room lights up blue again. I jump. I don't think I've ever had so many calls during one show. I have three minutes to talk.

'Stella McKeever,' I say.

'You knew I'd call, didn't you?'

'Who is this?' I ask.

But I know.

It's him. The man who has called four times already, every Friday since Victoria Valbon was found, and one Tuesday. I asked the first time if he had left me a book at the studio, how he got in, and what *Stella, this will tell you everything* meant, but he ignored the questions.

Should I ask again?

Do I want to know?

He speaks slowly, as if disguising his true voice, trying not to let his accent slip out. His voice isn't deep, but it's smooth, gravel-free, gentle, as though trying to lessen the menace in his words. 'You know who it is,' he says. 'And you knew I'd call, didn't you?'

'We can never know anything for sure,' I say.

'You hoped I would.'

I don't speak. Absolute silence at his end. Music at mine.

'Is it because of me that your last show is all about secrets?'

'Why would it be because of you?' Surprised at his arrogance, my tone is harsher than I intended. 'I thought it would make a juicy topic.'

'Of course.' He inhales deeply, and I wonder if he's smoking. 'I have the biggest secret ever. Don't you want to know?'

'No,' I lie.

'It could make your show the best yet...'

'Not interested,' I lie.

'I heard your announcement. You're leaving. I'm a bit disappointed.'

'Why is that?' I ask.

'I was hoping for longer.'

'For what?' I ask.

He doesn't respond.

'We have tonight,' I say.

'You'll be going soon,' he says.

'Not yet, I've a while.'

'I mean the song will end and you'll have to talk to the listeners instead.' He said that last week; sounded sad about it rather than put out. 'And you'll never hear what I know.'

'Tell me now,' I say, 'if you really do know something.'

'You can't just blurt these things out, Stella.'

'You said you know who killed Victoria Valbon. Is that your

so-called secret? You've said it four times now. It's getting boring. If you expect me to believe that, tell me who you are, and how you know.'

'I'm nobody. Really. But what I know is *everything*.'

I only have two minutes now.

'*Everything*? How can you?'

'I was there,' he says.

The line in the song that's playing repeats. The word pounds three times.

'You were *there*?' I whisper.

'Yes.'

'Why were you there?' I ask.

'What kind of question is that? You'd not make a very good detective, Stella.' He pauses. 'Ask what you *really* want to know. Go on.'

'What did you do?' I ask.

'I saw *everything*,' he says.

I frown. '*Saw*? You could just be saying that. Tell me something the papers haven't said.'

'I know that the killer *knew* Victoria.'

I feel sick. I close my eyes, swallow the nausea back. 'The papers *have* said it was personal. One of my callers mentioned that earlier. So, I think we can all assume that the killer knew her.'

'*Knew* is vague, though,' he says. 'Could be a work associate. Someone up the street. This was more than that. They were arguing. In the alley. It got very heated.'

'Do you know the person?'

He doesn't speak.

'Do you? Or can you describe them?'

'Not yet.'

I have only another minute until the song ends.

'I don't believe you,' I say. 'You just want airtime. Attention. Anyone could ring and tell me the same thing. Do you know how many cranks we get calling here?'

'I'm no crank.'

'Look, I've only got fifty seconds.'

'Stella, that's your loss.'

'Did you leave me a book in the foy—'

He's gone. The song fades out and I can barely concentrate. Have I cued adverts? Is it the news? No, it's me again.

I wonder if he's listening. As I move the fader up, my throat closes. I gulp, try to fill the fatal silence.

'This is WLCR and you're listening to Stella McKeever. That was—' The song title eludes me, and I look at my computer screen for help, but can't see it. 'Um … Let's get some weather, and then hopefully more … more music…'

I wonder if my mystery caller expects me to share his revelation with our listeners. Will he be disappointed when I don't? Because I'm not going to. Maybe he'll call back. Tell me more. My hands shake uncontrollably.

I go to the window and find my comfort in the stars.

7

STELLA

THEN

When I was ten, one of my mum's boyfriends bought her a bottle of perfume shaped like a woman's torso. She had moved the perfume bottle with a star-shaped stopper to the drawer by then. The new scent stood amid the chaos of rings and scarves and necklaces on her dresser, like a mistress insisting she be seen.

My mum caught me dabbing some on my wrist, the way I'd seen her do many times.

I froze. Her reactions to me were endlessly unpredictable; I both feared and thrived on them. I'm now sure her responses are why I need such intensity in my relationship with Tom. They're why I'm addicted to drawing attention to myself.

'I'm not sure I like it,' she said, in an offhand way, sitting on the padded stool. I loitered by the dresser, basking in this rare moment of attention. 'But Rob bought me it, so I suppose I'll wear it until he's gone.'

Just like every time, I thought.

'Go on, put more on,' she said, playful. 'It might suit you better than it does me. Perfume changes its smell, depending on who wears it, you know. Something about the skin and hormones.' She sniffed my wrist. 'It's kind of sweet on you. You can't have it, though. Well, maybe when he's gone...'

I had a box of perfume bottles in my bedroom, most half full, some barely used. Each time a boyfriend left, Mum tossed them my way. My friend Alissa said I was lucky; she said the bottles were so pretty, the smells inside so nice. I often let Alissa rummage through my collection and take one home.

Each cologne reminded me of a different mother. There was the sharp, bitter scent in the purple bottle, which she had worn when she dated Stephen. The light fragrance in the tiny bottle, which she'd dotted on her neck when Malcolm was on the scene. The flowery one she sprayed all over when it was Sean.

My mum fluffed her golden hair in the white vanity mirror and ran a tongue along her teeth. 'Think I could pass for twenty-one?'

I knew she was thirty because she'd had me young, at twenty.

'You always look beautiful to me, Mum,' I said.

It was true. Even without her usual blusher and long eyelashes, her skin glowed and her eyes flashed with the kind of life that only passionate people have. To me, she was prettiest without her make-up. When she stared off into space, a little sad. I loved her so much then that I thought I'd burst.

'You would say that.' She put on lip gloss. 'When you're older you'll realise that you can't ever be less than perfect. Not with a man, anyway.'

You are perfect, I wanted to say.

'And never bore him,' she said, very serious.

This I feared. I knew I bored my mother sometimes. When I was telling her my exciting tales – my day's adventures or who had sat next to me at school – she invariably stopped me halfway and said she didn't have time or could I run to the corner shop for her. What she meant was that she was bored. I knew it. Saw her eyes dim as her attention drifted.

'It's better that you get bored first,' she said. 'Better that you finish it, and then he leaves, wanting you desperately and wondering why it's over. That way he'll never forget you.'

I lapped up my mother's words, happy that she was giving them to me.

'Do you think I'll be interesting when I'm older?' I asked.

'I'm sure you'll try.'

'I *will* be,' I insisted.

'You're too...' She paused to consider. 'You're too wilful. Stubborn. You'll have to supress that. Do things you might not want to do to keep them happy.'

'Like what?' I asked, innocent.

She paused. 'Like washing their socks,' she laughed.

'Never!' I cried. 'Yuck. I've smelled Rob's socks in the bathroom. I'll never love anyone enough to do that.'

She laughed, then studied me for a long moment. 'Shall I style your hair?'

'Will you?' I jumped onto the padded stool as she stood up.

'We could sweep it up into a high ponytail.' She fiddled with my locks, her hands warm. 'Hold this part with a jewelled clip. Leave these bits loose to soften the look.'

When she was done, I looked fifteen. I wanted to sit there forever, luxuriating in her love.

She rummaged around in her bottom drawer and then took out a large black pouch. From it she extracted a camera, the kind with a huge zoom lens and all kinds of fancy functions. I'd never seen it before.

'I keep forgetting I've got it,' she said, as though hearing my query. 'It's one of those dead good ones.'

I presumed one of her many men had given it to her.

'Let's get a picture,' she said, fiddling with it.

I smiled, posed like the models I'd seen in magazines. Later, she would have the picture developed, but it would be so blurred she'd throw it away.

My mum's phone buzzed on the bedside cabinet and our rare mother/daughter time was done. She spoke flirtatiously to Rob while I unclipped my hair, and the years fell away with my heart. She hung up and chose what she would wear; silver top, tight black skirt and heels that made her legs beautiful.

'You know,' she said, spraying the woman's-torso mist on her neck, 'I think when a man buys me exactly the right perfume, he'll be the one.'

But I thought the star perfume was exactly right. I loved its smell because she wore it when there were no men around; when it was just us two. If that floral, sweet scent drifted around the house, I knew she'd have more time to talk. She'd smoke cigarettes in the kitchen with me, say that now it would just be us against the world, and that men were useless anyway.

I decided when I grew up that I'd never wear perfume.

When my mum disappeared the month after I turned twelve, she left the star perfume. I kept it with me. Took it everywhere I went. Wherever I lived after my mum had gone, I kept the bottle by my bed or under the pillow. At night, the star stopper glinted as though winking at me. I couldn't bear to waste the remaining perfume inside. I feared that even just sniffing it would somehow steal the essence.

So, I only unstopped the bottle and breathed in the scent when I missed her so much, nothing else would ease my pain.

8

STELLA

WITH TOM

Two days after the girl in the alley was found, they announced her full name on the midday bulletin: Victoria Valbon, twenty-six, single. Tom and I were sitting at the kitchen table, opposite one another, drinking coffee when Stephen Sainty spoke. Tom shook his head, looked sad. He swigged his coffee and went upstairs.

'Are you okay?' I followed him.

'It's horrible,' he said. 'A woman killed like that ... only miles from where we live. Your age too. That's what gets me.'

I held him tight. Let him know that I'm fine, I'm alive, not gone.

Despite his dark obsessions, Tom is sensitive. Kind. Thoughtful. That was the first part of his nature that I saw. Along with his skull. We met at a radio party. It was a fundraiser to get treatment for a local girl who needed life-saving surgery in America. All the hospital staff were invited. Tom knew the family. He shaved his head on the night and raised another three hundred pounds. I loved his generosity and how different he looked in just the space of five minutes. Long floppy hair gone in a flash.

Over drinks afterwards, I'd boldly touched his head. It was the first part of him that I touched. Before his hands, or arms, or stomach. I sometimes wonder if I tapped into his mind by doing so, because after that I could not get him out of mine.

'Well, that's it, then,' he'd said.

'What's it?' I said.

'We *have* to go out.'

'Do we?'

'Yes,' he'd said. His eyes glowed. 'You just touched me where no other girl ever has.'

I had smiled. And even though I'd never had a relationship, had sworn I would never submit to any man, we've been together since. His hair grew back, thick and tug-able. But I would forever be the only girl who had touched what was underneath

The day after Victoria's name was announced, Stephen Sainty shared the sad news on the midday bulletin that she had been almost nine months pregnant when she was killed. Twitter went crazy. *#BabyKiller* started trending. The local paper ran it as a headline in the late edition. Reporters said the frenzied attack was even more vicious because the murderer must have seen that she was pregnant. I threw up each time I heard her name on the news.

Perhaps it was to distract ourselves from the relentless headlines, but we finally talked about the playing-dead game that night.

The game had been like the one with the kitchen chopping board; Tom pretended not to care, I faked forgetfulness, and neither of us put it straight. He had shocked me, and I needed to reclaim my power. Most mornings when he gets up early, while I stay in bed, Tom dresses in the dark. I'll reach to pull the curtain open, so the half-light permits me a dim view of his beautiful body while he fastens his shirt. Seeing me watching, he'll smile, dress more slowly. If there's time, I pull him to the bed, take his cock in my mouth, and pleasure him until he abandons the shirt and joins me.

But during our game of *who's going to mention playing dead first* I didn't watch him. I didn't seduce him. I pretended to sleep, which was ironic in light of his dark-game suggestion, and made me smile beneath the covers. If Tom noticed, I couldn't see. But I knew I would *not* be the first to talk about it. If I surrendered, he'd get bored.

Then, the day of Victoria's pregnancy headline, Tom asked me if I knew what Beverley Allitt had used to kill those babies in Grantham. I didn't say anything. I was in bed – I didn't have to work that night

– ready to end another day with no victor in our game. Now, though, it looked like I had won. I knew what he wanted from me. A reaction; a question. I buried my face in the pillow.

'I know you're listening,' he said.

'She didn't *mean* to kill them,' I said eventually.

'You know what she used?'

'Yes. Insulin.'

I sat up. Tom's damp hair absorbed the lamp's glow, like a sponge in blood.

'I remember this documentary about her,' I said. 'She just wanted those babies to get ill so she could rescue them. She liked the attention. She wasn't a traditional killer – whatever one of those is. Grey was the same – he was only experimenting.'

Even with the shocking details of Victoria Valbon's murder – and having previously decided I wouldn't – the previous night I'd read some more of the Harland Grey book, perhaps hoping to find clues as to who had left it for me, and why. But I was no closer to knowing.

Grey was obsessed with getting everything on camera: sex, birth, life, death. I'd never heard of *cinéma vérité* until I'd read him discussing it. The term means Truthful Cinema; it's a style of documentary film-making in which the camera is acknowledged. Most films try and make the camera invisible, letting the story unfold as though the camera isn't even rolling, but with *cinéma vérité* the camera is – in a way – another character. One that seeks to share the full truth. Grey said he wanted to capture that truth.

Tom paused. 'Still, not a nice thing to do.'

'I wasn't justifying what she *or* Grey did.'

'Insulin is a miracle drug for those who need it.' Tom climbed into bed. 'It used to be a psychiatric treatment, you know; patients would be injected with it to induce daily comas. Allitt was just too heavy-handed with it. Those babies were probably too tiny.'

'Those poor parents,' I said, sadly. 'What must that have been like – never seeing your baby reach childhood?' I thought it must be like my mum not witnessing me change from a twelve-year-old into the adult

I was now. It had been her choice to leave, but I still pitied her. I pitied the teenage me.

And the baby inside the girl in the alley.

'Don't you wonder what it might feel like to fade away?' asked Tom, moving closer to me. 'Like being dead but coming back. And you'd never know afterwards what had happened – would you? I suppose the body might recall anything that had been done to it...' Tom smiled and turned off the lamp. He leaned over, tugged my earlobe and asked, 'And what do you think I might do with you while you're playing dead?'

I didn't say anything.

I knew what Tom wanted to do with me if I played dead.

And he realised I knew, because he said, 'It could be dangerous, of course.'

I said that there was something far worse than danger.

'And what might that be?' he asked.

'Boredom.'

'How could I ever get bored of you?' he said, kissing my neck. 'You're avoiding it.'

'Avoiding what?' I asked.

'My question. What do you think I might do to you while you're playing dead?'

My eyes became more accustomed to the dimness. I wrapped my leg around his, pressed myself against him. I had to surrender to this game. I had to keep him. 'Maybe you shouldn't tell me,' I whispered. 'Maybe we try it out, and you can do whatever you want.'

He shivered. 'How will you know that you'll like it?'

'I won't. But if you film it, I can watch afterwards, and I'll let you know.'

I was thinking of Harland Grey's obsession.

'*Film* it?' I could hear the smile.

'Yes.'

'You're sure?'

'No,' I admitted. 'But what the hell.'

'God,' he murmured. 'I think you're the sexiest woman I've ever met.'

'Only *think*?'

He kissed me urgently, his lips grinding against mine, as if he thought stopping might allow me to escape. Change my mind. I responded with equal ardour. *I* was afraid of losing *him*. When he pinned me to the mattress and entered me, hard, I realised I would do anything he asked. Did this shock me? It should have done. But for me, love and risk are bound. They are wrapped up in one another as absolutely as Tom and I were in our heat.

'I love you,' I whispered into his ear.

I did. No matter what.

'I *adore* you,' Tom whispered back.

Did he? No matter what?

'I do,' he whispered, as though hearing my fears.

9

ELIZABETH

THEN

I sometimes think I should have let someone else take Stella – right from the start.

I was cruel to commit half-heartedly to being a mother. She deserved much more. She deserved a hundred percent from someone. Plenty of couples can't have children. They would have loved my curious, wilful, opinionated girl. They'd have enjoyed reading her the same book over and over because she loved the abstract pictures and the happy ending. They'd have relished her describing the minute details of her day. They'd not have needed to paint their lips red and wear ever more revealing clothes to lure men to bed, just so they could cope with the mundane daily tasks.

The whole time I brought her up, I think I was waiting for an excuse to leave Stella. One that would take me away, somehow, somewhere, but without any guilt.

When she was twelve it came.

That morning, Stella was at school. For once I'd got up when she did. But she left after we'd argued. She said she hated high school. Said she missed junior school, the gentleness of those days. That's exactly how she said it. Always one for words, my Stella. I said she'd get used to it, that life was a series of different things that we got used to. She stormed out in a flurry of school bags and the long, tasselled scarf she had taken from my dresser.

I watched her flounce down the path. So young and vibrant. So unlike me, tired at thirty-two, smoking thirty a day, still clubbing when I had the energy, trying to hide crow's feet and bags with make-up, and working my way through men who now hardly ever bought me perfume.

Frumpy Sandra was pulling her wheelie bin out and made time, as she always did, to chat to Stella for a moment. Stella's face broke into a natural smile. A pang of jealousy gripped me despite my wish to escape. I didn't know then that it was the last time I'd see my daughter for four-teen years. If I had, I might have gone after her. Hugged her. Pushed her hair out of her face. Said sorry. Taken a photo of her with the good camera to keep the moment forever.

The post brought a letter.

Though I had never seen his handwriting, I knew it was from him. Just holding the envelope, electricity pulsed along my fingers. It was the first I'd heard from him since before she was born. I must have stood with it in my hands for five minutes before I finally opened it and read the words – fast the first time; savouring them the second. He wanted me. He had never stopped thinking about me. I was all he'd thought about for the last thirteen years. I don't know how he'd found my address, but I didn't care.

He wanted me.

But *just* me.

Because he didn't know about Stella.

I had worried that if he found out about her, he might disown us both. Though he had never given any indications that he felt that way – if anything he had once said a daughter might be nice – when I had found out I was pregnant I had worried he might not be interested in the dull aspects of life as a parent; in a needy and demanding child. I decided that I would rather let him go; that I would rather cherish the memory of our divine passion than share it with anyone.

But I had an even greater fear: if I told him about Stella, he might love her more than he did me.

Now I *had* to go to him. Alone. This was my excuse. This was the escape I'd been waiting for. If I went I would be my nineteen-year-old self again. I'd be free. I'd be vivacious. I'd be where I was meant to be, with the one I'd never been able to forget. It didn't matter who he was or what he'd done, only that he was my soul-mate.

It didn't take long to fill two bags. I only packed my good clothes, my classy underwear. Then there wasn't much else to do. Book a taxi. Buy a train ticket at the station. When you rent a house, there are no ties. My tenancy was due to run out in three weeks anyway. Usually I renewed it with a fresh signature. This time, the landlord would simply realise I'd gone and find new occupants. And a part-time job can be ended over the phone. I'd make that call when I got there.

Daughters are a little harder to desert.

I cried; I *did*. I pictured her coming home from school, her head full of some story, and I felt terrible. Would she simply think I was out late, and that I'd return in the morning, as I often had? How long would it take for her to realise I'd gone for good? Surely it was for the best. My heart had never been here, not really. I think she knew that. She was a sharp kid. Maybe it wouldn't hurt her, and she'd be glad.

In the end I wrote a note; it wasn't fair to let her think I might be back.

My Darling Stella,

I know this might come as a bit of a shock and I'm so sorry if it does, but I have had to go. I can't tell you why or where. But I think you will understand when you grow up. I think you're too young yet.

You deserve better. Better than me. You always have. You're a strong girl and I know you'll be fine. Go next door to Sandra. Show her this. She will take care of you, I know she will. I'll write when I get settled. I might even be able to come and see you. Yes, I am sure I can do that. Be good, my Stella. I do love you, I just don't think it's enough. One day maybe I can tell you why.

Mum x

I left the star perfume on the table next to the letter. I often caught Stella in my drawer, holding it, smelling the fragrance inside. I knew she would like it, and I didn't need the comfort it gave anymore.

Then I left with my two cases and a photo of Stella taken just after she'd been born. It started raining as I got into the taxi. There was another night, long ago, when rain had sent me into a taxi; into a cab that wasn't mine. It had been waiting for Stella's father. Now this one would take me back to him.

I didn't even look back as we pulled away. Not then, and not for the next fourteen years. I should have written to her. I occasionally started a letter, intending to finish it and put it in the post. But I truly thought that it might upset her. If she had settled with Sandra and was living a life of relative calm, I might disturb all that. Whatever kind of mother I was, I really didn't wish to cause her any further pain. And anyway, my life was full.

Until now.

Now, I'm trying to put things right.

That's why I came back to find my Stella. I knew she would no longer be the child I had left. She would be twenty-six. I could hardly imagine it. What would she look like? Had she found a man who loved her? Who was he? Where did she work? What did she do?

I moved back to where we had lived together over half her life ago, not even sure she'd still be in the area.

Then, on my first night in the tiny house I'd rented, I switched on the radio for company, and there she was. I knew her voice right away, before she said her name. I shivered. She had a voice that both lulled and fascinated me. She sounded so confident, so happy.

Somehow, she had learned, in spite of me, to be utterly self-sufficient.

10

STELLA

NOW

I call him The Man Who Knows, in my head – whenever I think of my mysterious caller. But *does* he know? I think again of the curious note left on the book: *Stella, this will tell you everything.* Does *he* know everything? Anyone could ring a radio station, implying they have intimate knowledge of the most serious crime the region has seen in years. Anyone could pretend they witnessed it – invent details so it sounds true.

But *why* would they?

If The Man Who Knows is a liar, what are his motives? What did he stand to gain? Airtime? I haven't given him any. Attention? I've been blasé with him. But what if he *is* telling the truth? What if he *does* know who killed Victoria Valbon?

What should I ask if he calls again?

I'm still standing, staring at my slither of a view, my stars. Just as I went to the window for comfort when I was a child – imagining where my mum was but trying to be strong without her – I go to this one to think. Has The Man Who Knows called me because I'm on the radio?

Or are there darker reasons?

And if he *did* leave the Harland Grey book, that means he somehow got in here.

I realise suddenly that the weather-reader is finishing, so I return to the desk. As I push the slider up I realise I've no idea what to say. That fatal silence looms. No music cued. No news. No adverts. Just me.

'So,' I say, after what feels like an eternity. 'You're all being very shy tonight. Come on now. We all have our secrets. I've said I'll share some of mine, but only if you do too. Let's have some give and take.' I say it for The Man Who Knows and imagine him listening, out there, in the dark. 'There must be things you've never shared before,' I say, my voice low and enticing.

I pause, check the time. Ten forty-five. Almost a third of the way through my show already. Not long until I walk away for good.

'Shall I tell you something before we go into a song?' I ask. 'Okay ... I never wear perfume. I love to smell it on other people, but I don't like it to put it on my own skin.' I laugh. 'That's not very exciting, is it? I'm sure I can think of something saucier, but I'd like to hear from you folks first. You know the number, so get in touch. Now it's "Living on a Prayer" by Bon Jovi for Gail Shaw in Orchard Park, who says she's living her life with new vigour after almost choking on a chicken goujon last week...'

I push my chair away from the desk and sigh hard. I'm exhausted suddenly. I imagine getting up and walking away now, abandoning the radio station early, leaving a long silence in my wake. Only half an hour ago I was thinking about shocking my sleepy audience with all the things I never say; now I'm all dried up. I only have two hours left.

I want to end it right.

I'm still not sure what made me hand my notice in. I thought it was boredom. When I was a kid, my mother told me that I should leave a man before he left me. Perhaps my leaving the station is the same: I'm leaving before I'm pushed out. Recalling my mum's advice makes me think of Tom, of course. I feel a little guilty that I haven't told him about my resignation. But I like the idea of going home tonight and saying that I want us to pack up and move. Be wild. Reckless.

A sound in the hallway stops my thoughts. A creak?

I frown. Did I imagine it? I move quietly to the studio door, heart thudding.

'Hello?' I call.

No response.

A passage from the Harland Grey book comes to me. He was quoted as saying that most films fall flat because lead characters do things no one would ever do in real life. Women go to investigate an intruder without turning on the lights or calling the police first. They're often scantily clad. Grey said realism was the most important aspect of film-making, and what he strived to create.

'Who's there?' I call, trying to sound confident.

In a mainstream movie, I'd now shed my clothes and bounce into the foyer. But this is no film; I go, fully clothed, switching all the lights on.

It's empty. I look at the table, half expecting another package with a strange note attached. Nothing. I look at the tiny CCTV screen that allows you to see visitors on the other side of the main door. No one.

'Anyone there?' I call up the stairs.

I climb the first step.

Out of the corner of my eye I see the studio at the other end of the corridor lighting up blue. I twitch, despite knowing what it is. The phone. I run to get it.

I've only a minute until the song ends, so I let the phone ring on while I cue another to get to the reheated news at eleven. My fingers are trembling. The Man Who Knows?

I pick up, heart still hammering. 'Stella McKeever.' I realise my voice is barely a rasp.

'It's me,' he says.

I know who me is. 'Tom,' I say. His voice thrills me, as always.

'I was listening in the car.'

'Oh.' So he must know I'm leaving. Shit.

'When were you going to tell me?' he demands.

I have to think. Get my head together. 'What? That I don't wear perfume? You *know* that.'

He tuts. 'Why the hell would you give up your show?'

'I was getting bored.' I glance at the door, glad all the lights are now on.

'Bored?' He's smoking. I can tell. 'What is it with you and *bored*? Everything gets less exciting after time.'

'Says the man who fucked me while I was unconscious and filmed it.'

Silence from Tom. The next tune starts. I want to turn it right up so I won't hear any more creaks in the corridor.

'I love that you're on the radio,' Tom says, sulky. 'I've always been so proud to tell people. You love that you are too. Why now? It can't just be boredom.'

'Honestly? I don't know. I feel like ... like a fraud.'

'A fraud?'

'Like ... I'm saying everything and yet I'm saying nothing at all.'

'You've lost me.'

'I don't quite understand it either,' I admit.

He pauses. 'Can't you retract it? Tell them you'll stay after all.'

'I don't want to,' I say.

'You don't know how impressed I was when we met and I found out you were the Stella McKeever I'd heard on the radio.'

'Are you saying you'll no longer be impressed with me if I leave?'

'No,' he cries. 'I'm just shocked you're giving it up when you get the most listeners of all the presenters. You even won that big award last year. Jesus, Stella.'

'Better to end it on a high.'

'What will you do instead?'

'I don't know yet.' I pause. 'I was thinking...'

'What?'

'Maybe we could travel? See the world?'

'Travel?' He laughs. 'With what? And I can't just leave my job, especially if you're leaving yours. Didn't you *think*?'

I concentrate on getting to the news, on fading Madonna's "Secret" at exactly the right moment so that it goes straight into Stephen Sainty's reheated bulletin without a gap, bang on the hour. A split second is forever if you miss a beat. I hear Stephen's familiar voice and relax.

'Look,' says Tom. 'We should talk.'

'Ooh, about secrets?' I exaggerate excitement. I don't feel it though. I'm still spooked. My pulse hasn't settled. 'Can I share it on the radio?'

'No, seriously: you and me, we need to talk.'

'Do we?'

'Not on the phone. When you get in tonight.'

Anxiety tightens my chest. He's going to leave. He got there first. I bored him after all. I played dead and he's still going to abandon me.

'Are you still there?' he asks.

'Yes,' I say, the word small. 'Is it because I never told you I was leaving the radio?'

'It's ... well...'

'At least tell me we're okay.'

He doesn't respond. My heartbeat picks up again.

'Shit, Tom, you can't expect me to finish the shift without knowing what it is—'

There's a sudden movement then, in the corridor. A heavy footstep. I jerk up out of my chair with a gasp, and the phone drops from my hand and clatters onto the desk.

Stephen Sainty is heading for the open studio door, laptop bag in one hand and a cling-film-covered plate of cookies in the other.

Thank God.

Just Stephen.

I didn't even hear the main door bang. His bulging frog eyes are more prominent than usual; his frizzy hair says he's angry. He's like a cartoon character – a villain. His rich voice fills the studio, telling listeners again about the girl in the alley, how there are still no new leads after three weeks.

'I have to go,' I tell Tom, and hang up without letting him reply.

I turn to Stephen. 'You're early.' I try to keep my tone steady.

'Why are all the lights on?' he demands.

We're supposed to be economical when there's only one of us.

'Sorry, I'll—'

He drops his laptop bag heavily on the desk next to me and perches his reedy frame against the edge, cookies still in hand. 'Stella, I'm not happy.'

I'd never have guessed, I want to say, but I bite my tongue.

'I think the secrets theme is getting a bit tacky.'

'It's just a bit of fun.'

'It's not like you.'

'Maybe I don't *want* to be me tonight.'

'It might be your last show, but don't take the station with you. I've had a complaint. A lady called Emma emailed me and said yours has always been a classy show, but tonight she turned you off.'

'What the hell? It's just a phone-in!'

'That bit earlier about the wife playing while the husband was away.' Stephen shakes his head, hair even more wild. 'It was sleazy, Stella. Who knows what else people will ring you about. You have to be *selective*.'

'That's the only call I've had,' I sigh. 'A little old lady bitching about her naughty neighbour.'

'Hmmmm. Well, maybe you won't get any more.' He shakes his head. 'Right, I've got stuff to do, so I'll leave you to it.' He looks at the cookies, seems to remember they are in his hand. He puts them next to me. 'I made these for you as a leaving gift. Coffee?'

'Thanks. And yes, please.'

He leaves to make it, and the news finishes.

'That was the news with Stephen Sainty,' I say. 'You're listening to me, Stella McKeever. This is WLCR, and you've got me for just two more hours, and then it'll be time for some love with Maeve Lynch. So, go on, make my final show fun. Call me now and tell me everything.' I smile, knowing Stephen can hear the radio in the kitchen. 'In the meantime, here's "Secret Lover" by Atlantic Starr.'

Stephen returns with two steaming cups, glaring at me.

'Lighten up,' I sigh. 'I'm not *stupid*. I'll be selective.'

'Hmmmm.'

'Anyway, someone complained about you, too,' I say, feeling annoyed with him.

'About *me*?'

'A woman called Chloe said you read the news too coldly.'

'Oh.'

I feel bad, so add, 'I told her you had to remain objective or else you'd never be able to do it.'

Stephen shrugs, looks sad. 'She should be glad we're the only local station to do our own news. I think people forget that we're unique and that I put it together myself so it's not the news everyone gets on bigger stations.' He pauses. 'And trust me, when I talk about Victoria it's hard not to lose it. It's really been on my mind recently. So horrible. She'd not even left home yet. And pregnant too. Did you see that in yesterday's paper? She was wrapped in her coat, they said. Was the killer being protective or just a coward hiding what he'd done?'

Stephen searches in his laptop bag. Watching him, I'm tempted to ask him if I should share that a man called to say he knows who killed Victoria Valbon. That he says he was there. Should that be on the airwaves?

Stephen finally takes a large red envelope from the bag and hands it to me.

'Anyway, there's been a small development in her murder investigation,' he finishes.

I stare at the envelope as though this new detail is contained inside it. My stomach flips over. I open the flap and pull out a large card with *GOOD LUCK* emblazoned across the front in gaudy gold letters. Inside all the presenters have written doodles and wished me well in my new endeavour/life/job.

I suddenly wonder if I've been completely stupid. What *am* I doing? These past weeks I've done so many things I'd never have imagined I would when I was small and staring out of my window.

And now Tom seems really unhappy with me and wants to talk.

I have such a bad feeling about it; my heart sinks.

'I was at a press conference today,' says Stephen, 'so everyone will have the same info. It's out of date really too.'

I close my card. 'What do you mean?'

'They told us only a few days ago that they interviewed her ex-boyfriend – ex-fiancé, actually, and father of her baby. But surely they must have interviewed him right at the start? Anyway, they were satisfied he wasn't involved and won't be questioning him further.'

'I expected her baby's father to be a prime suspect,' I say, softly. 'They always look close to home first.'

'We can't talk now.' Stephen glances at my computer screen. 'You've got thirty seconds until the adverts.'

'I know.' I hate when he takes over.

'Secret Lover' winds down. 'That was Atlantic Starr, it's five minutes past eleven, and you're listening to WLCR.' Then commercials.

'Anyway,' says Stephen. 'They're interviewing a new possible suspect. Not the ex. They've made it clear that no arrest has taken place, and that this person has gone to the station voluntarily, to help with their enquiries.'

'They didn't say who?'

'No. I guess they must be getting closer. Her poor family must be frantic.'

I nod. It's always the family that suffers when someone leaves.

'I still wonder if it was random, though,' says Stephen. 'If there's a murderer out there. Serial killers have to start somewhere – have a first – don't they? I don't let Deena walk anywhere alone after dark at the moment. I'll be bloody glad when they catch the bastard, I tell you.'

'Do you think they will?' I ask.

He shrugs. 'They have to, don't they?'

'Not necessarily. Think of all the unsolved murders. Missing people never found.'

'I 'spose.' He picks up his coffee. 'What do you think happens to all the missing people?'

'Well, it won't be the same thing, will it?' I laugh.

'No. You're right.' He studies me. 'Right I'm gonna go do my report upstairs. Be back just before midnight.'

The adverts finish. 'If you have any song requests,' I say, 'don't forget you can tweet me, message on Facebook, and text on the usual number. And if you love a particular track, tell me what dark reason lies behind it being a favourite. Personally, I love this next one. It's The Weeknd and "I Feel It Coming."'

And I play my life.

During the song, I fire a quick message off to Tom: *Please just assure me we're okay? I love you.*

Then I leave my phone on the desk, so I'll see if he responds. I sense him as though he is standing behind me. I often have this experience: it feels like he's incredibly close – and more so when he's actually far away. This is how we are bound. It's more than the physical. I often hear his voice in my ear and turn, half expecting him to be there. I even feel his pain. There was one night, here at the studio, when my knee throbbed all evening. No painkiller could touch it. When I got home, Tom was lying on the sofa, his knee all bandaged up. He'd fallen down some steps at work. And I'd felt it.

I'd known.

I used to get that with my mum. I'd know on the way home from school if she'd been crying. I sometimes said a word just seconds before she did. At school once, my nose wouldn't stop bleeding. I got home, and hers looked red too. After she left, this gift faded. At first, I'd be sure that somewhere she was crying, at night. Then either she stopped, or I lost my link to her.

I *can't* lose Tom too.

The radio phone flashes blue. I jump, still on edge. I've two minutes until the song ends.

'Stella McKeever,' I say.

'It's me again,' she says. 'Chloe.'

The woman who thinks Stephen Sainty reads the news coldly.

'I can't sleep.'

'Don't I usually help with that?' I joke.

'It's not just the girl in the alley on my mind,' she says. 'No. Usually your show is relaxing, but tonight you're different somehow. Like there's a different ... energy.'

Is she right? Stephen said a woman turned me off tonight.

'And you've got me thinking about secrets,' says Chloe.

'One you want to share?' I ask.

'God, no. But I do think you should be careful. They can destroy everything when they come out.'

'Are you speaking from experience?'

She ignores the question. 'People unburden themselves, make out they're doing the right thing. But they should shut the hell up because they're only doing it to relieve their own guilt.' I wonder what terrible revelation ruined her life. 'Keep it to yourself, is all I can say. We don't want to know.'

I can't think of any reply.

'Sorry,' she says. 'I guess your theme really got to me.'

And she hangs up.

Is she right? Is such sharing selfish?

The song comes to an end and I wonder what my last one will be tonight.

STELLA

WITH TOM

Tom kissed my thigh; he squeezed its dimpled flesh between his thumb and forefinger and bit me; I parted my legs so he would see how aroused I already was. He gasped, pushed his tongue up inside me, as though to compensate for the risk I had just taken. I shivered. He stayed there, fat and warm, and his fingers sought the rest of me. The top button of his jeans was undone.

I waited to see what would happen.

The salty taste rose in my throat again, mixed with vodka.

Tom said it would only take twenty minutes.

He had done his research – working in a hospital helped – and suggested that injecting me with insulin was too risky. So we decided to go for the more traditional approach: he ordered some GHB online. It had arrived two days before, in discreet white packaging, with refund guaranteed if not satisfied. We had both smiled and said for a hundred pounds there had better be some decent satisfaction. The clear liquid was 99.9% pure and 'perfect for insomniacs'.

I hadn't wanted to think about that 0.01%.

I'd just now swigged two capfuls, followed by vodka. Tom said I shouldn't take any more until we saw what happened. I might just feel sleepy, dizzy, confused. It was apparently very easy to overdose.

It was ten days since Victoria Valbon had been killed. I was about to play dead, and my boyfriend was going to record it all. Harland Grey said in the book I was now almost halfway through that his compulsion to film everything was because he wanted to capture the truth. I wondered what Tom was going to capture?

My breath began to slow. I felt calm. Sensual. Nice. I smiled at Tom. His edges were smudged. I was glad I had agreed to this game. Any fear I had melted as the drug began to work.

'Tell me why you *really* want to do this?' I asked, my words slightly slurred. This fall into a soft and sensual place made other questions whirl around my mouth, tease my tongue. I held them in place. 'What made you ... *want* it...'

A moan escaped from between his lips, like the tiniest piece of evidence that proves guilt. He undid the rest of his jeans' buttons and I saw how much he wanted this.

'It means you'll be ... fully and totally mine.'

'I'm already am,' I whispered.

'You know, when the muscles relax fully,' he said, 'they clench more tightly if they're stimulated.' His smile was blurred. 'That's gonna feel good. People think that taking someone by force is sexy, but I'm not interested in that. I'd *never* hurt you. Just give yourself *completely* to me...' He closed his eyes briefly, lost for words it seemed.

My eyes felt heavy too. I fought to keep them open.

'I love you,' he said. 'I'm going to love you while you're dead.'

'*Playing* dead,' I reminded him, the words thick and clumsy.

'Of course.'

'I love you too,' I said. 'And I want you ... to ... do ... this...'

I could barely concentrate. My fingertips tingled. I felt like the bed was trying to swallow me. Time slowed. I wanted Tom desperately. All questions died. He watched. *Kiss me*, I tried to say, but couldn't move. Lines from the Harland Grey book came to me. *If we do not record it,* he said, *does it even happen? If something isn't captured on film, we might say it did not exist. That we do not exist.*

I existed.

Then I didn't.

What led me to absolute darkness?

Flashes of light did. Tingling as though my body was lit by sparklers.

LOUISE BEECH

Tom asking how I felt. My tummy twitching in a strange dance.

How do you feel?

Were they Tom's words? Yes.

Stella, you will not escape from the truth in this oblivion.

Tom again? I wasn't sure.

Stella, you can't ignore me forever.

Less light then. More dark.

How do you feel?

Yes, that was Tom asking.

And then finally, Tom reaching into his back pocket, taking out his phone, and starting to film.

And then I knew absolutely nothing.

*

We watched it afterwards, on our blood-red sofa. Together, smoking, breath slow again. It had taken me five hours to wake up fully, and a good few coffees to chase away the grogginess. I waited excitedly for the high I'd experienced after almost drowning when I was seven. For the panic I'd felt after sinking to the bottom of a river and being swallowed by the black; for the exhilaration of seeing the light again when I resurfaced.

Tom's camera footage was high definition. My memory wasn't. I had no recollection of any of it. Tom hadn't said anything afterwards, he'd just kissed me tenderly once I was my usual self again, and said he loved me. We leaned in to watch the footage unfold, Tom's smile knowing, my heart tight with anticipation. My breath clouded the small screen; Tom had to wipe it away with his fist so we could watch.

'Did you enjoy it?' I asked as it began.

'Yes.' The word was a groan.

'Did *I*?'

'Your muscles said you did,' he smiled.

In our home movie I was unconscious, mouth slack, skin loose, all control abandoned to oblivion. The camera moved the length of the bed, up, down, up down, up down. Then a wobble, a flash of ceiling, as it was placed on the cabinet, where it viewed the room for a moment before being adjusted to show my body. Tom smiled into the camera and approached me, naked.

He asked the camera, 'Are you ready?'

Then he paused. Did he wonder what to do, or consider that he should not do anything at all? He rolled me roughly over so my face was in the pillow. He turned my head so I wouldn't suffocate, and then pushed himself inside me. His passion died fast; ten thrusts, some slaps, a moan. Curiosity remained though, and Tom flipped me back over and licked and kissed all my crevices and lines. He put his flaccid penis in my equally relaxed mouth, appearing to want to learn something rather than become aroused. He ran his hands over every part of me. Gently slapped my face. I didn't flinch. Finally, he lifted the camera and moved it along the bed, up, down, up, down, up, down.

I saw parts of myself I never would have otherwise or would again.

The film finished.

Tom was breathing heavily. I was surprisingly numb. Maybe it was the after-effects of the drug. Or was it too disturbing to see myself pretend-dead? Still the high of escaping death after almost drowning didn't come. I closed my eyes. Could recall my mum's rough hands drying me while my heart pounded with the elation of being alive.

'Let's watch again,' whispered Tom, gripping my thigh.

If we did would it thrill me this time?

'Go on,' he urged.

'You watch again if you like,' I said.

'You okay?' Tom's face creased with concern. 'Are you sorry we did it?'

'No.' I wasn't. 'I think I just still have that bloody drug going through me.'

Though I'd been keen to surrender completely to Tom, I now hated the lack of control I'd had over my own body. Must it feel that way to be killed? Would Victoria Valbon have felt that way? 'If we watch tomorrow, I might feel different. We have it forever.'

He touched my cheek. '*Forever.*'

I made Tom some toast, spreading extra jam on it to replace the sugars that our exertions must have burned. I put the chopping board a fisted hand's distance from the edge of the worktop; our eternal compromise. On the sagging sofa, he ate noisily; I watched quietly from the door.

'I never wanted to hurt you,' he said when he saw me. 'But I can't lie: it was a thrill to take a risk like that.'

I nodded, joined him on the sofa. 'I could have ended up like Rebecca March.'

'Who?'

'The woman Harland Grey killed in his last film. Everyone thought she'd gone missing – that she'd done her scene and then simply disappeared. But he'd buried her in cement under his film studio. He said he'd caught life on camera and he wanted to capture death too.'

'God, that's not what *I* wanted.' Tom kissed me tenderly. 'I can't deny that, once you were unconscious, I was overcome with desire.' He paused. 'Then I kept thinking about Duchess.'

'Duchess?'

'My cat.'

'What happened to her?' I asked.

Tom wiped his mouth, streaking burgundy jam across his cheek. I licked my sleeve and wiped it off; he pushed me away.

'We got her from a neighbour when she was days old,' he said. 'My dad called her Duchess. The first thing she did when I went to pick her up was scratch me. Six-year-olds don't realise that animals are driven by instinct. I tried again – the same. My father told me I was a wuss for crying. The next day, when my mother had gone to work and my father was at the pub, I put Duchess in a bag. She scratched and kicked but I wore my father's gardening gloves. And then I put her at the bottom of our bin. When my father came home, stinking of ale, he started looking for Duchess. I didn't say anything. I just watched the bin men driving away. I felt awful. I never told him where she'd gone. I was so sorry for what I'd done, but what good was there telling anyone?'

If we do something but we're sorry, can we be forgiven? My mother wanted my forgiveness. She never asked for it in words, but I could feel in every look and movement that she needed it desperately.

'Did you ever get another cat?' I asked.

Tom's eyes were teary. My heart melted. I held him.

'You were just a kid,' I said.

'We don't have to play dead again if you don't want.' He was serious, kind, holding my gaze. 'It's enough for me that you trusted me like that. There's no one like you, Stella. I don't think any other woman would have done such a thing with me.' He paused. 'How do you feel now?'

I felt like I did at WLCR; I needed to look forward not back – to the next song, the next beat.

But I didn't answer – instead I slipped into Tom's lap and permitted him to bury his face in my neck, like he might have done in Duchess's had she been less catty. I thought of my own childhood memory. Of almost drowning. Of rescuing myself. The thought of another woman loving Tom had me fighting again to climb a slimy riverbank with a mouthful of putrid water, and not giving in and sinking to the bottom.

That night, when he was asleep, I watched Tom. Now *he* was oblivious. Did I prefer it that way? No. I wanted us both to be absolutely present. Perhaps that was why I couldn't help feeling disappointed at the lack of thrill I'd felt after our game. At the start – as I fell into unconsciousness – I had been so excited. Now, I couldn't sleep. Now, I wanted to cry.

12

STELLA

NOW

My scattering of stars bring me no calm now that Stephen Sainty is wandering around the studio, criticising and interfering. I can't wait to leave, and it makes me sad because I wanted to make this a special show. Chloe's call has put a dampener on things. *Keep it to yourself,* she said of secrets.

Should I have kept my departure to myself and treated this show like any other?

Except it doesn't feel like it will be.

My phone buzzes. Hoping for Tom, I grab it so fast I knock it from the desk. It's a text from Late-Night Love Affair presenter, Maeve Lynch.

This is Maeve's husband Jim. She's left her phone here. I'll drop it off later if you think she'll need it.

I type back to him: *Thanks Jim, I'll ask her when she gets here.*

A moment later, my phone lights up again: *Isn't she there yet?*

I ask: *What do you mean?*

The response comes: *She left an hour ago.*

I frown, look at the words as though they might change. An *hour* ago? She only lives five minutes up the road from here – so close that she walks. I know her routine well. She usually arrives just before midnight to prep for her one o'clock show. She's a breath of fresh air; all swinging scarf, intricately detailed blouse, quilted jacket, bright eyes, and hearty Irish accent. Her accent is what the listeners love. What *I* love.

It's eleven-thirty, so she must have left home at ten-thirty. Why was she coming in so early?

As though hearing my question, another message from Jim pops up. *She was coming in with cakes for your last shift.*

I respond: *Was she going anywhere else first?*

His reply: *No. Where else would she go at this time of night?*

I'm concerned, but I want to reassure Jim, so I type: *Maybe she's already here and I didn't hear her. I'll let you know.*

Or *have* I heard her? Was she the sound I heard earlier? But why didn't she say hello before going straight upstairs? No. It can't have been her. She always chats to me.

The song comes to an end, and I have to speak before the adverts. My heart just isn't in it now. Tom hasn't responded to my text. Maeve should be here. Stephen Sainty isn't happy with my show. I'm leaving and I'm not sure now that I should be. What a mess. *I'm* a mess. I've done everything I could to make sure Tom stays with me, but why on earth would he now, after all this?

Somehow, the words come anyway.

'This is Stella McKeever,' I say, slow and velvety. It's so different to my life voice. All the presenters assume air-friendly tones when the world is listening. 'Don't go anywhere because we've still got plenty of great things coming up. We'll have "All About Lovin' You" by Bon Jovi for Ben Groves and his wife Hannah. Then the news at midnight with our very own Stephen Sainty.'

While the adverts run, I dash out into the lobby, shout upstairs for Stephen to come down and then return to the desk.

He saunters into the studio, obviously irritated at the interruption.

'I'm worried,' I say. 'Maeve's husband, Jim, just messaged – she's left her phone at home. But apparently she left over an hour ago to come here early.'

'And she's not here yet?'

'Yes. She's here – look, in the corner.'

Stephen tuts. 'No need for sarcasm.'

'It's not like her,' I say. 'Where would she go at this time of night?

She was coming straight here because she had cakes for my last shift.' Sadness swells inside me. I have a bad feeling in the pit of my stomach. 'I don't like this,' I add. 'She should have been here ages ago.'

Stephen nods. 'And if she doesn't have her phone, we can't even contact her. What do you reckon we should do?'

'Wait. There's not much else we *can* do.'

Stephen appears to think of something. 'Shit. You don't think...'

'What?'

'Well ... Victoria Valbon...'

'No,' I say more harshly than I intend. 'That was ... a one-off.'

'But can they be sure? They said personal, but, well...'

'For God's sake, Stephen, no one has killed Maeve!'

'Sorry. I didn't mean to be dramatic.'

'If that Chloe who complained about your coldness could see your passion now she'd be pretty happy,' I say.

'Stella! This is no joking matter.'

I take the adverts into the song and quickly check my phone for any more messages, feeling bad that I'm looking more keenly for something from Tom than an update from Jim.

Stephen frowns and gently knocks his fist against his pursed lips. Behind him, my thin window is black. No stars. The sky must have clouded over. Doesn't matter; they're not bringing any comfort tonight.

'We have to be practical first,' Stephen says, avoiding my eyes. 'What about her show? What if she doesn't arrive in time to do it?'

I realise that I don't want to leave until we know where Maeve is. But then I need to see Tom. Need to know what he wants to tell me. I decide I can try to call him.

'If she's not here, I'll do it.'

'I'm sure she will be.' Stephen doesn't sound confident.

'I'm here, so I'll stay,' I insist.

'Should I go outside and have a quick look?' he wonders.

'I don't think she's playing hide-and-seek.'

'For God's sake.' He starts to leave the studio. 'I'll be back down in fifteen minutes to do the news,' he says. 'Let me know if she arrives, okay? Straight away.'

As he speaks I know – somewhere in the dark place within me that has dictated what I do and know all my life – that Maeve won't be here for her show. Like I knew my mum wouldn't be back when I was a child, even though I wished and wished for it. And like I knew straight away – when I touched his naked scalp – that Tom was going to mean everything to me.

'I'm going to have to let her husband know she's not here,' I say.

Stephen pauses by the door. 'Maybe give it ten minutes, in case?'

I nod, knowing I'll be texting Jim.

Stephen slams the studio door after him and I yell for him to open it again, but he has gone.

The song finishes, and I speak. 'Sometimes,' I say, 'the things we want to hide come out no matter what we do. Like a crush. As we go towards the Late-Night Love Affair, why not tell me who you adore from afar. Go on, they might be listening. And, you never know, they may feel the same. Let's get some weather, and then I want your hidden loves!'

I grab my phone. No messages.

I send one to Jim: *Maeve hasn't arrived yet. I'm sure she will. Promise to let you know when she does.*

As I put mine down, the radio phone flashes blue. What if it's *him*? The Man Who Knows? Can I take the call? Stephen could come downstairs at any moment.

I pick up. 'Stella McKeever.'

'Stella,' comes a dry croak. For a moment, I think it's The Man Who Knows, but when the voice speaks again it's clearly female.

'That's me,' I say.

'I don't usually listen to your show,' she admits.

'Always good to get new people. Except you may have heard that I'm leaving.'

'It was the secrets bit that made me keep listening. I was flicking through the stations ... and that ... spoke to me...'

'Why?' I ask.

'What you just said about hidden loves…'

'You have one?'

'Yes.' Her words are quiet.

'You want to tell me your name?'

'No,' she says. 'I can't.'

'So, who do you love?' I ask.

'Jennifer,' she says.

'And why haven't you told her?'

'I can't.'

'Why not?'

'Because she's dead.' She says it gently.

'Ah.' I glance at my screen. I only have one minute. 'I'm sorry.'

'I loved her so much.' She sounds desperately sad.

'What happened to her?'

'I—' The word is strangled. 'It was me.'

'*You?*' I shiver.

'Me. I didn't want anyone else to have her.'

I look at the time; hate that the clock is ticking.

'She was with him. But I know she didn't love him. The way she looked at me. I *knew*.'

'So what did you—?'

She hangs up.

The weather finishes. I have to speak, but I feel sick. Was she a crank? Making up a story to get on the airwaves? Lonely? I guess I'll never know.

'A caller told me earlier,' I say to the listeners, 'that it's selfish to unburden ourselves by talking about our guilty secrets. That if we do we're only thinking of how it feels for us. Are we? What do you think? Let me know. You have the number.'

I take them into another song. My head throbs.

I realise I haven't checked Twitter or Facebook for requests, so I quickly skim-read the mostly negative comments ('shit show' 'glad she's going' 'getting desperate') and find the odd thing of interest. Nothing serious. Admissions of stealing chocolate bars as a child, white lies, buying handbags and telling husbands they were fifty quid instead of two hundred.

Stephen returns to the studio just before midnight for the news. When he asks about Maeve I resist being sarcastic again.

'Did you let Jim know she's not here?' he asks.

I nod.

'I'll get the news done and I might have a walk around the area.'

He takes the seat.

I go to my window, look for the stars. Just blackness. Must still be cloudy. I listen to Stephen. His tone is cool, on air, but it works perfectly well. He tells the region that new work on tidal barriers is expected to halve the chance of flooding. That extra government funding means an extension for our major theatre. And that local police have said they're interviewing a new suspect as part of the Victoria Valbon murder investigation.

The clouds disperse, and my stars return.

But I don't smile.

13

ELIZABETH

THEN

It was Stella's radio voice that made me think she was self-sufficient; that she had learned to be strong in spite of me. Of course, when I first heard it, I didn't know if it was different to her everyday voice. The last time I'd heard her talk, she'd only been twelve. Now it was deeper. Obviously female, but warm and kind to my lonely ear that first night in my new house.

I'd listened to most of the show before I found the courage to ring the number she had given out for listeners to make requests. I wasn't sure whether she'd answer or some kind of receptionist would.

But it was Stella. I asked if it was her, but I already knew. Her voice wasn't quite as rich as the radio one but hearing it was like déjà vu. She didn't reply, and I wondered if she also had a sense, somehow.

After a brief silence, I told her it was me. I used the word 'me', not the word 'mum'. And she said she knew. She didn't sound angry or sad; she sounded as if she had been expecting me.

The rest of the conversation was a bit of a blur. We talked about easy things, I think, like the weather and the area. I was just relieved she didn't hang up. It didn't seem long before she said she was working and had to go, so I gave her my address and invited her to come over the following Saturday. She didn't say if she would or not.

But she did.

I waited in the front-room window, hoping but not certain. The house was still bare. I'd only brought the essentials with me: a bed, one armchair, my few clothes. Moving had happened so suddenly.

Just after noon, Stella pulled up in a small white car. She didn't get out for ten minutes. When she did, she looked straight at me, still standing in the window. I thought about the last time I saw her; a twelve-year-old leaving for school in my tasselled scarf, not looking back. By the time she reached the front door, I'd opened it and welcomed her inside.

I apologised for the bareness of the place and offered Stella the one chair to sit in, but she followed me to the kitchen. I made tea and she looked out of the window at the overgrown garden. I said I had plans to sort it out in the spring. I expected her to have so many questions. But she didn't really ask much. I asked her instead. About what she had been doing, where she lived. She seemed happy to answer. I asked if she had a partner, and she shook her head. She hadn't met Tom then; that was a month after. She said she was happy on her own.

Not like me, I thought.

I hate being alone. That was why I turned on the radio my first night in the house. For company. That's why I went from man to man in my twenties. Why I rushed right back to the only man I've ever loved as soon as he contacted me. It was why I wanted Stella again as soon as I was alone. Why I came straight back here. I do love her. I *do*. I felt it as she sipped the tea I'd made and looked around and answered my question about why she went into radio work.

Stella shrugged and said most people were surprised since she's not the biggest talker, socially. Then she said she figured that doing something that felt so unnatural for her might be good. A challenge. She said she'd trained for almost two years with Simon Sainty. And it turned out that she loved it, and she was quickly given her own show. Her eyes glowed as she recalled this.

I liked seeing that.

And I knew what she meant about doing something that felt alien.

I told Stella how I'd recently finished training as a doula. She knew what one was. Said she'd had a guest on a show once who was hoping to recruit more of them. A doula is someone trained in all things to do with childbirth. They give emotional and physical support to a mother who's pregnant, in labour, or recently given birth. This mother is often alone.

Before moving here, I'd spent nine months on a doula training course run by the National Childbirth Trust. The whole thing had surprised me. It wasn't something I'd ever have thought of doing. I'm too selfish, I *know* that. My friend Allison – a drinker who had abandoned her kids years before – had started volunteering at Help the Aged. She said it eased her guilt. Something about Allison's face when she described helping the elderly made me want to do something similar.

Stella asked one of her few questions then: *What had made me choose to help pregnant women?*

I knew what she meant. Of all the people I could have helped, why someone who is carrying a baby? Why mothers? I could have lied and said I didn't know. But deep down I did, and I guessed she deserved the truth. Especially since she was at the core of it. I told her I knew what a lousy mum I'd been. That I got a leaflet about doulas through the door one day and thought I could be a better person by helping other women have their babies, especially if they had no one else. In nurturing them, I might learn how to be kind.

I had enjoyed the course more than anything else I'd ever done. Some nights, after a full day of study, I found it hard to sleep. Now I was just waiting for my first client here.

Stella didn't say anything. She didn't say that yes, I was a lousy mum, or no, I wasn't. She didn't insist I was kind or tell me how cruel I'd been to abandon her. She could have done. She had every right.

She sipped her tea. I tried to read her. Not easy when I'd not seen her grow up. Eventually she said she was sure I'd be a great doula; but her heart didn't seem to be in the words. I wanted to prove her wrong. Prove that I *could* be loving.

She saw my good camera then, in its black pouch, on top of an unpacked box.

I remember that, she said. *You took that photo of me all done up once and it was so blurred you threw it away.* She looked sad.

Let's take one now, I said.

Stella shook her head.

I said I was better with it now, had played around with some of the functions, but she still shook her head.

Then, after what seemed like only ten minutes, she said, *I have to go*.

I wished she would stay, but I didn't say it. Had no right to. We exchanged phone numbers, each of us tapping the new digits into our phones. Then she handed me her empty cup and I followed her to the door. Neither of us seemed to know what to say. I didn't want to be pushy.

You can text me any time, I said, *and maybe we could go out for coffee*.

As Stella took her car keys out of her bag, I glimpsed the star perfume inside, catching the light as it always used to. I gasped. It had been so long.

She handed it to me. I held it to my face, the cut glass cold against my cheek. Then I opened it and the sweet smell took me back. *Right* back. I thought I might collapse; my knees buckled. God, I missed him. Could feel him inside me, breathing, beating. And I realised I'd shown more emotion about the fragrance than about Stella. I could never help it. I was still a terrible mother. It didn't matter how hard I might try to be a good doula – to put things right now – my emotions still only truly soared for one person.

Stella said, *Have it*.

I wanted to. I *did*. So much.

It's yours, she insisted.

I shook my head, said she was my star girl, and *she* should have it. The words surprised me. I was thinking about how I'd recently read that Stella meant star. I was thinking about her being on the radio. About how thrilled I had been to first hear her voice. About the star quality I'd felt she had. 'Star quality': it was the kind of phrase a mother would use to a small child to make them feel special.

I was fourteen years too late with it.

After a while she put the bottle back in her bag, stepped over the threshold, and headed for her car.

Would she turn around? Would we see each other again? What if she never came back at all? What was she thinking? More words formed on my tongue. Not a question. An admission. But I couldn't say them. I tried again. Tried to tell her. Stella got into the car. She waved as she pulled away.

And it was too late to shout out that, for all these years, she had been carrying the first and only gift her father ever gave me.

14

STELLA

NOW

After reading the news at midnight Stephen goes to look for Maeve. I don't tell him that I feel in my gut that he won't find her; that I'm sure she's not wandering around in the dark, waiting to be found. I know he won't settle unless he checks for himself. I understand how he feels. As a child, even though I sensed that my mum wouldn't come back for a long time, if ever, I still prepared a little speech in case I woke up one day and she had returned, sorry and full of love.

I play 'Pillow Talk' by Zayn Malik.

Creak. Then another. Somewhere. In the hallway? I turn the song down, listen harder.

'Stephen?' I call.

Then, although I know in my gut that it's pointless, I cry, 'Maeve?'

I go into the foyer. Wait. For what?

Another creak. Above me. Upstairs. I glance back at the studio, aware I only have two minutes until the song ends.

'Stephen?' I yell up the stairs. 'Are you messing around?'

I head up there, determined to be noisy, show I won't be spooked. On the first floor is the kitchen, as well as a large open-plan area where the presenters relax. It's empty.

Of *course* it is. I shake my head at my fears.

I open the fire door behind one of the sofas and peer out into the blackness. The night smells of takeaway food and candy floss from Hull Fair – the travelling fairground. It leaves today, I remember. I'd enjoy that life – moving from place to place, opening a caravan door on a new world each week, fresh news, never reheated.

From this exit, metal stairs climb the side of the building to the second floor, where Stephen's office is, and where there's another fire door. Then to the third floor – our junkyard – and another fire door, and then up to the roof. The stairs going down from here were broken, so they were removed. We're still waiting for them to be replaced. Everything takes forever to get fixed here. But I suppose it makes this building even safer from intruders. With most of the windows bricked up, leaving only a thin sliver of glass, this place is very secure. No one can get in.

And yet they did. To leave the book.

I can't forget that someone – somehow – *did* get into the building.

I look above me, wondering whether to explore further. I wait for another sound. Afraid. But now there's just the pounding of my heart. It takes forever to slow down.

I realise the song might be finishing and hurry back to my desk. As the tune fades, I say, 'And so we're into the last hour of my final show.' It occurs to me that if Maeve doesn't turn up, this isn't my last hour after all. I could be here until 3am. But they don't know this.

'Speak to me people,' I say. With Stephen still outside, wandering the streets, he won't be able to listen in and monitor me. I can say what I want. 'You're all being very quiet tonight. Come on, why not share and make my last hour with you something special. Put in a request for your favourite cloak-and-dagger song and tell me something you've shared with no other.' I close my eyes, inhale. 'Maybe there's something you *wish* you knew. Something that's been kept from you all of your life.' I pause. 'Like the thing that's haunted me all of mine. I might tell you what it is after these adverts and another song.'

Sometimes *not* knowing something is worse than knowing something you wish you didn't.

The main door slams. I jump, but I know it will only be Stephen returning. Or Maeve? My instinct tells me not. I lean to try and see into the hallway. No one there. I frown.

'That you Stephen?' I call.

No response. I go back into the foyer again.

'You there, Stephen?' I call.

I look up the stairs, call out again. Nothing. I wonder if it *could* have been Maeve turning up, that my instinct is off. But she wouldn't hide without saying hello in that cheery, tuneful voice of hers. And neither would Stephen.

Shit.

Adrenaline pulses into my bloodstream. I savour it, the way an athlete might, before she needs to perform. It's similar to how Tom makes me feel; face hot, heart fast, stomach tight. I suddenly remember his call earlier – that we need to talk. Fear that he is leaving me heightens my senses.

The only sound is the commercials; a woman singing sweetly about removing her bikini-line hair. They are almost finished, and I have to queue in the next song. I hurry back to the desk – my panic is rising now, my breath coming fast – and do what I must. Then I return to the foyer.

'Who's there?' I demand.

What would I do if someone answered? If an eerie voice floated down the stairs. It could be my overactive imagination. But is it overactive? Haven't I been hearing a voice recently? Didn't I think I heard it again this morning, in the gush of water as I cleaned my teeth?

Stella, why won't you listen to me?

A voice that knows my name.

I could go upstairs again and check there's no one lurking behind any corners. But this is the real world, where a cinema audience don't need me to add to the tension, so I'd rather not know. If someone has got in, intent on harming me, let them come to me. Let them play a game.

Maybe there's a fault with the door. Maybe the electrics failed, and it opened and then swung shut again. Not much I can do, and I have a show to finish. I return to the desk and check my phone. No messages. I want desperately to call Tom back, but I only have a minute or so.

And if he's going to leave me, isn't it better if I finish the show without knowing?

As the final bars of the song die, I speak, burying all my emotions. 'That was "Brilliant Disguise" by Bruce Springsteen.' Opening some emails, I say, 'Let's get a few of your messages.' I skim them, quickly taking in the interesting ones, ignoring the rude ones. 'Frances Pearson says she's listening to the show in her car, driving back from a long shift at the hospital, and she often secretly wishes there was a drive-thru where you could pick up a man for the night, like you do a latte or a burger. You could be onto something, Frances. Stuart in Bilton says the only secret he has is that he can't stand *Game of Thrones*. Oh, and Lisa Lee wants to know what the lifelong mystery is that has haunted me.'

I pause.

'A few of you have shared things, so it's only fair I do too. And Lisa Lee really wants to know.' I pause. 'Now this is going to sound like a hook for a bad TV drama: *She never knew who her father was*. It does, doesn't it? But the thing is, it's true: I don't know his name. I don't know where he lives. I don't know anything.'

I wonder if my mum is listening. I remember asking her about him as a kid. Not often. Children have a good sense for when grown-ups don't want to talk about something. She always replied with the same thing: he was the kind of father that was better out of my life. I think now it's up to me to decide that for myself.

'I imagine some of you have gone through similar.' I have to control my voice, so it doesn't waver. It never has in five years of being on air; I can't let it now. 'That's probably why that TV show where families are reunited is so popular. We love a good reunion, don't we? But what if it doesn't have a happy ending?' I pause again. 'Right, let's get another song.'

As it plays, I wonder where Stephen is. He's been gone more than twenty minutes now. I can't leave the building. I try his mobile, but it goes straight to the message service. Shit. Annoying as he is, I wish he'd come back. Trembling, I go to the thin window to look for my stars. It's cloudy, like dark-grey candyfloss. No astronomy for me tonight. No comfort.

The studio lights up electric blue. The phone sets me on edge every time now. I answer it.

'I think you know who this is,' he says.

I do. The Man Who Knows. I don't show that I hoped he'd call again, let alone that I expected him; I won't give him the pleasure.

'Is that Stephen?' I ask. Despite my panic earlier, I now hope Stephen doesn't suddenly burst in. I'd have to hang up.

The man laughs. 'You *are* playful tonight. You know who I am.'

'Except I don't,' I say. 'You won't tell me.'

'You've seen me before,' he says.

'Have I?'

'Yes.'

'Where, then?'

'Outside here.'

I frown. 'Here? You mean at the station?' It dawns on me. 'Are you the man I've seen watching me? But you ... sound...'

'What, Stella?'

'Older.'

He laughs softly. 'Flattery won't get me to spill.'

'It's not flattery. The man I've seen around here looks like some kid in a scruffy hoodie, and you sound ... well, *mature.*'

'I suppose I am mature for my age. What I look like doesn't really reflect who I am. I could say the same about you though, Stella.'

'You think you can scare me, hanging around here?' I demand.

'I know you called your boyfriend. Got him to come and walk you home that night. I definitely spooked you.'

'Haven't you got better things to do than loitering around radio stations like some pervert?'

'That hurts, Stella. I'm no pervert.' He exhales. 'I have a hobby...'

'Oh *God.*' I glance at the computer screen. Two minutes until I have to speak. 'And what's that? Peeping in windows? Stalking people?'

'No. I like photography. Mostly at night. I like the lack of light then. Love the night sky. I love to capture the constellations. It's not as difficult as people might think. You just need good focus, plenty of practice, and the darkest of skies.' He sighs. 'Doesn't it make you feel insignificant? Looking up at the stars.'

I wonder for a moment if he knows me. *Really* knows me. Knows my love of the stars too.

'I'm not interested in prancing around, looking at the sky,' I say. 'And you didn't ring me to talk about amateur photography. So, quit bullshitting. You reckon you know what happened to Victoria Valbon – so spit it out and stop wasting my time.'

'I heard what you said about your dad.'

'I'm going to hang up,' I say.

'I understand it,' he says. 'I've never known mine either.'

I listen hard, hoping to recognise something in his voice, but I don't.

'My mum never knew who he was. At least that's what she said. But a woman must know. I think you're right about it not being a happy ending every time. People are so naïve. Not us. So, I understand how you feel.'

'Good for you,' I snap. 'Now are you going to tell me what you claim to know, because if you don't, I have a job to be getting on with.'

'You don't think I know anything, do you?' He sounds put out. 'What if I told you I had my camera that night? That I took pictures. That I had some printed.' He pauses. 'I have them with me now.'

'I'd say you're lying.' Is he though? 'If you did, you'd have gone to the papers by now – sold them for thousands and got all the glory you clearly want by ringing me.'

'Oh, Stella, let's be honest with each other. You're the one doing secrets on your show. Come on. Tell me. Why do you think I'm ringing you? You're the one talking about dads. Absent dads.' He pauses. 'Where was the father of Victoria's poor baby, eh? Where was *he*? Leaving a poor girl to bring up a child alone. To go through pregnancy alone.'

I don't know what to say.

Eventually, I say, 'Send me the pictures if you have them.'

'You sure you want that? Horrible pictures like these, dropping into an inbox that anyone could see? I don't think that lovely Maeve Lynch would ever get over such a sight.'

'And *I* would?' I ask softly.

'*You* asked me to send them.' He pauses. 'It wasn't too dark that night. There was a good moon. Would have ruined any chance of shooting the Milky Way. But that meant I caught what happened. I could bring the pictures to you. In person. At the end of your shift.'

I'm about to tell him I probably won't be finishing at one, but resist. I don't need him knowing. I look at the computer. Time's almost up. 'I think you're a fraud,' I say. 'And you don't scare me, if that's what you're trying to do.'

'Stella – you really *should* be scared. Of what I know.'

He hangs up.

When the song ends, my throat constricts. I can't think of anything to say. Can hardly get my breath. I let another song start straight away. The bassline is harsh, drowning out the lyrics. For some curious reason, the words from my teenage speech circle my brain like vultures looking for flesh. The speech I had planned for my mum, if she ever returned.

Mum, I'm happy you're back. I've wished for this. Every day. But you don't need to stay. I talk to you at night. See you in the stars. And that's enough. You're better up there where the light never goes. If I let you back into my daytime world you might leave again. So I'll be with you in the sky.

A gut feeling explodes inside me; so violently that I close my eyes and bend over as though to protect myself from physical onslaught. Every smell in the room is intensified; heat, cold coffee, electronic equipment. It's a feeling more powerful than the ones I had as a child, when I knew my mum was sad, or when I felt Tom's aching knee before I saw it.

It's a gut feeling that tonight is the last time I'll see *any* stars.

Anyone.

Anything.

And most of all I won't get to meet the father I've never known.

15

STELLA

THEN

The first night my mum was gone I slept under a pink-and-purple crocheted blanket on a thin bed and cried into the pillow until it was saturated with my tears, until my throat ached, my head throbbed, and I threw up in the bin. I fell into an exhausted sleep with her letter stuck to my chest. When I woke at dawn to an alien room, I felt empty.

The second night she was gone, I slept on top of the blanket, with her star perfume bottle under the pillow and her letter in tiny pieces in the drawer nearby, and I didn't cry. The tears froze somewhere between my heart and my eyes, like crystal worry beads. I shivered all night. I would not permit them to melt. The cold kept me safe. Immobilised by agonising grief. I opened the window wide and inhaled the night air. Reached out so it looked like I was cupping the stars in my palms. Became part of the sky.

Sandra, our neighbour, had read my mum's last letter wordlessly. Her hand shook; the piece of paper looked like it was floating across a lake. She looked at me with a thousand words in her eyes but said none of them. I wondered how many shone in mine. I closed them for a moment.

I had come in from school that day in such a good mood. I'd got an A for the first time in English, for a story about a killer who was stalking women at the local fair. He lured them onto fast rides and killed them while they screamed, their cries for help merging with shrieks of pleasure. Then he disappeared into the night. My mum didn't usually listen for long when I told her about my day, but this time she was going to hear it all. How Mrs Brown had said the story showed 'quite a lot of promise' even though she worried that it was 'rather too dark for a twelve-year-old'.

It was customary for my mum to be out when I came home. I often made our tea, eating my own and covering her portion so she could eat it later. But the letter on the table was a surprise. And so was the star perfume bottle sitting next to it.

For a while I didn't open the envelope. I stood there with it in my hand. Tried to sense what was inside, knowing it couldn't be good, knowing that she hadn't left me a shopping list or a love note. I sometimes felt things before they happened. It was like smelling a meal before it arrived. But sometimes my nose didn't work. It had a filter. Only certain things trickled through, and it never happened when forced.

I tore open the envelope and read the letter.

Once.

Then I went next door to Sandra as my mother had suggested. After she'd read the page, and looked at me so sadly, she put it back in the envelope and said, 'Well, now, let's not be hasty about this, young Stella. She might just need some space. So, let's get you some tea, lass, and let's get you a bath run. Your mum said she'd come and see you when she's sorted. I bet she's just gone to a stay with a friend for a few days. You know, to have a rest. It's hard being a mum, especially a single one. She'll be back by the end of the week, you mark my words. Now, do you want sausages or fish fingers? Have you got any homework?'

I let Sandra ramble because I sensed it made her feel better. That she felt she was doing good by whitewashing the harsh colours of my note. Even at twelve, I found it easier to imagine my mum had gone forever and to make plans for dealing with it. I felt bad for Sandra, having been burdened with me. So I let her fuss over me. Let her run me a bubble bath and cook sausages and apologise for the small bed with the itchy knitted cover in the back room.

In the evening, we watched all her soaps. During the adverts, Sandra was happy to hear about my A in English. She winced when I told her what my story was about, but said I should write mystery novels when I grew up. She made us both some Horlicks during the news and followed me upstairs when I said I was tired. She even followed me along the landing.

'What are you doing?' I asked, more harshly than I'd intended to.

'Tucking you in,' she said.

I knew her children were grown up and had left home, and that she had once fostered many youngsters. I also knew that some parents kissed their small children at night and read them stories. But I'd never had that. I'd always taken myself up to bed, pulled my own covers over.

'I'm *twelve*,' I said.

'Of course.' Sandra paused at my bedroom door. 'Sorry. I just thought ... well, you'd like the comfort. Nothing wrong in a hug before bed. I don't often get the chance to share one with anyone.' When I remained at a distance she said, 'She *will* be back. By tomorrow, I bet. Don't you go being sad, lass. Have you got a toothbrush? I've got a spare in the bathroom cupboard. Just help yourself.'

I nodded. After a moment I said, 'You can hug me if you want.'

She put her arms gently around me. It was nice, but I wasn't used to it. I was scared to enjoy it too much. Because nothing lasts.

Then I went into the room she'd allocated me. I hadn't brought anything with me except my school bag. Without turning the lights on, I undressed to my faded undies then I got into bed. After a while, I got my bag and took out the star perfume and my mum's letter and cried until I passed out.

The second night I took the letter and bottle out of my bag again. I knew I'd keep the perfume. It was the best of her. A sweet scent that only we had shared. The letter I tore into small bits. There was no bin, so I put them in the bedside drawer, scattered like large dandruff flakes. I took the star stopper out of the bottle and inhaled the whiff of her. I decided I wouldn't waste a drop. I'd never wear it. I wouldn't even smell it too often in case it evaporated altogether.

'Goodnight,' Sandra called through the door, making me jump. 'I'm going to bed now, but if you need me, just wake me up.'

Why would I do such a thing? I'd never woken my mum in the night. Even when I was sick – when I threw up violently in my bin. I'd just cleaned it up and gone back to sleep.

'Goodnight,' I called back.

I waited until I'd heard her door shut then got up and opened my window. I wanted to freeze. To turn into a loveless icicle. I thought then that maybe I might one day defrost again and look at my feelings – when I was strong enough. But the longer you deny them, the harder it becomes to find them again. In the end, you wonder if you ever even had them. In the end, you forget how you even *should* feel.

That night I wondered for a moment what it would be like to fall through the open gap. To land on my back on the concrete below. Would I smash or just splatter?

No.

I wanted to get another A in English. I wanted to finish school and do all the exciting things I'd seen adults do in TV shows and films.

Though I tried to ignore it, I heard my mum's voice.

Never bore them, she had said of men.

I had always feared boring her. I dreaded when I saw her bright eyes dim as her attention drifted, as my words fell flat and dull before her.

'It's better that you get bored first,' she had said. 'Better that you finish it and then he leaves, wanting you desperately and wondering why it's over. That way he'll never forget you.'

Was that why she had gone, left me first? She didn't want me to forget her. Then the worst thought of all came to me, making me collapse against the windowsill. I staggered back to the bed and dropped onto the crochet blanket. I couldn't look at the star perfume. I put it under my pillow. Covered my head with my arms.

I had finally done it. I had finally bored her altogether.

I would never bore anyone again.

STELLA

NOW

Gut feeling heavy in my chest, I go to the narrow slash of window, hoping to see my stars. I play the game so many of us play; if they're visible, I decide, all will be well; if they're not it won't be. The clouds must still be thick in the post-midnight sky. Not a single twinkle breaks through. My fatalistic gut feeling makes me maudlin. I put my forehead to the cool glass and try to prepare.

The main door slams.

I run towards the foyer. No one will fool me this time. No games. No mystery. My heart hammers with the fear of who – *what*? – I might find.

Stephen Sainty stands there, hair wilder than ever, unfastening his coat with one hand and holding a parcel wrapped in newspaper in his other. The thick odour of chips emanates from his package.

'It's just you,' I cry.

'Who else would it be?'

I frown. 'You got *chips*?'

'I'm starving. I got you some too.'

'You didn't find Maeve?'

'No.' Stephen hangs his coat on one of the pegs by the door and shakes his head slowly. 'I walked around the area a few times. Went up and down the alleys and tenfoots. I thought I saw someone in the car park here. I got excited for second. But it was stupid to think it would be Maeve. Why would she loiter there and not just come in? Then I smelt that chippy up the road. Couldn't believe they were still open, but the fair's on, isn't it? Loads of people in there. So I—'

'Who *was* it?' I demand.

'Who was what?'

Stephen goes into the studio and starts unwrapping the newspaper. I follow. I want to remind him that we're not supposed to eat in here. The pounding bassline prompts me to check how long I have; one minute.

'Who was loitering in the car park?'

'Oh, I don't know,' he says. 'They'd gone by the time I got there. Here – help yourself.'

'How can you *eat*?'

'What do you mean?' He pauses with a chip halfway to his mouth.

'Maeve's *missing*.'

'And because I'm eating I don't care?'

'You were suggesting the poor woman had been murdered earlier!' I cry. 'What are we going to do? Just carry on like it's all fine?'

He chews noisily. 'I'm only eating because I'm staying. Normally I'd eat at home, but I can't leave with Maeve not here, can I?'

'You can.'

I dread the thought of him staying and hovering over me; but I dread also the thought of being here alone again. Am I alone though? A question I don't want to consider. No, even with the unexplained noises and my overactive imagination, I want Stephen gone.

'I've agreed to do Maeve's show,' I say. 'I'll tell you if there's any change.'

I glance at the monitor. Time to speak to the listeners.

'Going on air,' I say, taking my seat. I move the slider up as the melody fades, and take a breath, like a swimmer preparing to dive. 'We've reached the other side of midnight where things get darker, folks.' Stephen glares at me. 'That was "Saving All My Love for You" by Whitney Houston, requested by Jon Murray in Bridlington.'

I remember that Stephen didn't hear any of the things I've said in the last half hour; the confession about my father. He definitely has to go, no matter what I have to face when I'm alone. I can't do my show the way I want with him here, interfering, irritating. I can't say what I want to say.

'We're not far from the Late-Night Love Affair,' I say on air. 'Don't go anywhere if you want to cosy up with a loved one to some of the biggest love songs of all time. Now, some adverts, and I'll be waiting on the other side.'

'Maybe you should have announced that you'll be doing the Love Affair.' Stephen scrunches up his empty newspaper wrapper. My chips remain on the desk, uneaten. I can't stomach them.

'What if Maeve turns up?'

'Do you really think she's going to now? How long since she left home? Over two hours.' He pauses, then says thoughtfully, 'We should let her husband know she still isn't here.'

'I said I'd get in touch if she *arrived*, so he'll know she hasn't.'

'The poor man must be worried sick. I'll call him.' Stephen heads out of the studio. 'Don't you want your chips?'

'No'

He shrugs. 'I'll be upstairs. Call me if she turns up.'

'I will.'

'If she doesn't come by ten to one you should announce that you'll be staying on for the Late-Night Love Affair.'

I nod. 'I will,' I repeat. Then, after a breath, 'God, where is she, Stephen? *Where*? I just have such a bad feeling...'

'Do you? Shit.' He studies me, frowning as though he's seeing something he's not seen before. A man sings about sparkling windows in one of the commercials. 'Look, Stella, maybe she's gone back home, and Jim just hasn't contacted us yet.'

'I doubt that.'

'I'll go and speak to him, find out. If she's still missing, I'll see if he has any ideas where she might have gone. And if he wants to contact the police.'

'They'll not be interested until it's been at least twenty-four hours.'

'Still, I'll ring Jim.' He pauses, then adds, 'What a last shift to have, eh?'

'I know.'

'Maybe you're supposed to stay?'

'No,' I insist. 'I'm supposed to go.' All this tells me I should.

He leaves, closing the studio door after him.

As the adverts conclude, I wonder what to say. Stephen is no doubt listening upstairs. I feel censored. Oppressed. And angry about it. But what is it I want to say that I can't with him around? I'm not even sure. The words are stuck somewhere deep in my stomach. When they do surface they will emerge in my everyday voice, not my smooth, syrupy radio voice; that much I know. But until he leaves, I'm Stella McKeever, radio personality. Star girl. The phrase comes to me, like a whisper. *Star girl.* For a moment, I think I can smell the sweet scent from my mum's antique bottle. I haven't inhaled it for weeks. Now it fills the room, as though it's rising up through the floor.

Then, only the stench of chips.

'As we head deeper into the night,' I say into my microphone, 'stay with me and there may be some surprises. Maybe from me, maybe from you, and definitely more of the best music. No other station in the region gives you all of those things. Stay tuned. This is WLCR, and I'm Stella McKeever.'

I take them into a song and push my chair away from the desk. My phone vibrates, and I scramble for it, hoping for Tom. It's a text from Stephen: *I'm listening up here. Less of the surprises stuff please.*

I type, *You want me to stay and do Maeve's show, so let me do things how I want.*

Then I dial Tom's number and listen to it ringing. Has he gone to bed and left it downstairs? Now that I know I'll be here for another few hours I have to find out why he wants us to talk. I won't be home until 4am and I can't wake him then, even if he doesn't love me anymore; and I can't wait until he wakes up tomorrow.

No answer. I hang up. No point leaving a message.

If he tells me it's over, I can change his mind. I may have done some intense things with him already, but there are many more things I'd do.

Before playing the last song of my show, I tell the listeners they have me for another two hours. 'The station isn't ready to let me go yet,' I say. 'Our lovely Maeve Lynch has sadly been taken ill, so you've got me instead. I know I've some beautiful shoes to fill and a big personality to live up to, so why not help me make it extra special and get your requests in for that favourite love anthem. And share your secret crushes. Is it that guy you keep seeing on the bus? The one who ignores you? Was it a teacher at school long ago? Is it a co-worker? You know the number.'

Then I play 'The Sound of Silence' by Simon and Garfunkel. It was playing the first time Tom ever said he loved me. I wondered earlier what my last song here would be.

It won't be this one.

17

STELLA

WITH TOM

I was ill the first time Tom said he loved me.

I barely had a voice so I hadn't been to work for a week. I lay in my bed, shivering and listening to Maeve Lynch covering my show; I was happy she was doing it so well but worried they might never have me back. I had kept Tom away as much as I could, not only to keep him flu free but because I couldn't bear him seeing me in such a state when we'd only been together five weeks.

He persisted. Kept messaging and saying he was worried about me. Delirious one evening, I relented. Let him in. Apologised for the mess and just made it to the sofa before I collapsed. He sat next to me and moved my damp hair away from my clammy brow. Looked concerned.

'I *never* get ill,' I croaked, almost as an apology.

'Don't speak.' He put his finger over my lips. 'Silence. Rest that gorgeous radio voice of yours.'

As though to back him up, 'The Sound of Silence' began to play on the radio. We both smiled. That haunting melody in the room with us was intoxicating; that famous first line about 'darkness, my old friend'. Tom's face was light though. Calm. The happiest I'd seen it. I'd already seen his dark side. We had explored how far we could push one another within days of meeting at the hospital fundraiser; how much we both liked to be held down, to be blindfolded and teased, to be made to wait for that exquisite release. The intensity was immediate. Like it had been waiting since the beginning of time, and now said, *hey, what took you two so long to meet*?

But now Tom stroked my forehead with the lightest touch.

'I *know*,' he said to me.

'What do you kn—?'

He shook his head, put a finger over my lips again. I felt anxious as his eyes probed mine. Had he seen all my flaws and decided it was over? Had he seen it all and decided I was dull?

'*What*?' I croaked. Was this another game? Another challenge?

He shook his head again. 'It's too soon.'

'What is?'

'To feel this way.'

'What way?' I whispered.

'Stop talking,' he said. 'I can tell it hurts you.' He paused. 'I *love* you.'

I didn't speak. Yes, it was soon. Very soon. But I was thrilled.

And I was sure I felt the same as he did.

'Seeing you like this. Vulnerable. I feel ... well, I just want to protect you. You have no idea. I feel like I'd ... do *anything* for you.' He exhaled. 'And when you know, you *know*. I've never felt like this before. And I never want to feel like this about anyone else. I mean it. I love you, Stella.'

I remained silent.

Silence was our sound.

Darkness was our friend, but lightness won that evening.

18

STELLA

NOW

As soon as I finish introducing 'The Sound of Silence', as if she knows I'll have ten minutes until we go into the news on the hour, my mum calls my mobile phone. It lights up, silently demanding. It's still odd to see MUM flash up on the screen. For ninety percent of my life this word hasn't been on my contact list. I've often thought that, if I were in an accident and someone found my phone, in the absence of a MUM or DAD listing, they wouldn't know who to call.

'Hello,' I say.

'I hope you don't mind,' she says, like she always does – eternally apologising for being here after so long away.

'No, I don't mind. It's late. You're still up?'

I don't know her routine so I'm not even sure why I say this. I've not spent a full evening at her house since she came back; we've only met up in town, shared phone calls, spent an odd hour or two at hers. She came to the radio station once, to look around, excited about the equipment and meeting Stephen.

'I couldn't sleep,' she says. 'I've been listening to you in bed.'

Usually she asks me if I want anything – eggs or bread – but then she's never rung me this late at night, or during one of my shows; aside from that very first phone call. I turn the music down so I can concentrate.

'You never said you were leaving.' She says it softly and yet it annoys me so acutely that I move the phone away from my ear for a moment.

Can the woman who never warned me she was leaving be so heartless as to say such a thing? Does she even realise the potency of the statement? *You never said you were leaving.* It feels like an accusation. That I've been cruel not to tell her. That I should feel guilty. That I've done something as bad as not telling a child that she's about to be abandoned, as bad as just leaving while she's at school.

I turn and look through the slither of window; it's still clouded over, as grey as cold stainless steel.

I bury my outrage.

'It's such a shame,' my mum continues. 'You're so good at it, and you're so loved by the listeners.' She seems to think for a moment. 'When did you decide to leave?'

'Oh, I've been thinking about it for ages,' I lie.

'But why?'

I try and think of an answer that makes sense. 'I'm just ready for a change.'

'Have you got a job at a different station?'

'No,' I admit. 'Nothing lined up.'

'Gosh, that's risky. What will you do?'

'I haven't decided.'

'What did Tom say?' The inevitable question. What my boyfriend thinks is what matters most.

'He—' I decide to lie; haven't the energy for the truth. 'He's supportive. We talked about it, made the decision together.'

'As long as you're both fine. You make such a lovely couple. I'd hate for anything to come between you.'

Like what? I want to ask.

'I know I'm not the best one to talk about relationships.' Is she referring to the many men who came and went during my childhood, or to her time away from me? I have no idea what happened in her fourteen years away from me. I haven't asked, and she hasn't told. 'But I do know when a man is worth keeping,' she says. 'When he's worth doing anything for.'

I hate that we sound alike.

But I'm *not* her. I'd never abandon a child.

'I'd have done anything for...' She pauses.

For the first time since we reunited I sense something before it comes; my gift returns. After eight months of having her back in my life, I smell the words before she speaks. I taste them too; citrus lemon on my tongue. Instinctively, I look back at my window again. The grey has given way to sparkle.

She says: 'I heard what you said earlier.'

I hear each word a split second before she says it, but what I said earlier is a blank. Then I realise that she might be about to answer the biggest question hanging over my existence.

'You have to understand,' she says. 'I always did it to protect you.'

She pauses but I'm not going to speak. My sound, again, is silence.

'You haven't mentioned it, you know, since we met again.'

I want to ask why it never occurred to her to bring it up; but instead I let her continue.

'If you had,' she says, 'I was prepared to tell you. I've anticipated the question every single time I've seen you. I'm surprised that you've never asked it. I don't know why you would say it on the radio before you've even asked me.'

'Say what?' I ask, determined not to make this easy.

'You know what.'

'Do I?'

'Say you don't know who your father is.'

'Why *shouldn't* I say it on my show? Just because I never brought it up, doesn't mean I don't wonder. Of course I do! Who wouldn't? But why is it *my* responsibility to mention it to you?'

I've never spoken this brusquely to her. Our conversations are gentle. I always consider her feelings; am mindful of topics that might hurt. Avoid anything that might send her scuttling from my life again. Once there was an episode of *Long Lost Family* on the TV while I was at her house for an hour. In it the daughter found her dad, and my mum just turned it over without a word. That's what we do – we switch channels. Ignore what's on the other side.

'You're right,' she says quietly. 'I never quite knew whether to bring it up.'

'Now it's out there.'

'It is.'

'So?' I demand.

'I can't just tell you on the phone like this.'

'Isn't that what you rang for?'

'No. There's something else I—'

'Just tell me his name,' I interrupt. 'Maybe summarise what he's like, where he lives...'

'He doesn't live anywhere.' I hear an intake of breath. 'He's dead.

This possibility has never occurred to me.

'Before I was born?' This will make me feel better. This could be a perfectly acceptable reason to keep it from me. Grief.

'No ... at the end of last year.'

'Last *year*?'

'Yes. I'm sorry.'

'You're *sorry*?'

I look up. Stephen is standing in front of me. I start.

'The news,' he hisses. 'If you're going into the national news, you missed the bloody start!'

I realise the song has died. That dreaded, forbidden silence fills the studio.

'Mum, I have to go!'

'But there's something else, that's not what I—'

'Not now!'

I hang up.

'Shit.'

I scramble for the fader. I could still go into the national bulletin, but no presenter wants to go from silence to mid-sentence news.

'You'll have to replay mine,' Stephen snaps. 'For God's sake! The bloody airwaves have been silent for half a minute!'

I play Stephen's news and put my head in my hands.

'What were you thinking?' he demands. 'Taking calls during a show?'

'It was my mum,' I explain. 'She ... It was important.'

'Unless someone died, it can wait.'

'Someone *did*,' I say before I can think.

Stephen opens his mouth, but nothing comes out.

'It's okay,' I add quickly. 'It was last year. I just didn't know. It's nothing. Sorry. I'm back on it now.'

'Are you sure?' he asks kindly. 'You don't seem okay? To be honest, you haven't all evening.'

'I guess it's a strange kind of night,' I say. 'Maeve is missing. We know they've got a new suspect in the Victoria's murder investigation.' I almost add that The Man Who Knows has called again too, but remember that one is my secret. 'Look, why don't you go home? Seriously. What good can you do staying all night too? Sitting here waiting for her won't bring Maeve in. And anyway, she's not going to come here now, is she? If she goes anywhere, it'll be home.' I pause. 'What did Jim say?'

'He's heard nothing. As you can imagine, he's going out of his mind. He's called everyone he can think of.'

'Poor Jim.'

'I guess I can leave,' says Stephen, not sounding altogether convinced. He checks the monitor. I follow his gaze. I have one minute.

'You can't do anything here,' I remind him. 'Look, I'm sorry about the call with my mum. I've a lot going on in my life at the moment. It won't happen again.'

'You're such a closed book, Stella. Five years of your show, almost two before in training, and I don't feel like I know you at all.' Stephen pauses. 'Will you come in and see us all again?'

I realise this is our goodbye. Unless I make the effort to come into the station I might never see Stephen again.

'Of course,' I lie.

'Good. Okay, I'll go. I'll keep my phone by the bed, so please, if you hear from Jim, let me know.'

He goes into the foyer, puts his coat on. I remember that Victoria Valbon was wrapped in her coat. It would not have warmed her or her poor child.

'I think we'll know by morning,' I call to him.

'Know what? About Maeve?'

The note that was attached to Harland Grey's book comes to me: *Stella, this will tell you everything.*

'About everything,' I say, not even sure what I mean.

The door slams after him. I have ten seconds until I become Maeve Lynch for the next two hours.

Five seconds until I fill in for a missing woman.

Two seconds.

One...

I close my eyes, take a breath, and slide up the fader. 'And so it's the Late-Night Love Affair. Are you all ready for some great music? Some love requests and dedications? Some passion? Because I am...'

19

ELIZABETH

THEN

If I thought I could become a kinder person by helping other women have their babies, then destiny, fate, or whatever you want to call it, decided to test me. I hadn't thought it would be an easy job – I chose to do it for that very reason. I just didn't realise how hard it would be, right from the start.

On the doula training course, we were warned that the job would mean being woken at all hours of the night, missing events, spending many hours in hospitals, and crying a lot. An experienced doula came in to chat to us during one session. She said she had missed her son's graduation day. She lost so much sleep she became ill. And at times she thought she might lose her husband. She said this was why it was best that doulas were already mothers themselves – mothers know what it is to be tired, to miss out.

I cringed then. Did I even deserve the title *mother*? I had missed most of my child's life. I was going to earn them, I decided – the title *mother* and the title *doula*. But, looking back, I didn't really have a clue.

I got my first client two weeks after my reunion with Stella. She and I had met up again just the day before. It felt right to meet away from our homes. On neutral ground. I called her. We had texted a little. Short messages. Polite. When I rang I wondered if she would answer. Wondered what she had called me in her contacts list? When she saw it pop up, would she ignore me?

She answered.

My first thought, after saying, *I hope you don't mind*, was to ask if she needed anything. Not sure where it came from. She thanked me but said no. I suggested we have lunch in town.

Stella picked the place. A café above a chain bakery. We both ordered the same jacket potato topping at the same time – tuna and mayonnaise – and laughed. It broke the ice. Stella ate slowly, as if she was savouring every bite. Like I do. I guess these are the innate habits that we can't control.

She didn't ask any questions. I expected her to: even though she'd only asked one at our reunion I thought she'd have come back with more. I was waiting for them. For a particular one. One I dreaded yet longed for.

Instead, I asked her how Sandra was. I almost called her Frumpy Sandra, as I cruelly had years ago, but I bit my tongue.

Stella looked sad. She sighed, said that Sandra passed away two years before. Had a stroke.

I almost said she was too young and then realised she'd have been more than sixty-five. Time is odd like that: your mind freezes things, but it passes anyway. I wanted to ask how life had been with Sandra, but I was afraid. Of what, I wasn't sure.

I enquired about Stella's life now. She admitted that, for the first time in her life, she thought it might be nice to meet someone. As soon as she'd said it she shook her head and wrinkled her nose. Added that it wasn't that she *wanted* to, just that she had this feeling there was someone there. Just around the corner. Waiting for her. Even though she didn't want it to happen.

God, those words pierced me. I *knew* them. Had experienced that knowing once, when I was younger. I'd wanted love so much that I looked everywhere for it. Willed it to happen. But it was just attention I desired. Until Stella's father.

I changed the topic. Told Stella I was still waiting for my first client. She said she was sure destiny would send me the right one.

When I got home, I had a message on my phone. A young single mum needed me. Sarah was nearly six months pregnant. Her partner had dumped her, and she needed support, mainly because she had learning difficulties, and none of her family were around. My agency felt that, since I'd been only twenty when I became a mum, and had also done it alone, I would be the most sympathetic to her needs.

My first thought was *I can't do this.*

My second was a guilt-filled: *How can I help her when I left Stella?*

My third was *this is why you're doing it.*

I remembered what Stella had said earlier. That destiny would send me the right one. I agreed to meet Sarah. It is recommended that doulas meet clients on neutral ground; it wasn't lost on me that that was how I'd just met my own daughter.

I met Sarah in the café where I'd met Stella, but I avoided the same table. We didn't get the same jacket potato topping either. She was thin, her twenty-five-week pregnancy barely visible under a thin T-shirt. Her hand was cool against mine. I knew she was twenty, but she looked seventeen. We talked about how she had been feeling, what kind of birth she wanted, and about eating healthily and what to avoid. She said her boyfriend had been mean. I opened my mouth to ask what she meant by 'mean' but decided she would tell me if she wanted to.

I paid for our lunch. This isn't part of being a doula, but I wanted to. I'd been told she had some learning difficulties, but I found her sharp and aware. I guessed her issues were more emotional than to do with any lack of intelligence. Her eyes were grey and sad. We agreed that I'd go to her next midwife appointment with her, and then to the scan. I said Sarah could call me anytime, about any concerns she had.

As we turned to part ways, she grabbed my arm and said, 'My mum has never bothered with me since I've been fostered. I want to be everything she wasn't.'

I wondered if Stella would feel that way one day.

Back home I wanted to call my daughter and share my experience. I didn't. I realised how many things she must have wanted to share with me over the years. I decided I should be the one to listen now, not to talk.

The next day I got a call in the middle of the night. Sarah had gone into early labour, and I needed to get there as fast as I could. I drove to the hospital, afraid of what might be waiting, rushing through two red lights. Again, I began to think I wasn't up to this. I might have given birth, but it was twenty-six years ago, and I'd been angry and uninterested.

I was too late to be Sarah's birth partner. Her tiny girl was already born, weighing only a pound and a half, and had been taken straight to the Neonatal Intensive Care Unit. I comforted her as best I could. Reminded her that these days they can do miracles. That her baby was in the best hands possible.

Over the next week I was with Sarah every day. She called her daughter Jade. Jade's world was an incubator, where tubes fed and monitored her. I watched Sarah do the cares, as it's called, for her. Watched her clean those spiky hands and thin body with a cotton bud. Watched her read children's stories to her, so Jade would know her voice, she said. Watched her stroke that hairless head. I took a photo of them with my good camera and had it developed so she had something when she wasn't with Jade.

The days were a round of cold cups of tea, waiting for medical updates, and watching Jade breathe, all accompanied by the beeping of a heart monitor.

Stella texted me one evening about meeting again. I was exhausted and realised I'd been wrapped up in Sarah. I felt bad. Neglectful again. Stella said she'd met a man. Said he was called Tom, and something felt oddly 'meant to be' about it. We arranged to meet the following Saturday in the same café; I said she could tell me all about him. I decided I would not burden her with what I was going through as a doula. I'd answer briefly if she asked, say yes, it's going okay. I'd make it all about her, all about her new man, Tom.

After a week, baby Jade became ill.

The doctor told us the infection was in her stomach. That they were doing all they could. The only thing about doing all you can is that there is a limit. A moment when nothing more *can* be done.

I held Sarah's hand as the nurse said Jade would definitely die, if not today, then tomorrow. I swallowed my own tears to give more space for Sarah's. The nurse asked if Sarah would like Jade to be taken off the machines, so she could hold her as she went. Eventually Sarah nodded. And then we went into a private room and waited for Jade to be freed from her tubes and brought to us. The tears I tried to stem as we waited were partly guilt-born. Partly selfish. Even being there for Sarah, for little Jade, was for *me*.

I can't change what I am. But in knowing it, I can actively try and do the opposite.

Sarah held Jade. The little mite tried to breathe by herself for half an hour. Then she became still. The pink faded. Wordlessly, a nurse listened for a heartbeat, held my gaze and left us alone. Sarah whispered to her cold daughter that she'd had so many things planned – Disneyland, Christmas presents, and all the love her own mother had never given her. After a while, a nurse asked Sarah what she wanted. Sarah said she'd like to bathe her daughter, as she'd never had the chance to do that. She did, in a small tub, cooing and whispering, so gentle.

They took Jade to the chapel of rest. I knew this was a kind phrase for a freezer, but I didn't say it. Sarah didn't cry. She packed the things she had brought to the hospital and I walked her out to the bus stop. I offered to drive her home, then insisted I come on the bus with her. But she said she really wanted to just go home and be alone. She thanked me for all I had done. Kissed my cheek.

And I watched her go.

I never saw her again. It was Sarah's choice, though I offered my continued support as a doula. I thought of Stella. Of how she must have felt when I left. It was too much. My heart contracted. I decided I was going to give it up, being a doula. There and then. I almost called them and said I had made a huge mistake.

But then I got a client who changed everything.

20

STELLA

WITH TOM

Fourteen days after Victoria Valbon's murder I got Tom a cat.

I hadn't planned it. His distress at Duchess being taken away by the bin men when he was a child must have been on my mind as I lingered over the small card on the radio-station noticeboard. Gilly Morgan had written an advert saying she wanted a new home for her cat, Perry, as she was moving in with her partner Jane, and Jane was allergic to them.

I collected Perry the next day. She was wash-powder white with a smudge of grey on her tail – as if it had been dipped in paint. Sweet and docile, she studied me when I picked her up, and barely grumbled about her short trip in a cardboard box in the back of my car.

I found Tom sleeping on the blood-red sofa, his hands together beneath his flushed cheek, as though in prayer. I watched him for a moment. Smiled at the way his eyes moved beneath their lids, hinting at dreams that in my head were deliciously illicit. I ran a finger along his back; it was damp. I sniffed his warm neck. He stirred. Turned to meet my lips with his.

'I've got something for you,' I said into his mouth.

'I hope it's *you*.'

'A pussy,' I said, reluctantly pulling free.

Tom laughed. 'My thoughts exactly.'

I took Perry from her box. She purred in my arms. The sound vibrated along my skin. 'For you,' I said.

Tom sat up; his hair was stuck to his head on one side. 'Really?' He took her. Held her at arm's length, facing him, as though to assess what she was about.

'Because of Duchess,' I said.

'Duchess?'

'You lost her, so I found you this one.'

'She's cute.' He nuzzled his nose to hers. 'Thank you. This is really ... *kind*. No one ever got me a gift like this.'

'Yes, they did.'

'What?'

'*I* did. The silver keys with our initials on.'

Tom studied me. I couldn't work out the expression.

'She's called Perry.' I sat next to him. 'I never had a pet when I was little, and your experience with one wasn't good, so we can change that together. We can make pet-having something unique to us.'

Tom put her on the sofa. Stark white against the red, she was a ghost – a figment of some past, here to change our now. He touched my cheek with featherlike fingers. I love Tom's soft side. I don't see it often, but I know it's there, lurking behind the bolshie boy like a shy twin. I think that's why I love him without condition, and why the thought of losing him kills me.

'You always surprise me,' he said then.

'Good.'

'Never stop,' he whispered, urgently.

'I won't.'

'I need that ... *danger*.'

'I know.'

Then he kissed me, carefully at first. But we rarely remain gentle. He must exude a hormone that fires mine. Some delicate but perfect scent that arouses me absolutely. I have often thought that this is why I've never worn perfume. I'm always waiting for his. I don't want anything to outdo it.

I don't want anyone who smells different.

Tom pulled me onto the sofa. He moved behind me, pushed me so that I was on all fours, catlike. Without even removing my underwear, he thrust into me, my gasp merging with his greedy grunt. His teeth in my neck heightened the exquisite pleasure. I clawed behind me, scratching whatever skin I could find. He tugged my hair, and whispered my name over and over, like a spell.

Stella, Stella, Stella.

For a moment, I tensed. Resisted. Was that him saying my name? It didn't sound like him.

Stella, why do you love him?

'Stella,' whispered Tom, urgent.

That was him.

Perry purred on the fur rug nearby. I cried Tom's name back at him, drowning out my own on his lips, overpowering his passion, and the voice I didn't want to hear.

Afterwards I asked him, 'What were you thinking earlier?'

'What do you mean? When?' His forehead was damp.

'When I mentioned our special keys and you looked … I'm not sure. Guilty or something?'

'Oh.'

'What?'

'I lost it,' Tom admitted.

It had only been a pair of cheap stainless-steel keys, but it was meaningful – the first gift I'd given him, and symbolic of us moving in together. It hurt that he'd lost his.

'I didn't tell you, cos I felt bad. It must have fallen off my keyring. I'm heartbroken, I am.'

I shrugged. 'Can't be helped.'

'It used to cut me all the time anyway,' he said. 'Shredded the inside pockets of my trousers.'

'*Thanks,*' I said sarcastically. 'I like mine.' I didn't admit it had also ruined the pocket in my bag. 'Admit it … you lost it on purpose.'

He laughed. 'We have Perry now,' he said, touching my cheek. 'An even better gift.'

'Have you watched the video again?'

'The *video*?'

'The playing dead one.'

'Oh.' He paused. 'Would you be bothered if I had?'

'No. I'm just curious.'

'Yes,' he said quietly. 'I've watched it a few times. If you want me to delete it, I will.'

Once we'd watched it just after we made it, I'd had no interest in viewing it again. Though I'd willingly taken part, now I wanted to forget it.

'Keep it,' I insisted. 'I don't mind if *you* still want to watch it, though.'

Perry jumped into my lap. I passed her to Tom, but she preferred me. I didn't want her to.

'Did you fix the washing line?' I asked him.

'*What*?' Tom laughed. 'God, you change the subject so fast, it's like your brain is this weird puzzle or something! I just fucked you over the sofa and you're asking about the washing line.'

'Did you? It seems lower again.'

'*Yes*. I was sick of not being able to reach it all the time. I loosened it a bit. Why?'

Coming home from the radio station the night before I'd cut through an alley behind the rows of terraced houses; forgotten laundry hung limp from a washing line in one of the gardens. I'd realised at that moment that I *liked* ours being just too high; I realised that I wasn't ever going to lower the line, even though it meant dragging a chair into the garden to peg clothes to it.

'It was the day after Victoria Valbon died,' I said, studying him.

'What was?' Tom asked.

'When the builders tightened the washing line. It came on the news that lunchtime. The line was too high when Stephen Sainty said what had happened to her.'

'You're such an odd girl, the way you link things. I don't get how your mind works.'

I didn't think Tom would understand.

But I didn't mind.

If he understood me, there would be nothing more to know about me.

What he didn't understand was that having to stretch for the washing line reminded me to let go of things I could easily reach. And now Tom had undone that. I *could* reach. I *could* touch it.

But I didn't want to.

It was all too close.

21

STELLA

NOW

And so, the Late-Night Love Affair begins.

I play a song dedicated to myself first, though I say that it's for Tom. Tom in West Hull. Tom who's likely asleep now.

Some songs are our favourites because of the lyrics; a certain turn of phrase haunts us for days after. Some are our favourites because of the melody; a tune that rises and falls with your heart. For me, though, a song can become a favourite because of an intense pause. A caesura, which in music represents a break. A breath. A moment to catch that breath. A moment between what was and what will be. I'm in that pause. My own show is over, and my leaving here will be next.

There's an almost-pause in this song: I play Madonna's 'Live to Tell'.

When it ends I say, 'Here we go into the darkest time of night. The time for the lovers and the restless and the insomniacs. Let me ease you into sleep, if that's what you want, or into romance if you're with your lover. But make sure you get in touch and tell me everything...'

I pause. I'm closer to knowing what I've always wondered about.

'Call us or message us on social media with your love secrets,' I continue. 'Or request a song for your other half. I'll be waiting. And in the meantime, some adverts, and then it's "The Ballad of Lucy Jordan" by Marianne Faithful. Not so much a love song as an anti-love song, I admit.'

The song is from one of my favourite films: *Thelma and Louise*. Marianne Faithfull once said her interpretation was that Lucy climbed onto the rooftop and was taken away by 'the man who reached and offered her his hand'. Others think Lucy jumped from the roof and died. She had been bored of being a housewife.

Poor Lucy.

I make a coffee while the adverts run into the song. Then I scan our Twitter and Facebook feeds for requests and comments. A handful of tweeters dislike me doing Maeve's slot. I'm too heavy-handed and not as soft-voiced as she is. I agree. Maeve's voice is perfect for the Late-Night Love Affair. But would they rather Stephen Sainty covered it?

I ignore them.

There are requests for a few of the cornier love ballads. I slot them into the next half of the show. And there are also one or two secrets. Simon in Hedon admits to a crush on Boris Johnson. I smile. Claire in Gilberdyke says she's always been in love with Bruce Forsyth. Honest admissions; not outrageous or wicked. Just routine daydreams.

Nothing, I imagine, like finally knowing your father's name.

Right now, I feel as if I have a forgotten word on the tip of my tongue. The consonants are heavy in my mouth. I just can't see their order yet. If my mum tells me, I feel sure it will be as familiar to me as my own name.

I wonder if she has any pictures of him. Will I feel complete when I see his face? Will the storm in me abate? Will it make me settle down, want children, security, marriage – all the things I'm supposed to long for?

Do I want it to?

'In the next twenty minutes,' I say to the listeners, 'I'll be playing Rihanna's "We Found Love" for Gemma Clark in West Hull. She dedicates it to Jason on their anniversary of meeting in the theatre where they work. Later we'll play Mariah Carey, and after three you'll have Gilly Morgan with you.'

Gilly isn't actually here in person; she's in Vietnam for two weeks. Listeners won't know this as she prerecorded some shows.

'Don't go anywhere,' I say. 'WLCR has everything you need.'

And I play the music.

I look towards the darkened hallway beyond the studio door. Is it my imagination or is there someone at the far end? I blink, twice, my chest tight. Nothing now. I stand, my legs trembling. I squint. Definitely nothing. Was it just a shadow? It *must* have been.

Am I losing my mind?

When the studio lights up electric blue just as the bassline comes in, I almost jump out of the seat. I answer, glancing at the monitor. I have two minutes. My hands won't stop shaking.

'You're still there, Stella,' he says softly. The Man Who Knows.

Did he somehow get in the building? Is *he* the shadow I thought I saw? I look again. No. Nothing.

'Who is this?' I ask.

'Where's Maeve Lynch?'

I frown. I don't like him asking this. Am I hearing menace in the words, suggesting he might know more, or is he simply curious? I won't show my concern. He wants me to.

'If you don't tell me who you are,' I say, 'I'm going to hang up.'

'No, you're not, Stella. We both know that.' He pauses. 'I didn't think I'd get to speak to you again tonight. I tried ringing again during your show, but the line was busy. I resigned myself to that being it. I was quite disappointed. I almost turned the radio off, but something made me stay tuned. Then you said you were covering for Maeve. Is she really ill?'

'Yes,' I say.

'I don't think you're telling the truth.'

'That's your problem.'

'I can tell when you speak the truth, you know,' he says. 'We have a connection...'

'I doubt that.'

'Don't be so hasty to dismiss it. I think by the end of tonight you'll be thanking me.'

'For *what*? Keeping me entertained? Making me laugh?'

'You can be as flippant as you like, Stella, but I know it's an act,' he says. 'So how come you're the one still there? Couldn't they have brought Gilly in early? I thought you were leaving.' He pauses. 'You know, I don't think you really will leave. I don't think you *can*.'

'You don't know me at all,' I snap.

'Maybe. But I do *know*.'

'So you've said. You've been saying it for weeks. And now you're saying you have pictures. But I don't just believe what some weirdo tells me without seeing the actual evidence. So, unless you're going to come and show me what you have, I'm done.'

'Is that an invite?'

'It is.' What the hell am I doing? 'I'm not scared of you. But I think you *want* me to be.'

'Actually, I don't.' He sounds sad.

'You ring a woman multiple times without giving your name, and act all cryptic about a horrible local murder, and you're *not* trying to scare her?'

'I needed to get your attention. It's for your sake, Stella. It really is.'

'For *my* sake?'

'Yes.'

'Why?'

'I've been listening to you for a long time.' His voice softens. For a moment, I think I hear a hint of accent, but I can't place it. 'You've got me through some really tough times. You were my glass of wine after a bad day at work. That's the best way I can explain it. Sometimes you'd say just the right thing at exactly the moment I needed to hear it. At night, I just have you and the stars when I go out with my camera.'

I'm tempted to ruin his speech with a brusque comment, but something stops me. I glance at the monitor; I only have a minute now.

'I knew when I first decided to call you that, if I just gave the usual request for a song, you'd not even take notice of me. I'd be one of many people you speak to every show. But I'm *not*.'

'So you decided to make up crap about witnessing Victoria's murder.'

'I didn't make it up. I saw what happened.'

'Okay, then,' I say.

'What?'

'Bring the pictures to me when I'm done here.'

'What time will that be?'

'Three.'

'You're sure.'

I'm not. I feel sick.

'I am,' I say. 'I won't be coming back to WLCR again, so this is your only chance.' I pause, then add, 'But first answer me this: you said something earlier about Victoria Valbon's baby's father. You asked me where he was. What did you mean? What do you know about that?'

He ignores the question. 'Are you alone there?'

'No,' I lie. 'What do you know about that baby's father?'

'We both know about not having a dad, don't we?'

Not anymore, I almost say.

'I was only commenting on the fact that poor Vicky was all alone that night. No one to protect her. If she had been walking home with the father of her child, who knows how differently things might have turned out. What hope do kids have when one parent isn't there?'

'I've done pretty fine,' I say.

'Have you though?' He asks it kindly.

Indignant, I shake my head. 'I have. I don't need some strong male to make everything okay.'

'I think you protest a little harshly.'

'Come here at three,' I say.

'I will.'

For the first time, I detect nerves. Now I've forced his hand, I have the power. I sit up a little straighter in my chair. I let it thrill me, chase away my fears. I look at the time. Just seconds left.

'I have to go,' I say.

'See you later, Stella.' He hangs up.

What have I *done*? I fumble for the fader, mutter over the dying song that our listeners can call in, and reminding them about our numbers and social media names. I take them into the adverts. Then I stand. I want to leave now. I head for the door. But I stop. Look into the shadowy hallway. Wait for a sound. A creak. Nothing. I could run.

Instinct is screaming that I should. But the feeling I had when I knew The Man Who Knows was nervous is overwhelming too; the feeling that I have to finish what I have begun.

So I turn and go back to the desk.

I'm not done. *This* isn't done. The show. The night. Me.

22

STELLA

THEN

There came a night when I woke on top of the pink-and-purple cro-cheted blanket on my thin bed in Sandra's back room with the star perfume under the pillow, and I didn't think of my mum straight away. A night when I didn't wonder for a moment if tomorrow might be the day she came back, and then, as fast as it had occurred, bury the hope deep with my tears. A night when I didn't whisper my speech for when she was sitting in Sandra's cosy lounge waiting for me.

Mum, I'm happy you're back. I've wished for this. Every day. But you don't need to stay. I talk to you at night. See you in the stars. And that's enough. You're better up there where the light never goes. If I let you back into my daytime world you might leave again. So I'll be with you in the sky.

The cold continued to freeze my grief at night. I opened the window wide every evening, even in midwinter. Sometimes I'd wake, and it was closed again. Sandra must have felt the draught and come in and shut it as I slept; but if she did, she never said. I never asked. I liked to feel I was part of the sky – an unfeeling star far from anyone, but bright and strong.

On this night – having been with Sandra a full year – I woke and, instead of the speech, I whispered: *It's just going to be me.* It made me feel I could do and be anything I wanted. I whispered it again. And again.

The next day at school the star perfume bottle fell from my bag while I was taking out my PE kit. I'd been carrying it around with me since my mum left. It wasn't because I wanted her – *no*, I fiercely told myself – but because of how strong I felt when it was with me.

I hated PE. Neither of my two friends, Shauna and Clare, were in my group. I was always picked last for the teams because I made zero effort to compete. I intentionally let the opposing teams' goals in and everyone would yell at me. In the changing room I pulled my kit sulkily from my bag and the bottle rolled along the wooden bench and fell into a pile of socks. When I reached to get it, pearly-pink-nailed fingers met mine. Beat them. Got it first.

It was Kylie Sandhurst, the most popular girl in our year. She was picked first for every team. Even though we were only thirteen then, she had the body of a twenty-year-old woman and wore immaculate pink make-up every day.

'What's this?' she asked. Her friends gathered around, eyes narrowed, immediately loyal to their leader. 'Looks dead expensive. Did you nick it from Boots?'

'No.' I tried to snatch it back from her, but she hid it behind her back. She'd coated her lashes in blue mascara and glossed her lips – hardly dressed for hockey.

'Where'd you get it, then?'

I wasn't going to say. It had nothing to do with them. I should've been scared. Kylie and her cronies had beaten up bigger girls than me. They had picked on smaller girls too. Weak girls. One girl, Jane Temple, had asthma and they tormented her by stealing her inhaler, chasing her until she couldn't breathe and then throwing it in the bin. I had got it out for Jane, cleaned it on the corner of my skirt and sat with her until she was okay. I hated people who tormented anyone vulnerable. It incensed me, made me get up and fight.

And my rage at Kylie for taking my star bottle was similar.

I could freeze my grief with an open window, but this was harder to control.

'Not gonna tell us, eh?' sneered Kylie. 'Thinks she's fuckin' better than us.' She squinted at the star-shaped stopper. 'Thinks she's *somebody*. Friggin' weirdo. What's so special about this bottle?'

'I reckon some boyfriend got her it,' said one of Kylie's friends, a girl with dyed red hair and fierce eyes.

'Nah, who'd go out with *her*?' Kylie spat the words out; her friends laughed. 'Unless it was some knobhead in chemistry or physics. Ha, probably that fat ginger lad. That's about all she could get. What do you reckon, girls?'

They noisily agreed.

Kylie raised the bottle. It glinted in the fluorescent light above, spat tiny stars on the wall nearby. I lurched forward to get it, but two of her friends stepped in and held me back. I suddenly saw my mum and me, at the kitchen table: her smoking, me listening, no men on the scene. The bottle sitting between us. I could bury my sadness as much as I wanted to, but the rage that they were trying to steal my precious thing grew, becoming bigger than I was.

'Does it smell good?' she asked. 'Let's see.' She pulled out the stopper. The sweet, sad scent filled the fusty changing room. It entered my pores, fanning the flames of my anger. 'Not bad. Bit like that Chanel one my mum has. Funny, cos I never smell it on *you*.'

'Yeah, Stella just smells of shit,' jeered the red-haired girl. 'Shitty Stella.'

'Ha.' Kylie studied me, sniffed the air. 'Yeah, she could do with a stronger perfume than this. So why would you carry it around but never wear it?'

I didn't answer. Fury simmered in my stomach, rising like the bubbling fat when Sandra made us a Sunday fry-up.

'Freaky weird *fucker* with perfume that she never wears!' Kylie edged closer to me, her eyes glittering. 'What if I poured it all out?'

The bubbling fat rose from my stomach, into my throat. I felt like I might vomit, and they would all dissolve in my acid.

Kylie tipped the bottle a fraction and then stopped, a cruel smile ruining her pretty face. 'What if I did, eh? All over this crappy floor. What you gonna do about that then?'

'I'll rip every bit of your hair right out of your head,' I said.

Instinctively, she touched her blonde locks as though it might protect them. The other girls looked at one another.

'Oh, will you now?' Kylie tipped the bottle so far again. The liquid edged towards the rim. 'Do I *look* scared?'

'You should be,' I said, trying to control my words so I didn't scream, 'because if you spill any, I'll smash the bottle and use it to rip your fucking throat wide open, you cunt. I'll cut through your windpipe and your bone and watch you choking on the floor in agony in your own blood.'

Kylie's face paled. Those pearly-pink-tipped hands fluttered by her throat as though she imagined it happening. I even saw it for a moment. Blood spilling over her fingers.

Her friends stepped back, and I moved closer.

'Give it to me.'

I held out my hand.

She wordlessly put the bottle in it, and then the star stopper. I popped it back in the hole, my eyes never leaving hers. Then I put the bottle back in my bag and left them all, mouths open like a row of Os.

I went back to Sandra's. I often walked out of school when I felt like it. She frequently came in to see the headmaster, trying to defend my absences, to explain that my mum had gone, and the school should have some compassion. That day she made me a sausage sandwich and sat with me as I ate it.

'Stella, I do understand, I really do, but only *you* lose out if you miss too much school,' she said. 'The better your exam results, the better your chance at getting a good job one day. Have you thought what you'd like to do?'

I shook my head. All I knew was that I wasn't going to be dull. I didn't want an ordinary life. And I wouldn't need anyone.

'What happened today?' Sandra asked.

I wondered if she'd still let me stay with her if I told her I'd threatened to cut a girl open with my perfume bottle. Now, I felt calm again. The girl who'd done that was another person. A hot, angry person. But

I was sure that, had Kylie poured her scent away, in that moment she'd have carried out her threat.

'Just some stupid girls,' I said. 'Bullying this other girl. I hate bullies.'

For the rest of the term, Kylie and her gang mostly avoided me. Kids whispered about me as I passed in the corridor, looking the other way when I turned to confront them. I liked that they now held me in high regard. My friends Shauna and Clare even viewed me differently.

'Me too,' said Sandra. 'Nothing worse than picking on those less fortunate.'

'Hate that phrase,' I said.

'What? Less fortunate?'

'Yeah. Bloody insulting.'

'I suppose,' she mused.

'We shouldn't judge, should we?'

'No. I guess we shouldn't.'

She hadn't mentioned my mum for ages. What was there to say? A year on and no phone call or visit; it must have shocked Sandra. Sometimes I caught her looking at me, tears of pity in her eyes. I hated it. No need to feel sorry for me; I was not 'less fortunate'. If I could freeze my hurt with an open window, then no one needed to help me. There was nothing to comfort.

So, I went to bed that night. Slept under my stars. Embraced the chill. I took the perfume bottle from my school bag and stood it on the bedside table. I liked how it flashed in the orange streetlight outside my window. It should never be hidden away. Never be taken away. I'd kill anyone who destroyed it.

Once again, I didn't whisper aloud the welcome-home speech for my mum. Not then, and not any other night, ever again. It tried to find its way into my mouth sometimes though.

Mum, I'm happy you're back. I've wished for this. Every day. But you—

No. I won't think it.

—don't need to stay. I talk to you at night. See you in the stars. And that's—

I said no.

—enough. You're better up there where the light never goes. If I let you back into my daytime world you might leave again. So I'll be with you in the sky.

No. I am the sky.

23

STELLA

NOW

Back at the desk, I take deep breaths. Was it stupid to invite a man I don't even know to come to the studio with God only knows what kind of photographs when I'm here alone? When Maeve is still missing and Victoria Valbon's killer has not been caught? When someone left me a book about an enigmatic murderer.

I notice my phone flashing the name that is always on the tip of my tongue: Tom. I don't care how much time I have. I must answer. I line a song up for after the ads, in case we're still talking.

'Hey.' He sounds sleepy. I can picture him, sticky hot, hair mussed. I ache for him. Always the ache.

'I tried ringing you back,' I say.

'I fell asleep.' I hear the soft whoosh of flame as he lights a cigarette. 'Kept the radio on, now I know it's your last show. You lulled me to sleep.'

'Charming.'

'When I woke just now and saw it was after one, I couldn't understand how your voice was still there. Thought I was dreaming. What's going on, Stella?'

'Maeve Lynch is missing,' I say, the words hurting more each time I say them. I should ring Stephen, check he hasn't heard anything more. 'She just didn't turn up tonight.'

'That's odd.' Tom pauses. 'What do you think happened?'

'No idea. I'm very worried. Her husband is too. I said I'd cover her

show, so I'll be here until three, and probably not home until four.'
Depends if The Man Who Knows turns up, I want to add.

'And you thought you were leaving the place.' He inhales. 'Maybe you're not meant to. Maybe it's one of those things that you would call a sign. Have you rethought leaving?'

'Why would I?' I might make rash choices, but they are absolute when I make them.

'It's just not what I expected from you,' he says.

'Good. Bloody good. I thought you liked the unexpected!' Then I realise our important talk could be imminent and I regret being so harsh.

'Are you okay?'

'What do *you* think?'

We pause. This is our caesura. I want to ask what it is we need to talk about. It's unspoken between us. But I'm afraid. Afraid that he's going to leave. Going to tell me he's bored, that he's packed his things, and he's going.

'So should we talk?' I say softly.

'Not on the phone.'

'Do we have any choice?' I say. 'Tom, I can't wait until tomorrow. I have so much on my mind. Maeve, you, my father...'

'Your *father*?'

'My mum rang. Brought him up. I think she's going to tell me who he is.'

'Oh, Stella.' Tom's words are gentle.

'So if you don't love me anymore ... well, I just need to know *now*.'

'Of *course* I love you. Is that what you think it is? God no.'

'Oh.' I close my eyes, relieved. 'What is it then?'

'I was interviewed by the police.'

My eyes widen reflexively. My mouth drops open. This is not at all what I expected him to say. This is a song I've never heard. For a moment, I think I've *mis*heard. But the words are clear. *He isn't leaving me.* That's all I can think initially. *He still loves me.* Then I refocus. Realise what he has said. The police. He was interviewed by the police.

'The police?' I repeat.

'A week ago.'

'About what?' I ask carefully.

'Look, I don't want you to get upset. I really should have told you. I would have done, but then ... with what happened ... well, it would have just seemed so ... much darker. It changed everything.'

'Tom,' I say firmly. 'You know I'm not some hysterical woman. You *know* that. So just spit it out.'

'Victoria Valbon was my girlfriend.'

I don't speak. The room holds its breath with me. I realise the silence needs filling so quickly cue in another song, the first I can find. I hope Stephen isn't listening. I should be speaking again. Listeners will have to wait.

'Your—'

'Not just my girlfriend,' he says. 'My fiancée.'

There are many things I want to say. Many things I want to ask. I turn to my window. To my stars. The clouds have stolen them again.

'We were only together a year,' he says.

'A *year*? And you never thought to...'

'I did, oh, I did. I just...'

'And you were engaged to *her*?' Jealousy rips through me.

'We were too young to get engaged so fast, I know that now. It was *nothing* compared with what we have.' These are clichés and I'm momentarily disappointed in Tom – my lover, whose mouth follows his heart more than anyone I know, whose words are usually like nothing else anyone ever said. 'Remember when I first told you I loved you? Said I'd never felt that way? It's true. I never felt that way wi—'

'And the police?' I ask, to stop him saying her name.

'Okay. They called me two weeks back. Not long after she was ... you know.' Tom can't seem to say the word 'killed'.

I say it for him. My jealousy says it for him.

'I finally went in to speak to them a week ago,' he continues. 'Her family had given them my name. I guess I understand why they needed to question me. I was the last man she went out with. But, Stella, our relationship ended amicably. It *did*. We had grown apart. There was no fall-out or anything. We haven't spoken since we split.'

More clichés.

'What kind of questions did the police ask then?'

'How it ended,' he says. 'Why it ended. When I last saw her. All of that.'

'When *did* you last see her?'

Tom doesn't answer.

'I'm not the police,' I say. 'You can tell me the truth.'

'I last saw her when we split up,' says Tom. 'That's what I told them, and that's the truth.'

The phone buzzes in my ear, disrupting his passionless words. A message. I move the device from my ear and hit the home button. It's from Jim. I feel sick. The text blurs.

'I have to go,' I tell Tom. 'I'm working. And Maeve's husband has sent a message. I need to read it.'

'Are you angry?'

'What about?' I ask.

'Victoria. The police. All of it.' I can tell he is shocked at my calmness. That he didn't expect it. He doesn't know how worried I was about losing him. He doesn't know that this is easier to deal with. What's *wrong* with me?

'I'm not happy you lied,' I say. I have not been completely honest with him, but that part is truthful. 'Tom. She was pregnant.' I feel sick. Like I often do. But I can't let it rise. Not here, not now.

'I know,' he says softly. 'And yes, I suppose it could have been mine.'

'You *suppose*?' I repeat with ill-hidden disbelief. 'I'm not angry about the fact that the police saw fit to speak to you. Or that you went out with her. But I can't *stand* being lied to. So just fucking tell me.'

'Okay. It was my baby.'

I close my eyes.

Victoria's poor baby.

Only a coat wrapped around her mother.

'But she only found out about that *after* we had split up,' he adds.

'I'm not some awful absent dad.' I know he's thinking of me. Me and my poor lack of a father. Me and the father who I now know died before I could meet him. 'I found out from a friend that she was pregnant,' continues Tom. 'She told him it was mine. But I figured that, if she needed me, she would get in touch. Then she never did. And now...'

'You never thought to tell me you'd fathered a child?'

He doesn't speak.

'I have to go,' I insist. 'We can talk about this when I get home, if you're still awake. If not, in the morning.'

'Are you okay?'

'I suppose.' I pause. 'You can hardly give *me* grief that I kept it from you about leaving here.'

'I guess not.'

'Goodbye, Tom,' I say.

'That sounds so ... final.'

'Does it? I didn't mean it to.'

'You're coming home then?'

'Why wouldn't I?' I wonder who I'm asking.

'I don't know.' I picture him frowning; the small line between his brows like a single no-parking line. 'I just suddenly felt ... like you might not. I'll try and stay awake. If not, wake me when you get in...'

I'm glad he seems edgy. Means I'm keeping him interested.

'Have you got your key?' he asks.

'I have. It's you that doesn't.'

'*What*?'

'Nothing,' I say.

'You're still pissed off that I lost our special key, aren't you?'

I suppose I am. Having our initials engraved on each one cemented the way I felt about Tom. That he could have let it go seems careless. Cruel.

'See you later,' I say and hang up.

Then I turn to read Jim's message.

24

ELIZABETH

THEN

It's difficult being sad and happy at the same time. It pulls you apart. I was still so sad about my first client, Sarah, losing her tiny daughter Jade – it was on my mind all the time; it woke me in the night. But then I'd turn on the radio and my Stella's voice would filter into the bedroom. And that made me happy. Which made me sad again. Because I could have her voice anytime. I could listen to her on the radio website's playback feature. Yet I'd left her without mine for many years. I never even rang her once. I could lie now and say I'd wanted to. But if I'd really wanted to I'd have found a way, wouldn't I? We all find a way to do the things we really want to do. I found a way to be with the man I loved.

Luckily, Stella seemed happy now. She had met a young man called Tom. It was all she could talk about. How they'd met, what he did, where they'd been. And I was glad to listen because this was something I understood. She spoke my language. The language of adoration. She kept reminding me that she didn't need Tom, not really. That she could live without him. Like all of us with an addiction, she insisted she could end it any time.

She just didn't want to.

Tom sounded a lot like Stella's dad. How powerful must genetics be if we seek out the familiar without even knowing it. She said he was a bit of a loner. Had a lot of friends but no one close, just like her. That he had his own special way of looking at things. I hadn't met him then, and I've only met him a few times since, but I had to agree – he sounded special.

In our favourite café, at the table we always chose, she showed me a picture of him on her phone. It was hard to hide my emotion. He looked so like her father that I couldn't speak for a moment. Black hair. Very short because he had recently shaved his head for charity. Dark eyes simmering with intensity. Handsome in an ugly way. A scar above his eyebrow. Shadows beneath his eyes. These flaws added to his beauty.

Pain ripped through my heart. God, I missed my love. I wished I could smell him, kiss him, one last time.

Stella asked what I thought.

Nice, I said. *Very nice.*

And I sipped my coffee.

I was never sure if meeting Tom just a month after our reunion was what prevented Stella from asking me the questions she must have wanted to – about our time apart. About her childhood. About her dad. She must have had them. But once she fell in love, I guess her joy quashed that curiosity. If one man had torn us apart it seemed another would now join us.

I finished my coffee. Wanted to ask why she never invited me to her house. I had hinted at it a few times. Asked questions about what kind of colours she had painted the walls, what the street was like. But I didn't say it. I knew I had no right. I was lucky Stella even saw me.

Stella then asked how my doula role was going.

It was a few days after I'd last waved goodbye to young Sarah. I almost told Stella I'd decided to give it up. That it didn't ease my guilt about leaving her as a child. That I was going to call the agency at the end of the week. Seeing that tiny baby dying in her mother's arms only highlighted how little I deserved to be a mum, and each birth I witnessed was likely to do the same.

Instead I said, *It's going okay. I'm between clients. The first was tough.*

Stella said the first one was never the right one.

I asked what she meant. She said the first time we do anything is just the practice run. Like when she first did a show at WLCR and it all went wrong. None of the faders worked, she missed the news and no one called in. Then, when she came back the second time, it was like she had earned her position there. Everything fell into place.

When I got back to my empty house, those words stayed with me. I wondered if I should see who the agency would ask me to help next, then decide. I didn't have to wait long. They called the following morning and said they had a woman who was quite early on in her pregnancy – only twelve weeks along. And she had indicated that she only wanted a doula who had been a single parent, who had done the whole pregnancy alone.

I was apparently perfect.

It was a freezing late-March afternoon when we first met. I hadn't slept a wink the night before. Even listening to Stella's show hadn't helped. It seemed again that somehow she was perfectly in tune with my life. She asked listeners to call in with their experiences of being a lone mother or father as it had just been National Single Parents' Day. Most people had positive stories to share. Or maybe Stella kept the negative ones off the airwaves. She had often grumbled to me that Stephen Sainty wanted things to be permanently upbeat there.

But that isn't real life, is it, she'd often said.

I decided to ask my new client if she'd heard the single parents on the show. To try and make her feel she would be fine doing this alone.

We met in West Park. She arrived first. She was sitting on a bench beneath the still-bare trees as I approached, wrapped in the bright-red coat she had told me she'd wear, with golden hair flying like kite strings from her head. She turned at the sound of my feet on gravel and gave me the loveliest smile. Her eyes shone emerald green in the soft, spring light.

My first thought was: *Who could abandon such a sweet girl?*

My second was: *I could. I did.*

But this time I wouldn't. This time I would make sure the petite young woman who invited me to sit next to her and who offered me a toffee from a bag (because she had such a craving for them, she giggled) had someone at her side when she gave birth.

She told me her name, though I already knew from the agency. Victoria Valbon.

Then she said she wanted me to call her Vicky; those closest to her called her that.

And after that I always did.

25

STELLA

NOW

With Tom's words, my mum's words, and the words from The Man Who Knows whirling around my head, I open Jim's message.

I remember reading once that when singers sing in unison, their heartbeats often synchronise. My heart pounds now in time with the wild drums of the heavy-metal love song chosen by Sean in Gilberdyke for his wife. I try to concentrate instead on Jim's words; to read; to *know*. But the text blurs into a mass of grey cloud, so I shut my eyes, open them, look over at the sky, and then try again.

Jim again. Sorry. Said I'd only message with news but have to ask if you've heard anything? Am desperate.

'Shit,' I whisper.

Where the fuck *is* she? It's been hours now.

I type my response: *So sorry, haven't heard a thing. Promise to message the second I do. Please try not to worry.*

Time to go back on air.

'It's just after one-thirty,' I say, 'and you're all very quiet out there. I hope you're all snuggled up with the ones you love. Sleeping. Oblivious. If you *are* awake, do you wish you weren't? Who wants to be awake at this hour? Maybe I can play a song to help you drift off. Or you can tell me all the things we only talk about when it's dark. I'll be here until three. Don't be shy.'

As we go into the next batch of adverts, the studio lights up electric blue. I'm afraid to answer. Not because of the stranger who might be out there, but because of those close to me. They have all the secrets tonight.

'Stella McKeever,' I say.

'I'm awake,' says a sleepy female voice. 'Maeve usually helps me to sleep. But you sound so...'

'What?' I ask.

'Edgy,' she says. 'You're making me nervous.'

I smile. Can't help it. 'Am I? I don't mean to.' Are my own feelings tonight pulsating out across the airwaves, carried on my words? 'I admit no one quite has the magic touch of Maeve Lynch.' I pause. 'You sure that's all that's keeping you up?'

She doesn't answer. 'You're playing ridiculous songs too.'

'Is there one you would like then?'

'That "Ballad of Lucy Jordan" was all wrong.'

'It was a request,' I lie.

'You should ignore requests for the wrong song.'

I laugh. 'How do I know they're *wrong*?'

'Maeve only plays *love* songs,' she says. And she will again, I insist to myself. 'I don't want stuff about suicide and depression. I don't want your edgy tone. I want to sleep, for God's sake.'

'Maybe you have a secret?' I suggest.

'What?'

'Something to get off your chest. Then you'll sleep easily.'

She hangs up. I must have hit a nerve.

I wonder if Tom is sleeping; if he is managing to stay awake until I get home like he said he would. If he's still listening to my 'edgy' voice. He's been falling asleep earlier this past week. I was worried he was avoiding talking to me. But now we have so much more to talk about. We've only scratched the surface. I've so many questions about Victoria – some Tom probably can't even answer.

What was she like? Did she wear perfume? What was her favourite? How did she like to be kissed? Had she thought up names for her baby? Did she know the gender?

Did Tom ever ask her to play dead?

No. That was our thing. I know that.

I remember our conversation about the odd years being the best ones. 'Odd year, odd stuff,' Tom said. We met this year – 2017. When did he and Victoria meet? He said they were together for a year. That would mean they met at the end of 2015. An odd year also. I don't want their relationship to have been anything like ours. I don't like that she had him before me. That she got a part of him I don't have. His child. I don't even know if I want a baby, but it hurts like hell when I imagine Tom having one with someone else.

But that poor infant is gone.

That poor little mite died before he or she could exist.

I close my eyes; feel sick.

No time for sadness. I push the nausea away and play another song. A slow love song. One with gentle, syrupy words for those who need them tonight. Then I go into the hallway. It's dark. Stephen turned the lights off. Should I turn them on? I wait; listen. How much would have to happen for me to run out of the building? The door banged shut and I'm still here. Someone got in and left a creepy book and I'm still here. Maeve is missing and I'm still here. A sound. I hold my breath. Nothing. It's me – it's my imagination. It *has* to be.

Everything lights up electric blue behind me. Shit. The phone. I rush to it and pick up.

'It's me,' she says. My mum.

'I know.' I have three minutes.

'I was waiting for another song so I could call again,' she says.

'There have been a few songs since we spoke.'

'I know. I've been sitting here, mulling everything over. I was going to ring you tonight about something anyway, before you went to work, but then I was busy.' She pauses. 'And then you made the comment about not knowing who your father is. I've been waiting since we met for that question. It seemed more powerful somehow with what I was ringing to tell you...'

As my mum speaks I wonder: did I reveal the mystery of my father on the show because I *knew* she would hear? A subconscious part of me must have known she often listens. Must have known that, if I put it out there, it would prompt her to call with an answer.

But what's the other thing she wants to tell me?

What on earth else can there *be*?

'First there was what you said about never wearing perfume,' she says.

I've forgotten I even said that. How long ago it seems now.

'I'd never noticed,' she says. 'And then I thought about it. You definitely never smelt of the star perfume. I would have known that one.' She pauses, then inhales as though actually smelling the fragrance now. 'And I realised it's true. You don't wear any scent. You always just smell like ... *you*.'

I laugh. 'Oh dear.'

'No, it's nice. I know it now. Your smell.' She sounds sad. 'So why don't you ever wear perfume?'

'Not entirely sure,' I admit.

'But it's unusual.'

'Yes. I decided a long time ago. When I was little.' I pause. 'When you were still around.'

'Really?'

'Yes. You always had different perfumes from different men. The star one was the only one you wore when they weren't around.' My throat feels tight. 'When it was just us,' I add.

'Oh Stella. I was terrible, wasn't I?'

I don't like her self-pity. I'd rather she was cool and indifferent. I don't know what to do with sadness other than bury it. I ignore it. 'I just decided I'd never wear any at all. No one would mark me with it. I wouldn't even be marked by the star perfume, though I adore the smell.' Should I tell her? I do. 'I couldn't wear it now if I wanted to.'

'What do you mean?'

'I lost it.'

'*No*?' The self-pity is gone.

'Trust me. I'm sad about it. You know I've had it since I was twelve. But what can I do? I looked online for something similar but couldn't find anything at all like it. And even if there was, it wouldn't be *that* one, would it?'

'No. That one was ... special.'

'Why?' I ask.

I remember how she saved it, only wore a tiny dab of it each time. It feels like the song has gone on forever and I realise I only have one minute. It's so frustrating.

'Why was it special?' I ask.

'Stella ... your father bought it for me.'

I don't know what to say.

My *father*.

It makes him all the more real. He chose it. Touched it. And now it's gone.

'Who *was* he?' I demand.

'I'll tell you,' she says. 'But not on the phone like this. It should be done properly, when we're together. You deserve it that way.'

I think hard. I can't wait until we next see one another. I feel I must know everything tonight.

'Come to the studio,' I say. 'Soon. Now. You can be here in ten minutes. I'll make the first twenty minutes of the next hour all songs so we can talk. Stephen Sainty will be asleep now so he won't even know I've done it.' I need her to be gone before three though, before The Man Who Knows comes. That meeting needs to be private.

'Can I ask a question?' she says

'I've only got thirty seconds. Can it wait?'

'Why have I never been to your house?' she asks anyway.

There simply isn't time to explore such a question now. I'm not even sure I know the answer. I know that I've occasionally thought about inviting her over and then found some excuse not to: the house isn't clean enough or I want time alone with Tom. But I guess if I really wanted her in my home, I'd have made it happen.

'What was it you wanted to tell me?' I ask instead.

'I so want to see where you live,' she persists. 'You let me come and see the radio studio that time...'

This is futile – I have seconds until I must speak.

'Hold on a moment,' I say, and slide up the fader and speak to the world. 'That was "Everything I do" by Bryan Adams, and it's almost one-forty-five. For my anonymous caller who can't sleep and misses Maeve Lynch, I hope you've found peace now. If anyone else wants peace, call and tell me about it. I'm a good listener. After the adverts, I'll look at tomorrow's weather...'

'You still there?' I ask my mum.

'Yes.'

'What did you want to tell me earlier?' I repeat.

'I was Victoria Valbon's doula,' she says.

'*What?*'

These are the last words I expected to hear. It knocks the wind out of me.

'I called her Vicky, though,' she says softly. 'All those who knew her did.'

'You were...' I can't finish.

'Yes.'

'But ... how? ... When?'

'I've never really talked to you about my doula stuff,' my mum continues. 'I don't like to bother you with it, I suppose. When we're together, I'm trying to make it all about you and not about what I'm up to.'

My mum knew Victoria Valbon too.

Tom *and* my mum.

Shit.

It's like Victoria is getting closer to me. I turn around, almost expecting to see her standing there, by my window, tiny baby in hands. And for a moment, she is. The green eyes that stare sadly out of so many newspaper pictures are bright with life; her throat is bloody, the red spilling down a frilled blouse, along her fingers, and onto her baby's golden head. Dripping scarlet stains onto sweet skin. I shut my eyes. When I open them, she has gone.

'But you...' I can't find the right words. 'But she ... How long?'

'Her doula? Since March.'

'Six months?'

'No. I wasn't her doula until … the end.'

'Why not?'

'I just … we fell out.'

'About what?' I ask.

'Look,' my mum says gently. 'You've asked me to come into the studio. Let me do that. I'll leave now. We'll talk. I know we won't have long, and it seems there is so much to say.'

She's right. I have to do the weather. I have to get my head together. Line up some songs so we can talk after the news on the hour.

'What was she like?' The words jump out before I can think.

Silence from my mum. In one of the adverts, a man describes his accident and how his huge claim changed his life.

Eventually she says, 'She was a sweet girl. She *was*. I really … I couldn't … She just couldn't…'

'Couldn't *what*?'

'Stella, I'll leave the house now. Come to you. We'll talk. Okay?' She hangs up.

When I read the weather for tomorrow, I again have the gut feeling I might not see it. Might not feel the unseasonally mild temperatures or see the haze of clouds that will depart to leave a sunny afternoon. Might not leave a coat at home and enjoy the light October breeze.

26

STELLA

WITH TOM

It turns out I told Stephen Sainty that I was leaving WLCR at about the same time as Tom was being questioned by the police about Victoria. Stephen ranted at length about my not giving him enough notice, even though I reminded him I had three weeks of holiday remaining so only had to work one more week. I didn't know that while I was hiding my imminent redundancy from him, Tom was in a room with two police officers, sharing intimate details about his one-year relationship with Victoria Valbon.

Did he take time off work to go?

Did he go when I was at the radio station?

I don't suppose it matters.

I do know that during those days Tom was more tender with me than he ever has been in all our time together. I thought Perry had caused the softness; that her purring had imbued us both with calm. That my gift – my wanting to undo Tom's sadness about his childhood pet – had peeled yet another layer away from his façade and shown me more of the real boy I loved, the child beneath the man who liked danger.

We let Perry sleep with us, her warm body between our feet. She preferred me though. I'd wake with her curled up in the curve of my back and pick her up and put her next to a snoring Tom. Hazel eyes glared at me in the dark, said Perry was not amused, but she would stay there if she must.

Some mornings, Tom held my gaze so long, I felt he could see everything I thought, and I had to break the connection.

'What's up?' he'd call as I went to the bathroom.

'Nothing,' I'd lie.

'You'd think you were hiding something,' he'd say. 'Not like you to be the first to look away!'

I'd compose myself, look in the bathroom mirror, study my eyes. Wait for strange voices to rise up from the gush of water.

Stella, Stella, you know what you see in your eyes.

Then I'd go back to Tom, say, 'Nothing to hide here.'

In truth, I loved to get lost in Tom's dark eyes; loved to fall into the autumnal browns that changed like dying leaves. At times, I was nervous about what he would see in my lighter irises. But I could cope with that. It was what I might see in *his* that I sometimes feared so much I felt sick.

That he might leave me.

I never cared what he might do.

Just stay with me.

'I'm gonna make an omelette for breakfast,' was all I'd say those mornings.

Our chopping board game ceased around this time too. Tom didn't play anymore. Instead of leaving it wildly diagonal he left it exactly where I had put it – further back so the crumbs didn't hit the floor. He wiped up his mess too. He washed his dishes rather than leaving them on the side for me. He emptied bins and ashtrays. He made the bed if he was the last one out of it.

My heart constricted.

I loved our conflict. Our sexual games. Our fight to dominate in the bedroom, on the floor of the bathroom, the kitchen table. This game of Tom being submissive unnerved me. Like he had given in, somehow. Surrendered. And I wasn't sure what that meant.

So I created the conflict by turning into him. I was the one who left crumbs scattered like mouse droppings on the kitchen worktop. I left the duvet hanging off the end of the bed. I swilled coffee all over the stairs when I carried a full mug to the bedroom. Had I known he was being interviewed by the police about his relationship with Victoria, I would have smashed every cup in the kitchen.

If Tom noticed my slovenliness, he never said anything.

Did I no longer incite him to battle?

Was he *bored*?

Four nights ago, four nights before my last radio show, I was reading my Harland Grey book in bed. I was almost finished with it but still dipped in and out of it, occasionally opening it at random pages. Tom had gone to a work meeting – or so I thought, but who knows now – and it wasn't a radio night for me. Perry curled up in my lap beneath the hardback.

I read about Harland's obsession with detail. How in his films he used actual things rather than props. If a cup was to be smashed, he liked the sound of thick glass not the sugar glass they used for stunt crockery. This brittle glass is less likely to cause injury. But Harland didn't care if an actor was cut or bled profusely. He liked it. It was all about the reality. About real blood. About really feeling it.

When Tom walked into the bedroom, it took me a while to notice. I jumped when I looked up and saw him studying me from the end of the bed.

'How long have you been there?' I asked.

'About a minute.'

'You okay?' I asked. He was still staring.

He shook his head, said, 'Yes, sorry. Fine. Long night.' Then he went into the bathroom, pulled off his sweater and jeans. I wondered if he would discard them by the sink like he usually did but he hung them on the back of the door. My heart sank. He returned to the room in his shorts and climbed into bed. Without even a kiss, he turned the other way, and closed his eyes.

'Is something wrong?' I asked, my heart hammering.

'No,' he said, sounding sleepy. 'I'm really tired, that's all. Sorry. Did you want to talk?'

'No. Not particularly. It's just you...'

'What?'

'Well, you *never* just go to sleep.'

'I thought you liked it when I didn't do what you expected?'

What could I say to that?

'Goodnight then,' I said softly.

'Goodnight,' he said.

I sat for a long time, listening to his gentle snoring. I could no longer see the words in my book. I put it aside and turned off the lamp. I didn't know then that he'd spoken to the police. But I did wonder if he had been to work that night. I wondered, and it killed me. But if not, where the hell *had* he been? Was I just worrying because of the change in his behaviour? Or because of mine?

I should never have played dead.

This came to me hard as I sank back into the darkness. I had given Tom too much. I had given him everything. And when you give someone that, what else is left? I had used real glass, not stunt sugar glass.

I only had one thing left. One thing that would show him no one would ever love him more.

Perry purred by my ear, as though she knew my torment.

'You're supposed to be Tom's cat,' I whispered, stroking her. 'Go sleep on him.' But she stayed at my side all night.

All I could think was, *He lost our special key and I have lost him.*

Did you ever really have him, Stella?

The words came up in the rustle of bedclothes as I turned over.

Yes, I did. He's mine.

But I was so scared I'd lost him.

27

ELIZABETH

THEN

Vicky and I loved meeting on our bench in West Park. It became our place, I suppose. We watched the world go by there. We saw spring turn into summer. Saw the snowdrops die, and the carnations and roses blossom. Vicky blossomed too. I saw her pale cheeks turn as pink as the flowers we enjoyed. Her tummy slowly swelled too. I guess I acted like a surrogate mother to her, even though her real mum was alive and well and loved her very much. I also found that I enjoyed her pregnancy. I hadn't enjoyed mine. It had felt like a hindrance. Something to be done with as quickly as possible.

That made me feel bad now.

I tried to be everything to Vicky that I never had been to Stella. I went along to scan appointments. I went to all the midwife check-ups and to see various doctors with her. Vicky was monitored more closely than the average woman due to her underactive thyroid. She had been taking levothyroxine since she was diagnosed at twelve years old, and the condition meant she had to have regular blood tests during her pregnancy to adjust the dose accordingly. She never showed any discouragement though. She just shrugged it off. Said there were many worse off – women who had lost babies or couldn't get pregnant.

I wondered many times why Vicky had even requested a doula. To me, she seemed to be coping incredibly well. The absolute antithesis of me, who twenty-six and a half years ago had been angry that I had found out I was pregnant too late to have any choice about it. Vicky seemed to have been put on earth to be a mother.

At least it seemed that way at the start.

I suppose we all *act* like we're fine.

Until we're not.

In the hospital once, while waiting to see her baby on a scan monitor, she said she didn't want to find out the sex of her child when the opportunity arose. She said she wanted a surprise when he or she was born. Vicky turned to me then, with those emerald-green eyes, and said I should be the one who told her. That I should look to see whether she had a son or a daughter and tell her.

I didn't deserve to be that person.

I remembered how blasé I'd been when the midwife told me I had a daughter. I'd actually wanted a boy. Felt a boy would be easier to love. And that's how I'd known that fate would give me a female.

Vicky grabbed my hand then, in the middle of the hospital waiting room, and said excitedly that she had planned to do it that way with the father – to let him find out the sex. Then she stopped. That simple word drained her of all colour; father. She must have realised the enormity of the thing she was asking me to do, and who it really should have been.

Are you okay? I asked.

Vicky nodded but didn't speak.

I asked if she wanted to talk about the father of her child.

But Vicky didn't want to talk about him then, and not for a good while after. She was, however, endlessly fascinated by my story. By how I had ended up as a single mum. Questions spilled out of her. Who was Stella's dad and why hadn't he been a part of her life? Where was he? Had he ever seen her? What *happened*?

Until then, I had never been able to talk about him to anyone. Since I'd come back to Hull, I'd had to carry him around secretly inside me. Back when we first met, and later, after what then happened, I could hardly tell anyone either. He just wasn't the kind of man anyone would understand.

There have been times since I met Stella again when I have longed for her to ask me who he was. Yes I've dreaded telling her, but I've also yearned for the opportunity to speak about him – say his name; explain; excuse. *Remember*. I dropped hints. Oh, I dropped hints.

When she didn't, I found that I loved how hungry Vicky was for my story. If I was her doula, she became my listener. My counsellor. I can't lie. I preferred when it was about me. Always have. I could feel compassion for Vicky, I really could, but when she turned those green eyes on me, craving *my* story, I blossomed. When she teared up over her own sadness, it affected me less than when her tears spilled for mine.

Of course, I could not be fully truthful about Stella's father. I could not tell Vicky all of it. How I'd abandoned Stella to go back to him. What kind of doula would that have made me? Vicky would never have seen me again. But I told her how we met, when I was just nine-teen and he was thirty-five. I told her the things I could.

About our love.

We were not on our West Park bench the day I first told her about him. Rain fell heavily and even the trees didn't protect us. It was the end of April and I'd been seeing Vicky for five weeks. It felt like longer. She was such an amicable and easy-to-like girl. She was always early when we met. She always mentioned some new top or item of make-up she'd bought recently, and showed me it, as excited as a small child. She incited motherly affection in me. It surprised me. It was not unlike the feeling I once had when men looked my way.

The sad thing was that she provoked that feeling in me more than anyone else ever had – even my own daughter. And what made it even worse was that Vicky was about to learn more about Stella's dad than Stella knew.

Could I forgive myself?

On this rainy April afternoon, we found a café – not mine and Stella's favourite – and we sat opposite one another in a booth. Soaked customers crowded in after us. A tub by the door was full of dripping umbrellas. I knew what Vicky would pick from the menu; not eggs, never eggs, not prawns, never prawns, but plain cheese sandwiches. She said that she must have needed the dairy as she craved milk and cheese all the time.

When our food came she studied me.

She said, *Tell me about Stella's dad.*

She insisted that if it was still a difficult subject, I didn't have to tell her, but she just thought it would help her cope with being alone too.

I shook my head and admitted that it would feel good to talk about him. I confessed that he had not been the kind of man likely to make a great father, and so Stella had never known him.

In the privacy of that booth with Vicky I went back in time. When I told her how we had met, I could no longer hear the clatter of teacup in saucer, or the door banging shut after new customers.

It had been raining the night we met so the smell of damp coats only brought the memory more vividly to life. I was free as a bird then, unattached and happily so. Cutting hair during the day and partying at night. I didn't want any more than that. I never felt so alive as when I had men's adoring eyes on me in the pubs and clubs. Such a simple thing to crave. Such an easy thing to achieve. The moment I had them though, I no longer wanted them.

I'd had a sense he was coming, I admitted to Vicky.

Of course, she wanted to know what I meant.

I'd visited a psychic with my friends. Each of us egged the other on at Hull Fair, where colourful, ornate caravans lined the street – home to many a fortune-teller. We'd all crowded into one, but the gold-adorned, wrinkle-faced woman had immediately targeted me. Said he was coming. We'd all giggled of course at the rudeness of the phrase.

She said my twin flame was on the way.

What the hell's one of those? I'd asked.

The fortune-teller explained that, unlike a soul mate – which is our perfect match – a twin flame is our perfect mirror. Relationships with them tend to be on-again-off-again, often painful, always intense. They ultimately serve to show us who we truly are. She said mine was close. That I would know him when we met. And that we had known each other many times in previous lives.

I laughed and said *bullshit*, and we all flounced out of the caravan. But her words stayed with me.

And now I know she was right.

A week later I had a bad experience on a date. It's not even fair to call it a date. It was simply an evening in a pub with a man I'd known for an hour. A man whose initial attention I'd liked, but whose insistence that I have sex in the toilets with him irritated me. I'm no prude. I'd done this before. But I got a bad vibe from him.

Vicky interrupted here to ask why I put myself in so much danger.

I didn't have an answer. I sipped my coffee and admitted it was all about the conquest. I'd collected men the way others might collect stamps or coins or oddly shaped stones.

Go on, she said.

I did. I told Vicky how I'd staggered from the pub, with this man's vile words following me. Outside, it was raining so heavily that my hair stuck to my face in minutes. I needed to get home. Vanity meant I could not be seen by anyone looking such a wreck. This was long before we had mobile phones, so I looked up the street for a taxi. As though hailed from heaven, one arrived. I opened the door and asked if he was free, but he said he had a pick-up. He must have seen how miserable I was and he promised that if his passenger didn't arrive in five minutes, he'd take me home, and I could wait in the car until then.

Vicky interrupted my nostalgia with a big smile, and asked if it was *him*, the taxi driver.

I laughed, said, *No, though he was memorable.*

I could still recall the name in capitals on his dashboard: BOB FRACKLEHURST. I mentioned to him how unusual it was, and asked if he knew its history. He said he believed there was a very old house on the North Yorkshire moors called The Fracklehurst, and that his great-great grandfather had owned it. He was just explaining how the place was said to be haunted by a little blind girl when the car door opened.

He got in.

My twin flame.

I knew.

I didn't really take in what he looked like. That came later when I'd got my thoughts in order. That was the only way to describe it; he messed up my thoughts. Disabled my ability to think straight. It was like when a famous person arrives on stage and you know well before because of the way the audience screams. Except it was my heart that screamed.

He opened his mouth to ask what the hell I was doing in his cab – I knew that was going to be the question even though he didn't say a word – and I saw the same scramble occur in his eyes. Saw that he too felt it. He held my gaze. It could have lasted a minute, could have been a second; but it felt like an hour.

I heard Vicky say *wow*, bringing me back to earth.

I wished she hadn't.

For that brief moment, I was there. Back with him.

So what happened? she asked.

I closed my eyes. Tried to feel it again. Recall how he nourished me, simply by being close by. That first time we met, he said to Bob Fracklehurst – without tearing his eyes from mine – that we should take me home first. For the entire journey, we drank one another in. I was vaguely aware of Bob saying he was sure he knew him from somewhere. Asking if he'd been on TV or something? I thought then that it must have just been his aura. That this man's hypnotising presence must have been felt by others too. Made them *think* he was a somebody.

I didn't ask his name, though. Not that night.

And he didn't ask mine.

My breathing slowed, merged with his. It was then that I took in the slick black hair, thick and powerful around his face. His heavy face – one that someone else might say almost crossed the line between formidable and ugly. I studied his dark eyes, the fine lines at their corners, the large nose, as though I knew I'd have to rely on just my memory of him one day.

When we got to my house, he paid Bob Fracklehurst and got out with me. I hadn't asked him. Bob looked worried. His concern was natural. He knew we'd just met. That we'd sat in the back of his car without uttering a word. And now this man was coming into my house.

I leaned in through the car window. Said Bob didn't need to worry about me. This was my twin flame. The two words came out before I could think about it. Bob must have been an open-minded kind of guy. He didn't even blink. Gently, he said he had only been driving cabs for three years, but he already got a strong sense about people. And he whispered to me that this man was bad news.

I didn't listen.

I watched Bob drive away, and went inside with the man, having still not exchanged a single word.

So what happened that night? asked Vicky.

I opened my eyes. Snapped back to our booth in the café. The rest of my coffee was cold. Vicky had finished her sandwiches. I shook my head. Some things are sacred. Not to be shared with another. How can you describe, without resorting to clichés, a night so violently passionate, that you felt the next day you had been in a car crash?

I told Vicky simply that from then on, I was obsessed.

So what happened? Vicky wanted to know.

I asked if she meant when I got pregnant, and she nodded.

That part of our story I didn't want to explore. Because it was the moment I lost him the first time. Let him go. I'd found out I was pregnant too far along to do anything other than go ahead with it. I decided I'd rather keep the memory of what we'd had than share his love with our child. A needy kid might dilute what he felt for me.

I didn't care that Bob Fracklehurst had been right.

My twin flame was bad news.

But someone who is wrong for the world can be perfectly right for you.

Vicky said she would have to go soon. Her mum was taking her shopping in Mothercare. I looked at the café's clock and was shocked to see that we'd been there for two hours. What kind of doula was I to unburden my issues on this young woman? She seemed buoyed by my words though. As we put our coats on she said I had given her courage.

Made her see. She said she would tell me about her child's father. When she was ready.

Soon, she promised.

And she admitted that, once the child had arrived, and when she was up to it, she was going to do absolutely everything to get him back. That she thought he was *her* twin flame too.

I smiled. I said I would help her.

That I understood love like that more than anyone.

28

STELLA

NOW

As we head towards the news at 2am, I'm tempted for a brief moment to leave the studio; the radio station; the whole town. I imagine lining up enough songs to take listeners into Gilly Morgan's prerecorded show at three; imagine saying my final goodbyes and turning out the lights and going.

No. I must speak to the listeners. But my throat is parched. The song dies; Lionel Ritchie's hello becomes goodbye. I remember Tom saying earlier on the phone how final my goodbye sounded. Despite his strange behaviour recently, his new habit of falling asleep early, he was clingy when we hung up. Afraid I wouldn't come home. The weird thing is that, although I feel like my world will collapse if he deserts me, I could quite happily be the one to go.

I slide up the fader.

'We're heading for the news on the hour,' I say. The reheated news, I want to say. Same old shit; all the stuff you've already heard. 'And after that, I bet you lovers who are still awake want some peace. Some time together without me interrupting. So I'm going to give you that. We'll have seven love songs, one after another, chosen by you. Thanks for all the requests. See you on the other side.'

One more song will get us to the news. I barely look at what I select. And I've all but forgotten to keep to the secrets theme. Now there are too many in my real life. I'm going to find out who my real father is.

Did I select such a theme for my final show because I knew this was going to happen?

Was it a gut feeling I missed?

Do I really want to know? What if knowing who my father is leads to regret? Is it better to fantasise about a mystical figure, as I often did when small? Am I heading for the greatest disappointment of my life?

Something crashes outside. I leap to my slither of window. It's cloudy again so I can't see a thing. Do I *want* to? But it could be Maeve. What if she's out there and in some sort of trouble? I turn, approach the shadowy corridor. Feel for the light switch. Flick it. Nothing. *Shit.* Now what?

I feel my way along the passage and into the foyer, praying the light in there will come on when I flick the switch. It does. I exhale hard.

The door buzzer sounds and I scream.

I daren't approach the little screen that shows who's on the other side.

My mum? Surely. She's on her way, after all.

Or what if The Man Who Knows is here early?

What if he heard me announce that several songs were coming up and thinks it's so he has a chance to speak at length with me. On cue, electric blue flashes at the end of the corridor. I'm torn between getting the phone and answering the door. The buzzer sounds again, urgent.

I run back, pick up the phone, and say, 'Stella McKeever, one moment please,' and then head for the door. It's my mum on the screen.

Thank God.

She looks small. I remember how she filled a room when she was dressed up to go out. How, as a small child, I felt warm in her dazzling light, even when she shone it in another direction.

I open the door. The light from the foyer momentarily makes her look young again. Like we are the same age.

'I hope you don't mind,' she says, as she always does, eternally apologising for being here after so long away.

'Not at all.' I close the door after her.

'Are you okay?' She studies me, concerned.

I must look a state. 'It's just … been a hell of a night. One of the presenters hasn't turned up and we're worried sick. Then I heard something outside and was a bit spooked.'

'Oh, that was me, sorry. There are no lights on out there and I fell over the bin.'

'Yeah, they've gone out in the corridor too.'

She has a carrier bag in her hand. When she sees me looking at it she says, 'It's for you. But not yet.'

As in my game with Tom, I ask nothing. 'Come in.'

I go into the studio. She follows. She may not have been to my home, but she's been here. This has been my second home for five years, really, seven if you include my training, so she has seen where I mostly exist.

'Do you want a coffee?' I ask.

'No, I'm okay.'

I see the phone's receiver off the hook and remember there's a caller waiting. 'Just need to get this,' I tell her, and then say 'hello' into the mouthpiece.

'Stella,' he says. The Man Who Knows.

'I can't talk now,' I whisper.

'Do you have someone there?'

I frown. Has he been watching the building? Is he already here?

'You do,' he says. 'Are you sure someone should be there when I bring my photographs?'

'No,' I hiss, turning away from my mum. 'It'll just be me. Don't ring again. I'll see you when we agreed.'

I hang up and try and compose myself.

'Who was that?' asks my mum. 'Are you okay, Stella?'

I nod. Lie. I realise that, even though I've lined up seven songs – something Stephen will *not* be happy about when he finds out – we still only have about twenty-five minutes. It isn't long; a pathetic amount of time for a life-changing discussion. I decide that, since she doesn't want a drink, I'll get straight to it.

'I can't believe you were Victoria Valbon's doula,' I say.

'It's true,' she admits.

'It's just ... why didn't you tell me when she *died*? I even mentioned it to you, the day after, when it hit the news. When they announced her name, you said *nothing* about knowing her!'

My mum perches on edge the of the desk, still clutching the carrier bag, as though, if she puts it down for a moment, I'll snatch it and pull out the contents.

'Before she died she was...' she begins '...just another client. Just another girl. No, that's not fair. She was more than that. We got ... *close*. And then when ... when it happened ... well, I was in shock. I just couldn't ... I didn't know what you'd think. What *anyone* would think. But then ... now...'

'What?' I ask.

'I'm telling you in case you find out.'

'Find out *what*?'

'What I wanted to tell you earlier on the phone.' She pauses. 'You deal with the news here so you're bound to hear it. I know they haven't said who it is yet. But they might.'

'Said who what is?'

'I'm being interviewed by the police. About Vicky's murder.'

'*You*?'

She nods. 'It's because I knew her.'

'Yes, but ... it's *you*? The new *suspect*?'

I wonder if she knows that Tom was questioned, too. Did Victoria tell her who the father of her baby was? She *must* have done. This all races through my head, but I don't want to ask any of it. Don't want her to know Tom was questioned. Surely if she knew, she would say so? But she didn't tell me she'd known Victoria. I glance quickly at my window to find calm; it doesn't work.

'I'm not a suspect,' she says. 'That's something more official. Even if they say that on the news, I'm not. I'm just helping them with their enquiries. It's all voluntary. Lots of people who knew her have done that. I was at the station yesterday.'

'What did they want to know?'

'Just about my time with her,' my mum admits. 'You know, our relationship.'

'You told me earlier that you fell out.'

'Yes,' she says softly. 'We did. But I won't tell them that. It doesn't make me look very good, does it? And it has *nothing* to do with her death.'

'You're going to *lie*?'

'It isn't lying if you don't mention something, is it?'

What can I say to that? Is she right? And aren't we all liars, then?

'I have to go again in a few days,' she says; 'and I think that should be it.'

'*Should*?'

'I've nothing to hide.'

Except she has. She has hidden my father from me all of my life. Hidden herself from me for most of it too. She seems to realise the weight of her words.

'With regards to Vicky,' she adds.

I sigh heavily. 'What if her family knows you fell out? She must have told them? What if they tell the police, and you don't? How will that look?' I pause. 'How *did* you fall out?'

'It doesn't matter,' she says. 'Don't we have more important things to talk about?'

'We do.' I glance at the monitor; we have nineteen minutes now. 'But I'm still curious.'

'Let me tell you another day,' she says. 'When we have more time. If we get into that, we won't have time for...'

My father, I think.

'Tell me about the star perfume.' The words leave my mouth before I know I've put them together.

My mum closes her eyes and inhales as though smelling it again. The gift I once had for knowing how she felt – for feeling it myself – floods through my system. Carrie Martin's "Maria in the Moon" plays; my favourite song this month. The haunting words narrate my emo-tions. *You left your story up in space*. It's coming down now. My mum is bringing it down. I feel childlike joy rise up through her. Thinking about him makes her feel this way. It's familiar to me. Tom makes me feel the same.

'It was the only thing he ever gave me,' she says. 'That's why I cherished it so much. Why I only wore the perfume when it was just me and you.'

'I'm sorry it's gone,' I say.

'Where did you lose it?'

'If I knew that...'

She nods. 'I know you looked but you won't find it online. It was a one-off. He had the scent specially made. He chose all the ingredients. Said it was perfectly me. The bottle belonged to his grandmother and was made of the finest glass. When he was little she used to say that the crystal stopper had actual stars trapped in it. He got it when she died because he was the only grandchild. He told me he kept it for the day when he found a woman who deserved it.' She strokes the carrier bag. 'He gave it to me just a month after we met. Stella, there's no explaining the love between us. I couldn't fight it. And I couldn't share it.' She looks at me. 'With you.'

'You kept him from me because you didn't want him to *love* me?'

'I thought it would dilute how he felt about *me*.'

The song ends. Another starts.

'He'd gone anyway,' she adds. 'He had to leave just when I found out I was pregnant.'

'Where did he go?' I ask.

Ignoring my question, she says, 'So I decided to let him. I thought I could live with the memory of what we'd had. Thought that would sustain me. I dated so many men when you were small, I know that. I think I was looking for something – anything half as powerful as what we'd had would have been good. But I never found it.' She pauses. 'Until he wrote and asked me to go back to him when you were...'

'Twelve,' I finish. 'I carried that perfume everywhere.'

'I know.'

Finally, I say what I've always wanted to. I speak softly, my pain quiet.

'You *left* me. It was the cruellest thing anyone has ever done to me. Not a word for fourteen years and then you come back. No warning. And I let you in. I let you back into my life. I asked for nothing.'

'I'm sorry.'

'Are you though?'

She doesn't answer. 'I *am* sorry that I've hurt you so much,' she eventually says.

'You went back to be with him. He wrote to you and you dropped everything. Your life. Me.' I glare at her. 'Did you ever think of me? Feel bad that you'd left me with our neighbour while you fell into the arms of your *great love*?'

'I did,' she insists.

'Was he worth it?'

She doesn't answer; her silence says it all. There's a break in the music – a caesura. Time seems to stop. In the space, something occurs to me.

'Now I know – it was because he died, wasn't it? You were alone, so you came back. If he was alive you'd still be with him and I'd still be more or less an orphan.'

She doesn't deny it.

'And you have the nerve to ask why you've not been to my home.' I turn my back on her and go to my window. Clouds have suffocated all the light. 'Do you really want to know why I never asked you over?' I pause; she doesn't speak. I'm thawing, the hurt is thawing, and I don't know what to do with it. 'I didn't know why at first, but I do now. I didn't want to give you the opportunity to come to the place I called home and leave me all over again.'

'That's fair enough,' she says sadly. 'I deserve that.' After a moment, she adds, 'Did you ever look for me when you'd grown up?'

'Not once.'

'I don't blame you.'

I think of the speech I prepared long, long ago. The words I planned to say to her if she returned.

Mum, I'm happy you're back. I've wished for this. Every day. But you don't need to stay. I talk to you at night. See you in the stars. And that's enough. You're better up there where the light never goes. If I let you back into my daytime world you might leave again.

But I don't say them.

'Who is he then?' I turn to face her again. 'My father.'

My mum pales. If she has prepared for this moment, she's not ready enough. 'I gave you clues,' she says.

'Clues? That's not fair. This isn't a game.'

I want desperately to cry.

She comes over to me. She takes my hands when she speaks. They are cold. Mine warm them. She looks me in the eyes for the first time. Her irises flash blue, like the phone, like they did when she was young and full of life. It occurs to me that they flash when she thinks of him.

She tells me about the biggest clue.

And I know who he is. She doesn't need to say his name.

I know.

I let go of her and run to the toilets and I'm violently sick.

29

STELLA

THEN

I used to pretend my father was Buck Rogers.

When I was little, and my mum was still around, I'd sit and watch an old video of the TV show *Buck Rogers in the 25th Century,* while she was out partying. Sandra-next-door lent it to me. In the end, I wore the tape out and as his image faded in my head too, I pretended my dad was someone else. Sometimes a pop star; sometimes a film star.

Once at school, I was dumb enough to say that my real father was on the telly. I endured weeks of ribbing. Weeks of finding posters of random celebrities stuck to my cloakroom peg with the word DAD scrawled over them. Children are so clever; they can spot the vulnerable kids. It all died down after a while, when they found someone new to mock, but I kept quiet about my father's identity for the rest of my school days.

Until Sandra.

Once I had lived with her for a few years and I loved her the way you love people who have accepted you with utter kindness, I told her about my fantasy fathers. Neither of us had mentioned my mum for a long time. A social worker visited a few times in the months after Sandra had to declare I now lived with her, but she must have found the home – and Sandra – perfectly adequate for an abandoned child, because she left us to it.

Sandra and I were sitting at her kitchen table one afternoon, a place we often drank our coffee or ate sausage sandwiches and caught up on the day's activities. I must have been about sixteen because I was in the midst of my exams. I hated revision, mainly because there were no subjects I enjoyed, and I had no idea what I wanted to do or be.

'It'll all soon be over,' said Sandra, stirring sugar into her coffee.

I drank mine strong, unsweetened. She always joked about me being sweet enough already, to which I'd raise my eyebrows, because we both knew it was the last word anyone would choose to describe me.

'What *are* you going to do, Stella?' she sighed.

'What do you mean?' I could be sulky with Sandra and she never rose to it. Never lost her temper, as though she felt I'd been through enough already.

'Are you going into sixth form? You'll have to decide, you know. Or do you think an apprenticeship might be the way for you? Learn a job while you're doing it?'

I shrugged. I just didn't care.

'What are your friends doing?' she asked.

'Clare's staying on in sixth form. Shauna's going to work at her dad's double-glazing company.'

'Shame you don't have—' Sandra stopped mid-sentence and shook her head.

'What?' I asked.

'I didn't think,' she said.

'*What*? Tell me.'

She looked sad. Eventually said, 'I was going to say that it's a shame you don't have a father with a thriving company and the chance of a job there.'

I laughed. Couldn't help it. All I could see was Buck Rogers. A job with him would mean futuristic space adventures in a skin-tight white suit, with a squeaky-voiced robot as our sidekick. I laughed some more.

'What?' she asked.

'Remember years ago, when you gave me that old video cassette with episodes of Buck Rogers on?'

'Oh, that. I always wondered where it had gone.'

'I kept it. Watched it over and over. I used to...'

'What?' Sandra asked softly.

'Pretend he was my dad,' I admitted. 'Daft, I know. I suppose I thought it would be cool to have a dad like that, who was famous. A hero, I guess.'

Sandra reached out as though to touch my hand and seemed to think better of it. She knew me well. Knew that I often rejected physical comfort, simply because I didn't know how to respond to it.

'Did your mum never even hint who he was?' she asked.

I shook my head. 'I asked her a couple of times, when I was little. She told me he was the kind of father who was better off out of my life.' I paused. 'Who was *she* to make that decision?'

'Maybe it was a genuine choice,' suggested Sandra. 'Maybe he hurt her, and she was protecting you?'

'I don't think that's it. She talked about him like he was someone … godly almost. I never got the feeling he'd done anything like that.'

'Do you wish you knew him?'

I wasn't sure. That my mother had seen fit to keep him a mystery, that she had clearly idolised him, meant he remained an enigma. The reality might be dull. Ordinary.

And I didn't want that.

'Do you know which saying I hate more than anything,' I said, suddenly angry and not sure why. '*It's better to have loved and lost than never to have loved at all*. Our teacher quoted it in English. Some knob called Tennyson wrote it. No thanks. I'd rather not bother. Then no one can hurt you.'

'You might change your mind one day,' said Sandra, softly.

'I *won't*,' I insisted. I hated it when adults told me what I might or might not do. How the hell could they presume to know me that well?

'Shall I put some chips on?' Sandra always offered me food when she didn't know what else to say to me.

'Not hungry,' I snapped, and pushed my chair under the table.

Sandra stood too. Looked at me. I knew the look. It was the one that meant she wished she could change things. *I wish I could get your mum back. I wish I could make it all good for you.*

But I didn't want her to.

I went to my room. Opened the window. It was the end of May so not cold enough to freeze my feelings. I preferred to see my mother as part of the sky; I saw my father there too; and myself. I was some fascinating, distant star that lit up the sky but would disintegrate if it ever fell to earth.

30

ELIZABETH

THEN

We were on our West Park bench when she finally told me about her baby's father. Vicky and me. Doula and client. The sun was hot and high. The August roses were vivid in the glare. So many colours – pink and red and yellow. She was as swollen as a balloon by then. I had watched her blossom over the last five months. Watched the small, curving tummy grow into a fully fledged pregnancy.

When I first arrived that day, Vicky seemed somehow different. I think it was a Sunday, because when I play it over in my head now, I remember she said she wasn't bothered about missing her mum's Sunday lunch on such a hot day. She said she was sick of seeing happy family life and feeling separate from it. Sick of being alone. A single mum. There are new things I recall each time I think of that day again. New details, like a child running past us and falling over and crying for her mum as her grandad cradled her.

I think of it a lot, you see. That afternoon. I think about our whole relationship a lot. Because two weeks after that Vicky was dead and neither of us had any idea it was coming.

I bought us an ice lolly each from the van nearby, and when I returned with them, Vicky asked if I remembered what she'd said. I must have looked blank – she had said many things during our time together – so she reminded me; asked if I recalled that rainy afternoon in the café when she had said that she was going to get her baby's father back once she'd given birth and felt up to it?

I licked cherry-juice drops from the back of my hand and nodded.

Vicky said she felt she was up to it now. *Why wait*, she said. She might be knackered after the birth if it was difficult. She would look tired and washed out. Have hormones pulsing through her. Leaking breasts and saggy belly. She laughed and said it would hardly be her most seductive moment, while now she felt good. Her hair was full of bounce and her cheeks were glowing.

I had to agree. Sometimes I couldn't tear my eyes from her. Even now, I see her as an angel. Glowing from the inside.

What are you going to do? I asked.

Vicky finished her lime ice lolly and sucked on the stick. Juice stained her chin. I remember wanting to wipe it off, almost licking my sleeve and dabbing at her, the way you do a messy child. She said she was going to see him the next day. She knew where he lived. There was just one big problem: he had a new girlfriend. She studied me to gauge my response.

I thought about Stella's father. Imagined him with another woman. What would I have done to get him back?

Anything.

I asked if this other woman was pregnant, and she said she didn't think so. She admitted to having gone past the house, seen her coming out.

I told Vicky that having a child together meant *they* had something he and this other woman didn't. I knew she hadn't told him about the pregnancy. She said once that they split up just before she found out – one of the other ways that her relationship paralleled mine with Stella's father. Vicky had said a few times that they had lots of mutual friends who'd have passed the news on.

Now Vicky said that she didn't like the idea of breaking up a relationship, but she had realised that family was everything. That he deserved the chance to be a dad to his child. And that the story of my passionate love for Stella's father had made her realise Tom was the one.

A crisp leaf fell from the tree above us and landed in her lap. She turned it over and traced her finger along its ridges. Then she looked at me. Hesitated. Said she was hoping that, if he took her back, then he could be with her at the birth after all. There was time. She had another month. She wanted him to be the one to tell her whether they had had a son or a daughter.

Do you mind? Vicky asked me.

She'd asked *me* to be the first to know her child's gender. This meant she would no longer need me to be her doula. In a sense, we'd be over. I realised I'd have no one to talk to about Stella's father. No one to drink in my words and ask for more.

As though she had seen all of this flitting across my face, Vicky quickly added that I had been everything to her this year. That without me she would not have left her bed. I licked the corner of my sleeve and wiped the green juice off her chin. I couldn't recall ever doing such a thing for Stella. Vicky smiled. I told her she should go get her man back. Go get her twin flame. Do anything.

And I meant it.

Until she said his name. Showed me a picture of him. It was at my request, so I could hardly blame her.

I said, *Tell me about him.*

And she did. She said they had only been together a year, but they got engaged quite early on. She flushed when she admitted that it was the most intense thing she'd ever experienced. That at times he was so demanding it wore her out. And that's what had caused the split – he exhausted her. But now she said she was beginning to realise that Tom's traits were merely his passion. How he expressed his love.

Tom's traits.

The words made me frown. A coincidence? Yes, that was all it was, I thought. Both my daughter and Vicky – two women the same age – had a Tom. I asked if Vicky had a picture of him. She pulled out her phone and swiped through images, stopping at one that made her eyes fill with tears. She showed me. At first, I thought my eyes were playing tricks on me. That the sunlight through the leaves had bounced off the screen and distorted his face.

It was our Tom. *Stella's* Tom. Tom who I'd only met twice but whose striking face was permanently stuck in my head. Tom who Stella had sensed was coming.

Had Vicky clicked on the wrong picture?

She was looking at me. Asking what I thought of him.

A million thoughts crashed into my head. How was it possible? Why did it have to be *him*? I couldn't let it happen. I had to stop Vicky trying to get him back. It was imagining my daughter's man being taken from her that finally ignited maternal passion in me. This was how I should have felt when she was born. When she cried, when she needed me. This was how I should have felt when her father got back in touch. I should have turned him down and stayed with her.

It didn't matter. I felt it now: I was a lioness protecting her cub. At long last the glory of motherly love engulfed me. And I knew I could not let Vicky take Tom from my daughter.

Under any circumstances.

Are you okay? she was asking me.

I told her, *Yes. I just feel a little unwell. Maybe the ice lolly gave me acid.*

I composed myself. Then I told her that Tom was handsome. But maybe she shouldn't be too hasty. Maybe she was heading for heartbreak if she went looking for him. What if he was happy in his new relationship? What if he rejected her? How much would that hurt?

Vicky frowned at me. Asked why I'd changed my mind. Said I'd only just insisted that having this baby meant they had something Tom's new girlfriend and he didn't. Then she put a hand on mine and asked if I was sad that she might not need me at the birth if Tom took her back and decided to be there.

Another leaf fell, this time into my lap. They were turning golden early this year. I studied it to give me time to think up a response.

Eventually I told Vicky that I cared deeply about her and it wasn't about whether I was at her birth or not. That what we had shared was about more than me being her doula. I wanted her to be happy. And I was concerned that she might be heading for more heartbreak.

What if Tom loves his new girlfriend deeply? I asked her. *What if the upset affects you and the baby?*

Vicky looked thoughtful.

After a while she whispered that, if Tom and she were meant to be, then it would happen. She reminded me that he could be her twin flame, just as Stella's father had been mine.

What could I say to that?

I had to come up with something.

I suggested she wait until her baby was here, as she'd initially planned. That would buy me time to think of a way to change her mind. I added that, if she turned up with his child in her arms, Tom might find it hard to resist her.

Vicky suddenly let out an *oof* sound.

Just the baby, she explained, rubbing her tummy. *Kicking again.*

I'd felt those kicks many times in the last few weeks. I'd stroked her belly more than my own when I'd been pregnant. She put my hand there now. I felt the ripples of flesh as her child wriggled and squirmed. A baby I had no idea then would never exist outside her womb.

Vicky said that she was determined to give Tom the chance to see his baby being born. That most of the women at her antenatal group had said they couldn't imagine not having their husbands or boyfriends with them for that life-changing moment.

But he's not your man, I wanted to scream.

He's Stella's.

I knew if I pushed Vicky she'd begin to wonder why. I couldn't have her know who Tom was to me, because then she'd know my efforts to stop her were selfish. She'd end our relationship and pursue Tom without restraint. She had incited motherly affection in me, had given me the chance to talk freely about the love of my life, but now she was threatening to destroy my real daughter's love life, and *that* I couldn't permit.

Why don't you wait? I said. *Think about it for a few days and then see how you feel. If by then you still feel strongly that you want to go and see him before the baby comes, I could take you. Wait in the car in case it doesn't go how you want it to. I couldn't bear to see you hurt.*

Vicky nodded. She admitted that the pregnancy hormones might be making her behave rashly. She said she hadn't told her mum that she wanted Tom back because she thought she would disapprove. She hadn't particularly liked him.

Mums know best, I said.

Vicky laughed.

I asked if she wanted to walk for a bit, to go and see the birds in the aviary. I needed to get her thinking about something else. As we strolled around the park, I thought about the last time I'd been with Stella and Tom. We had gone for a drink at the marina. Sat on a wall with our beers. Every time he spoke she held his gaze so intently that I knew nothing else existed. I knew that look. She told me once that he had a way of saying the most ordinary thing and making it sound like poetry. She had that gift too and I don't think she knew it.

I had abandoned Stella and would have to live with that for the rest of my life. But now I could stop it happening again. I could stop Tom deserting her for another woman.

And I would do absolutely anything to make sure he didn't.

To make sure that Vicky kept well away.

31

STELLA

NOW

I think of *cinéma vérité*. Truth cinema. I'm in the middle of my own film, but there is no camera to record the moment; no camera to capture my vomit swirling like a whirlpool down the toilet. Hunched over it, I grip the seat and then sit back on my heels.

My mum taps on the door and asks if I'm okay. I want to ask whether she has the good camera with her, the one with a zoom lens and all the fancy gadgets and functions. If she takes a picture of me right now it will be the most truthful one ever taken. My face will tell my whole story.

I open the door. She stands there, sheepish, concerned, hair messed. 'The *camera*,' I say, realising something else.

She looks confused. 'What about it?'

'It was *his*, wasn't it?' I pause, readying myself to say the two words I've been reading repeatedly for the last few weeks. The two words on the cover of the book on my bedside table. 'It was Harland Grey's. My father's.'

'It was.' She speaks softly. 'It was Harland's. I can't use it the way he did. My pictures used to come out all blurry, as you know. I've practised since but they're still not the best. I can't part with it.' She seems to have an idea. 'Would *you* like it?'

'No,' I snap. 'I bloody wouldn't.'

I push past her, stagger into the foyer. What time is it? How long did I throw up for? How long do we have left? I look at the clock above the door. Just ten minutes until the songs end. I can always talk for a bit on air and then resume the conversation with my mum, but now I know who my father is I realise I want to deal with it on my own.

The way I've always dealt with things.

'Harland fucking Grey,' I say. 'No. *No*. I reckon you're making it up. Using some local celebrity's name so you don't have to tell me that my dad's actually boring John from up the road, or the postman.'

Even as I say the words, I know they're not true. Now that I know my mum left the book here, it all makes absolute sense. I want to deny it, but there was something that felt right when she revealed he was my dad. I can't explain it. Reading the book did at times feel like I was reading someone's diary. Someone I knew.

Stella, this will tell you everything.

That note.

'It's him,' she says. 'He's really your father.'

'And you thought that leaving a book about him would just make me think, ahhh, *this* is my dad!'

'I don't know,' she admits.

'How the hell did you get in here?'

'That time I came to the studio with you – I remembered the code. And I just sneaked in and left it.'

'Some other presenter could have taken it.'

'That's why I came during your show,' she says. 'And left the note on it.'

I go back into the studio. The song is a love ballad from the eighties, the title of which I can't recall. The clichéd words mock this moment; a totally inappropriate soundtrack. I go to my window. One star shines alone. I'm there with it, like when I was small.

'Tell me about him,' I say. 'We've got less than ten minutes now. What do I need to know that isn't in that bloody book? What more is there – other than the fact that he was this reclusive, obsessive film-maker?'

'Why don't you just ask me what *you* want to know,' she says.

'Okay then. How did he like his coffee?'

'You're being facetious, Stella.'

'Are you *surprised*?' I compose myself. Turn to face her. 'Did he ever know about me?'

My mum shakes her head. 'I thought it was for the best that he didn't.'

'The best for who?' I demand.

'For me,' she admits.

'Fair enough. At least you're being honest. Why best for you?'

'Don't you think it's odd,' she says, ignoring my question. 'He tried to capture the truth and, in a way, you speak the truth on a radio station. You have a way of talking that's so like him. I can't describe it, but it's there. You're alike. You *are*.'

She might be right.

I don't want her to be.

'He *killed* a woman,' I snap.

'He did,' admits my mum. 'I can't forgive or condone that. But it didn't stop my love. Nothing could. That's the thing, Stella; it was like nothing you can imagine. He committed a brutal act, but he wasn't a serial killer or anything. It was...'

'Art,' I finish, sarcasm dripping from the word. 'I know. He was quoted in that bloody book as saying that Rebecca March was part of the art he created. What was it now? Oh yes ... he was just the *catalyst* of the situation. He was capturing the truth of her death. But who was *he* to decide when she died? I can understand murder driven by passion. By people who are angry or jealous or blinded by the intensity of their emotions. But to coldly kill a young girl as part of a film, and then call it art?' I shake my head. 'No. That I don't get. How can you make excuses for what he did? How could you go *back* to him?'

'I loved him.'

The three words used by many humans over the centuries to justify a bad relationship. *Love is all you need*, croons the singer on the radio. Why all the fuss over romantic love? Why do we glamorise it? Excuse horrific crimes because of it?

How far would I go for Tom?

I've surrendered to every one of his desires so far. I've kept myself interesting. I've played all the games to keep him utterly enthralled. And I *love* him. Like my mum loved my father?

No.

I do not.

Do I?

'I'm guessing my father went to prison?' I say. 'That it's where he went when you got pregnant with me?'

She nods.

'And when you left me when I was twelve it was because he was freed?'

She nods again.

'Harland can't have been his real name,' I say.

'It was. It was the only one he ever gave me.'

'I imagine he'll be dead proud that you're a murder suspect too? Two peas in a pod, you are.'

'Stella,' she sighs, 'I'm not a suspect, I told you that. I'm just answering their questions. And Vicky's murder was nothing like Rebecca March's. That was a crime of passion.'

'Was it? How do *you* know that?'

'The papers. The news. How do you think?'

I hold my mum's gaze. She looks away first. 'I can't imagine Vicky or Rebecca cared how it happened,' I say. 'They probably both just wished it *wasn't* happening. They probably both fought to live.' I come back to the desk and lean against it. 'What was he like then? In everyday life?'

'Fascinating,' she says. 'Intense. In our early days, he often went off to make his films and take his pictures. He always had one project or another. I never went along, but when he came home he sparked with energy and we...' She closes her eyes. I close mine. This, I don't want to know. Am I afraid it will be similar to Tom's and my passion? 'Anyway,' she continues, 'as a young man, he was vigorous and passionate about everything he did. About me.' She pauses. 'Prison changed him.'

'It's supposed to,' I say.

Ignoring me, she continues, 'After his time there he was more subdued. He'd lost some of his spark. I brought a bit of it back, I think. But he never made another film. He still took photographs. Always liked the human form.'

'Alive or dead?' I can't help but ask.

'Stella, he killed once, and he paid for it. Served his time. That was part of an experimental film he was making, and yes, he took it too far. But I was never afraid of him. *Ever*. He never hurt me. And no one ever made me feel more alive.'

I glance at the monitor. We have just five minutes until I must speak to the listeners. Are they out there waiting, or have they all fallen asleep by now? Is Tom awake?

'Harland *never* bored me,' my mum finishes.

'But I did,' I say softly.

'Did you?' She frowns.

'Yes. I could tell. Your eyes always wandered when I chatted as a kid. I could tell you wanted to be anywhere but with me.' I rub my arms. 'Now I know where you wanted to be.'

'I'm sorry,' she whispers.

'You're not,' I say.

'I *am*,' she insists.

'If we could go back,' I ask, 'would you stay with me instead of going to him?'

She doesn't answer.

'Exactly,' I say. 'You're not sorry. But I don't mind. I was always terrified I'd be dull as a kid. But having that sort of thought only makes us strive harder to resist whatever we're scared we might be, doesn't it? Tell a kid they're ugly and they'll spend their whole life dieting and wearing loads of make-up. If you knew me, you'd know I'm not dull.' I pause. 'God, if you *knew*.'

I glance at my mum and tears are streaming down her cheeks. I think of the many that I've held back over the years. I'm not bitter. I'm not angry. I don't wish her any pain, in fact I hate to think of her hurting. I still love her. But her sadness isn't my responsibility. *She* isn't. She has chosen her life just as I have chosen mine.

'Don't be sad,' I tell her. 'I'm not. We're here.'

She sniffs and nods.

'We're almost out of time,' I say softly.

She holds out the carrier bag. I take it carefully from her. Our fingers touch briefly. Hers are still cold.

'It's just a few pictures of Harland and me,' she says. 'They won't be like those formal ones they used in that biography. These are the real him, I suppose. The man I loved. Your father.'

His *cinéma vérité*, I think, in photograph form.

'I'll look at them later,' I tell her, knowing she expects me to open the bag now. I pause. 'Do you think he might have been a good dad?' I ask. 'Do you think he would have cared about me?'

My mum rolls up the carrier bag as though to occupy her hands. A new song begins. I know it's the last one I lined up. We have three minutes.

'I think he would have been, yes,' she says. 'I think he'd have adored you, but that's what I was scared of. My selfishness has denied you your dad and I can't undo that.'

'You should go,' I say. 'I need to be on air soon.'

I walk her into the foyer. We stand, awkward, by the door. The phone flashes blue in the studio behind her. It will have to wait. It's like lightning. I almost count in my head, waiting for the thunder to sound, like you do as a child.

'I did miss you sometimes,' I admit. 'So much that it was painful, physically I mean. I denied it to myself, but it was there. That was when I'd smell the star perfume. It revived me somehow.' I shake my head. 'Then I got used to it just being me.'

'You must miss the perfume now it's gone.'

'I do. More than I ever missed you.' I don't say this to be cruel, but because it's true. 'That bottle was the one thing I've known all my life and now it's gone.'

'Can you forgive me?' my mum asks.

The phone stops and the blue light dies.

'I can let the past go,' I say. 'Is that the same? I think it is. I haven't done too badly after all. Look at me. I'm well. I'm here. I have made a success of myself.'

'But you're *leaving*,' she says, clearly still shocked by it.

'Isn't it better to end on a high? You taught me well, Mum.'

'My star girl,' she says.

'You're making me sound like some book again.'

'I mean it. *You are*.'

'I really have to get to the studio,' I say. 'Will you keep the radio on when you get home?'

'Yes. Why?'

'Not sure yet.' I'm not. I don't know where the words come from. I just have a hunch again that she should tune in. 'Keep listening. All night.'

'I don't think I'll sleep anyway.'

'Guess I'll see you soon,' I say.

I open the door. Cold air trickles in. The fading smell of chips and candy floss from the fair follows it. Another gut feeling hits me so hard I gasp and clutch at my chest. My mum reaches for me, but I push her away, shake my head and insist she goes. As she walks away, I suddenly know she is going to see something terrible.

Tonight.

Soon.

I want to warn her. Find the words. Something. Anything. But she reaches the end of the carpark. She turns left and goes up the street.

It's too late.

I could be wrong. Maybe the gut feeling is for me?

But I don't think so.

32

STELLA

NOW

I close the door. The phone is flashing blue again. I rush into the studio, but I can't answer it. I'm out of time. The song dies, so I have to speak. I slide the fader up and open my mouth.

Nothing comes out.

Find the words. Something. *Anything.*

'This is Stella McKeever standing in for Maeve Lynch,' I say after a fatal second or two. 'It's almost two-thirty, and for those of you who are still awake I'm with you until three. And that was a whole lot of love for you there with our string of beautiful ballads. After the adverts, I'll return with some of your dedications. Make them juicy, now...'

Immediately, the phone flashes blue again.

'Stella McKeever,' I say.

'Why didn't you answer before?' he asks. The Man Who Knows.

'I couldn't,' I say.

'But you weren't on air.'

'I was busy.'

'With that woman who came to the studio?'

My heart stops. He must be outside. I glance at the window. He can't get in though. Can he? He didn't get in here to leave the Harland Grey – my *father's* – book, I know that now. And so he doesn't know the door code, surely. I want to demand if he knows where Maeve is, but what if he's nothing more than a desperate fan? Then I don't want him knowing she's missing.

'It's not three o'clock yet,' I say, hiding my nerves.

'You still want to meet?' He seems surprised.

'Yes.' My heart screams *no*. 'I want to see those pictures.'

'I told you, they're not pretty,' he says.

'*Life* isn't pretty.'

I suddenly feel brave. Have I been emboldened by what I've learned in the last half hour? That I'm the daughter of a murderer. I'm the daughter of a man who was a genius, who was interesting, who was *someone*. In the brilliant light of my true ancestry, I need to examine the truth in these pictures taken by The Man Who Knows. I'm not afraid. The truth is not something to fear.

My *father* knew that.

'You sound ... *different*.' The Man Who Knows is unnerved.

'It's all different now,' I say, more to myself.

'Is it? Has something happened?'

'Are you being absolutely honest when you say you have pictures of that night?' I ask him.

I *need* to see them. I won't be alone. By three Gilly Morgan will have arrived for her show. I don't want her to know about this meeting, but she'll be inside the building if I need her. Then I remember: she's in Vietnam for two weeks. Her show has been prerecorded.

I suppose I don't have to let him in. I can speak via the intercom at the door. Tell him to post the photos through. But what if he won't? No time to worry now. Face that when the show finishes.

'Absolutely honest,' he says.

'Then I'll see you in half an hour.'

I hang up and go and look out of the window. Why would I be scared of him being outside when I've invited him here? When I might let him in? I realise I'm not afraid of the outside world.

It's what might be in here that scares me.

The adverts finish and I tell the listeners about some of the upcoming shows this week. While I'm talking my phone flashes. A message from Jim. Desperate to read it, I rush my speech, and open the text.

I'm at hospital. Maeve hit by car. She's fine just shaken up. Cracked ribs and bruising. Keeping her in overnight. Thanks. Jim.

'Thank fuck,' I say to the empty studio. 'Thank *fuck*.'

And I cry. With relief. For Maeve. For me.

Then – despite her minor injuries, and what must have been a terrifying experience – I smile. Whisper 'Thank God' aloud. Maeve is okay. My gut feeling was for an accident, not an ending. The lovely, vivacious Maeve, who always makes time to talk, is okay. It's one thing I can stop worrying about.

I message Jim: *That's wonderful, give her my love! X*

But if I was right about Maeve, is my gut feeling about never seeing the stars again true too? Or does it mean one star in particular? The star perfume bottle?

I haven't seen it for weeks.

But I don't want to think about that right now.

At least knowing about Maeve makes room in my head for all the other revelations tonight. It means I can concentrate on getting through the show and then do what I must afterwards. Over the current song, I hear other lyrics; lines about fathers' identities, boyfriends' past fiancées, and mothers' insomniac admissions.

I send a quick message to Stephen about Maeve being okay, and then move the fader up and speak to the world again.

I realise someone might have to cover her show tomorrow night, and it definitely won't be me, or Gilly. I smile when I think of Stephen doing it, and the complaints he might get. There's a text from him on my phone.

So glad Maeve is okay. Couldn't sleep until I knew. Will call Jim in the morning. Thanks, Stella.

I stand and stretch, think about perhaps making coffee.

Then my phone flashes with Maeve's name. Probably Jim with an update. As always, I look to see how much time I have until the song ends. It's a habit that now infiltrates my everyday life. If I'm microwaving something at home, I check to see how long I have before answering a ringing phone. If it rings while I'm stirring pasta sauce or boiling an egg, I look at the clock. I wonder now if I'll still be doing it when I'm long gone from this place.

I swipe my phone's screen.

'Stella,' comes that gorgeous Irish voice.

'Maeve,' I say, feeling teary again.

'Yes,' she says.

How often I've secretly wished she was my real mum. It's a craving I've hidden even from myself; when the longing arose after we chatted each evening here, I buried it, cursed myself for being needy.

'How *are* you?' I ask. 'What happened? Shouldn't you be resting?'

'I'm trying to,' she says. 'Jim's just left and I'm on a ward with a serious insomniac who keeps trying to jump out of the window, and a woman who's snoring like a horse.'

I laugh. How she cheers me. I stand and move to my thin slither of a view. Outside, the sky is clear. Clearer than it has been all night. The stars look as though they are competing to burn the brightest.

'What on earth happened?' I ask.

'It's a bit of a blur,' she says. 'I was on my way to you. Had a plate of star-topped fairy buns for your last night. Those stars are spread halfway across Anlaby Road now. Anyway, I must've been miles away because I stepped out onto the road – and that was it. Next thing, I'm coming around, my ribs hurt, I've a corker of a bruise on my head, and some man is bending over me, looking worried.'

'We were worried too,' I tell her.

'Anyway, I just wanted to thank you for covering my show. I've been lying here listening. You're doing a wonderful job.' She pauses. 'Why are you leaving us, Stella? You're a fantastic presenter. It won't be the same.'

What can I say to her?

'Why do I think you won't stay in touch,' she says sadly.

'I will,' I lie.

'Well, I just wanted to say...' Maeve sighs. 'I wish we'd got to know one another better. Outside of the radio station, I mean. All of us are too busy, and that's sad. You're an elusive one, Stella, but I've grown very fond of you.'

'And I have you.' This isn't a lie.

'Sorry to miss your last night. Take care, won't you?'

'You too,' I say.

When we hang up, I turn away from my stars and return to the desk.

Victoria Valbon is standing in the foyer.

My knees almost give way.

Not Victoria, says the voice in my head. *She liked to be called Vicky.*

Golden hair flies away from her head. Then, like Medusa's curse, they become silky snakes, hissing and writhing. Her throat is bloody. Thick drips fall onto anaemic hands. Hands that cradle an infant; her golden-haired child. The baby grips her finger and opens its pink mouth to swallow the rich droplets. Others splash onto the floor by Victoria's feet, spreading like crimson lava.

Not Victoria, says the voice in my head. *Vicky.*

I close my eyes.

Whisper, *No, no, no, my mind is playing tricks on me.*

When I open them, she is gone.

But I can still see her, the way you still see the sun after you've foolishly stared at it for too long. I sink into my chair, heart hammering. My mum and Tom have made Victoria Valbon too real. Brought her to life for me. They *both* knew her. The girl Stephen Sainty has mentioned over and over on the news is no longer just a headline. She's real.

I can't look back towards the foyer. I want to close the studio door, but daren't approach it.

All the sounds I've been hearing – were they her?

But they were real, and she is not.

Weren't they?

I feel light-headed. When I started my show hours ago, I felt the thrill had gone. Now it's back. Goosebumps crawl up my arms and spine. Breath tickles my neck. I turn, half expecting Victoria to be standing behind me.

Stella, I'm not behind you. I'm beside you.

I shiver, look to my left and then my right. No one there.

It's just me.

Me and all my terrible gut feelings.

33

ELIZABETH

THEN

Vicky said she would wait. And then she didn't. She said she would have her baby before going to see Tom. And then, one day in the middle of September, she told me that she could *not* wait. That she sensed this baby might come before its due date in two weeks, and she wanted him to be at the birth.

We were not on our West Park bench the afternoon she told me, but in a café we'd never gone to. I'm not sure why, but we never returned to our bench after she revealed that Tom was her baby's dad. Something changed that day. She no longer shared small details with me. Didn't show me the make-up she'd bought or new clothes she was excited to get into one day. It was like she was working up to letting me go.

But how could I be angry about it? Hadn't I done the same to Stella?

The doula agency called me the morning of our meeting in the café. They wanted to know why I'd missed her recent appointments. Said that I should be going to every single one with her. But I hadn't known about them. Vicky hadn't told me. I tried to explain this to my manager, but she wasn't happy. She suggested things must have deteriorated somehow if Vicky felt the need to keep them from me. That I should be placed with another woman. I promised to work something out that day and headed to the café with my emotions all over the place.

I was angry that Vicky had deceived me, yet sad that I had grown really fond of her and now she wanted me gone. Now I knew how Stella must have felt; what I must have done to her.

It's no good trying to feel something if you haven't experienced it yourself. You can imagine it. You can analyse it. But you can't actually *feel* it. I've only ever cared how *I* feel. It's true. I still do, really. So now I knew first-hand how it felt to be abandoned – and this only gave me more determination to stop Vicky messing up Stella's relationship. It mattered far more than being Vicky's doula now.

Vicky was waiting at a table by the window. She often arrived at our meetings before me. Her usually pink cheeks had lost their glow. I wondered if it was guilt for how she had deceived me. I sat down, and before we could speak a very eager waitress flounced over to take our order.

After a while, Vicky asked about Stella.

She didn't often mention her, and I wondered if it was to avoid talking about what we'd really come here to discuss. Previously, when she had asked about Stella, in order to avoid admitting how new my relationship with my daughter was, I said that being a doula meant it was really just about Vicky. One time she'd suggested I'd been happy to talk about Harland, and yet my daughter's name hardly came up.

Now I simply said that Stella was fine, thank you very much.

I'd seen her yesterday. I didn't tell Vicky that. Didn't tell her we'd gone shopping for a rug to cover my cold kitchen floor and that we'd laughed at the fussy saleswoman who tried to get us to buy a bright pink one. That, while we giggled, I'd put my arm on Stella's arm and she hadn't pulled away. She usually did if I got too close. I could still feel her slender wrist beneath my hand. The silky sleeve of her shirt.

Does your daughter have a boyfriend? Vicky asked.

I frowned. Was it a loaded question? Did she ask because she *knew* the answer? No – her green eyes were bright only with curiosity, not with knowing.

I told Vicky that she did.

Of course, she wanted to know what he was like.

I said he was the kind of man you would never let go.

Our food came then. Two steaming bowls of soup and warm bread. I tore into mine. Vicky didn't seem to have the same appetite. She sipped slowly from the bowl. After a while she said she had decided that today was the day. I could have asked her what day, but I think we both knew I had a clue.

I'm going to see Tom tonight, she said.

I nodded because I wasn't sure what I might say.

Vicky told me she'd been awake most of the night, thinking about him. About what future they might have together. She'd been imagining that he might be out there, knowing she was pregnant, and actually hoping she would come back to him. And what if she didn't? What if she didn't and she missed her chance? So she was going to eat tea with her family, excuse herself and go upstairs, and then sneak out while they were watching the soaps.

She paused, and I knew she was waiting for my response. I finished chewing my bread to buy time. Then I told her that I thought she was heading for heartache.

Is that your instinct? she wanted to know.

I said yes, it was what my gut told me would happen.

Mine tells me the opposite, she said. *And I have to go with that*.

What could I say?

Vicky said she didn't care who disagreed. Whether her mother thought it was foolish, or if I did. She was going to Tom's house tonight to tell him she still loved him, that she always had, and she wanted the three of them to be a family. She said she had been asking around about him; and a friend had said his girlfriend was some radio presenter and worked evenings, so hopefully she wouldn't be around.

I don't want to hurt her, Vicky said to me. *I really don't*.

Then don't go, I said.

I have to, she whispered.

I looked out of the window. It had begun to rain. The water was making the crisp leaves soggy. The waitress took our plates away. The bread was heavy in my stomach.

This is it, isn't it? I said.

Vicky frowned.

Come on, I said. *You went to appointments without me. You're going to get Tom back. What have I done to make you turn on me like this?*

Nothing, she cried. Those green eyes looked hurt, but I didn't care. *I didn't mean to exclude you, but I just thought if I do end up with Tom, it's better I get used to not having you to help me. Because you won't be around, will you? You've been amazing, you really have, but it's time for Tom to be there. There are loads of other pregnant women who are going to love having you around.*

As she said this, I realised I would not do it again.

Being a doula would end here.

I'm going, I said.

I stood up and put on my coat without looking at her.

Don't be mad at me, she pleaded.

I'm not, I lied. *We're done, aren't we?*

Vicky said she wanted to stay in touch. Wanted me to see the baby. That not being her doula didn't mean I couldn't be her friend.

I knew there was absolutely no point trying to persuade her not to go to Tom's house. To Stella's house. She was clearly determined to do it. So, for me, it was over. I put my money on the table and walked away, ignoring Vicky's cries for me to wait, to let her walk to the bus stop with me. I could not tell her what to do, but I could try and think of a way to stop her doing it.

I turned at the café door and said goodbye.

She looked crestfallen.

But I didn't care.

I didn't want to wait for a bus in the rain, so I went to the nearest taxi rank and got into the one at the front of the queue. As we headed to my side of town, the driver sang merrily along to the tune on the radio. Something in his smile and in the tone of his voice triggered a memory. Harland. The first night we met. It was raining then too. I leaned forward. The same name on the dashboard: BOB FRACKLEHURST.

It was you, I said to him.

In a cheerful voice he asked *what* was him.

I explained that he had picked me up about twenty-seven years ago. It had been a miserable night and I'd waited in his car because he had another pick-up, so he couldn't take me anywhere.

Bob chuckled and said that I must have a bloody good memory.

I told him it was a special night and so his name had stuck in my mind the way a man coming into my life had. I said I'd met the love of my life simply because I'd stepped into the cab that was his – Bob's *and* Harland's.

Bob admitted he didn't remember, but that he had seen a lot of people in his time as a taxi driver. He had taken pregnant women to the hospital, been in collisions, comforted the bereaved, counselled the depressed and laughed with those celebrating. He said that tomorrow night would be his last shift. He would be retiring after thirty years of driving cabs around the city. Thirty years of being part of important journeys, and in between that just the radio for company.

You've probably listened to my daughter, I said. *Stella McKeever. She does the 10pm show most week nights.*

He smiled and said he always tuned in. That she had a no-nonsense way about her that reminded him of his Trish when she was younger. He had even given Stella a lift a few times. He said she was a bit quieter in real life, but he liked that. Said she had that air about her that you knew she would treat you as you treated her. Either very well or very badly.

How proud I felt.

My daughter.

We pulled up outside my house. I gave Bob a tip and wished him well in his retirement. He said he was sure he would miss it terribly and probably come back part-time. I got out and waved goodbye.

Just as I had said goodbye to Vicky. Goodbye to me being her doula.

Even though I didn't intend for it to be the last time I saw her.

34

STELLA

NOW

Ellen Devonport in West Hull says on Twitter that if she revealed all her secrets they would be made into one of those three-part dramas on the BBC. It makes me smile, despite the intensity of the night. I read her tweet to the listeners and play her request: 'Who's That Girl' by Eurythmics. Then my smile fades.

I go to my thin window. I wish I could open it and feel icy air on my face. In a way, I'm grieving. I've been given a father and yet I'm not able to have him.

Before I know it, the song is dying.

I return to the desk, slide the fader up, and say, 'That was the divine Annie Lennox, and you're listening to WLCR. I have been Stella McKeever and I'm afraid that's it from me tonight.' I pause. 'My *last* night. Thank you for sharing my final show with me.' A lump rises in my throat, threatening to crack the words. This is it. It's over. Really over. I'm leaving. 'Thank you for the requests, and for the secrets you've dared to share. Thank you for the last few years. If you're still up, or you're working that nightshift, don't go anywhere because after the news it'll be your fave Gilly Morgan with plenty more classic hits. After this tune, we'll get the news on the hour.' I smile to myself, and add, 'The reheated news as I call it. If you heard it an hour ago, you already know everything there is to know. There won't be any dark surprises.' I pause. 'Well, that's it, then. Goodnight. Let's end it with "Stargirl" by Lana Del Rey and The Weeknd...'

I shove my chair back with my feet as I have so many times before. Then I stand and push it firmly under the desk. I look at the clock; I have five minutes until The Man Who Knows comes. *If* he comes. Perhaps it's all a game. Perhaps he's never had any intention of actually coming. But even as these questions occur to me, I know he is already here.

I make a coffee, but I don't drink it. I watch the steam rising and then dying. The final lines of the song rise and die too. *I just want to see you shine cos I know you are a Stargirl.* I lean over and start the adverts. Notifications draw my attention to the monitor. Someone has tweeted about my reheated news comment.

So no big reveal about #thegirlinthealley tonight, then? God bless poor #VictoriaValbon #WhoDidIt #BabyKiller

I don't respond.

Instead I pick up the carrier bag my mum gave me.

I open it carefully.

Inside is a faded photograph pouch, the kind you used to get when you had to have your pictures developed by a professional. It contains three photos. They are all of my mother and father – Elizabeth and Harland. She looks just how I remember she did – vibrant, glorious, full of life. He looks completely different to the stiff and posed pictures used in his biography. Though he is heavy-featured, almost ugly, his eyes are also full of life. When he looks at my mother in one of the pictures, it is as though he can't get enough of her. Cannot drink her all in. I'm not sure how it makes me feel. Happy that they had such love? Sad that it was more important to her than I was? Angry that I never got to meet him?

Disgusted at the pair of them?

I look more closely. There's something else. Harland looks a little like Tom. In the simmering intensity of his gaze. In the light of his darkness. Is it possible I can only love a man who is similar to the one I have never known?

I realise the adverts are ending.

No time now for brooding.

I time it carefully and take the listeners into the reheated news for the last time. At that exact moment, the door buzzer sounds. I put the pictures in my bag and go into the foyer.

Am I ready for this?

Yes, I am.

On the small screen, I see him: The Man Who Knows. The small, nondescript man I've recently seen loitering around the building. I open the door. He blinks in the glare of the fluorescent light as though it burns him. I suppose he's a creature of the night; a man who takes pictures of the dark. He's wearing a grey hoodie and has greasy hair and gaunt features.

He's not menacing; not mysterious.

'Come in, then,' I say.

He steps into the foyer. He's in *my* world now. He has surrendered his power. A Nikon camera hangs around his neck, not unlike my mum's (and my father's) good camera. Now and then he fiddles with the strap.

'This place is smaller than I thought,' he says. The voice is still mature, much more powerful than his physical appearance. He hasn't looked at me yet.

'Yeah, they all say that.'

I go along the still-dark corridor and into the studio, expecting him to follow me. He does. He looks around, at the fading carpet and walls, and I'm sure I see flickers of disappointment in his eyes. I understand. It's the same when people meet Stephen Sainty – they expect him to be a hunk because of his rich voice.

You'd fit in here, I think.

The Man Who Knows is just like a misleading radio presenter or scruffy studio. Finally, he looks at me. I see in full the pale face, delicate cheekbones, and pointed chin. I see his eyes light up, the way my mum's did when she was bathing in the sunny rays of some man's attention. I do not disappoint him. Whatever he hoped to see, he sees. I smile.

'What?' he asks.

I shake my head. 'Did you bring them?' I ask.

He takes a large envelope from inside his coat but doesn't open it. He really has them. Or at least he really has *something*. I feel a little sick.

'I know I shouldn't have scared you by hanging around outside those few times,' he says.

'You didn't,' I say coolly.

'I want to explain that I'm not some weird stalker. I'm out most nights with my camera anyway, and I just wanted to...'

'What?'

'To see you properly,' he says. 'To get a picture of you, maybe.'

I laugh. 'And you don't think that's stalker-ish?'

'Not really. All fans want a picture of their idol.'

'I'm hardly a celebrity,' I say.

'You are to me.'

I don't know what to say.

'So many things disappoint us, don't they?' he says. 'When I started listening to your show, you became my saviour – you were there at the end of every long day. I'd have your voice in my ear and my camera in my hand and the sky up above me. It was like it was just the two of us.' He sighs. 'But I wondered if you were real. I mean, I knew you were *real*, but I thought, is it just a persona that she assumes on air? I came here to check. I hid by the trees, but I know you saw me and I know I unnerved you. But you were glorious.' He pauses. 'You *are*. You're exactly like your voice.'

'Glorious?'

'Yes.'

What can I say to that? It's exactly how I thought my mother looked in her pictures earlier. No one has ever called me glorious. Not even Tom. He's whispered sweet obscenities in my ear, and said there's no one like me and that I'm beautiful. But glorious? Not that.

'And then that night happened,' he says.

'That night?' I have almost forgotten why he's here.

'Victoria Valbon.' He holds my gaze. 'It's like I was supposed to be there at that exact moment. To bear witness. To be able to call you and make the connection with you.'

'Show me your pictures then,' I say.

'These are not the only copies.' He takes them out of the envelope.

'Well, of course,' I say. 'We live in the digital age. There's no such thing anymore.'

He holds them to his chest as if, now the moment is here, he doesn't want to share them. I think of Harland Grey's final film, *In Her Eyes*. No – my *father's* final film. When I read about it in the book, I looked online for it, but it wasn't available anywhere, not to buy on DVD or to stream. I was glad. I didn't want to have to decide if I could watch a girl die before my very eyes. See the colour fade from her irises like paint watered down.

'You didn't come all this way *not* to show me,' I say. 'Harland Grey was compelled to share his work. And you're the same.'

'Harland *Grey*? What's he got to do with this?' The Man Who Knows looks confused.

I smile. Something profound occurs to me. 'Quite a lot. Don't you see? You're pretty similar. You both caught a murder on camera.'

'Yes, but I didn't *commit* one,' he cries. 'I didn't set one up!'

'I suppose not.'

'*That's* what you call creepy. Murdering a girl and recording it. I'm *nothing* like him.' He pauses, fingering his camera strap. 'What made you put that together?'

'He's my father,' I say. It's like I want to test the fact on someone. Gauge what kind of a response it gets.

'Your *father*? But I thought you didn't ... you said on air you didn't...'

'Know? No, I didn't. But I do now. I'm not going into the details. Those are private. But he is.'

'Wow.' He slumps against the wall. Studies me as though I have changed before his eyes. 'That must have been ... wow. I remember it being on the news that he had died last year. My mum loves true crime and she was telling me what he'd done. There was talk of them making a film about him, wasn't there?' He pauses. 'Kind of makes me not want to go fishing and find out who *my* dad is after all. Maybe it's better to keep the fantasy of a perfect father, eh?'

I shrug.

'How do you feel that it's Harland Grey – of all the men in the world it could be?'

'I'm still processing it. It'll take time.' I pause. 'Like the best photographs do, you could say? So, show me yours.'

The Man Who Knows hands them over. Our fingers briefly touch. Like mine, his are warm. There are three pictures. I peer at the top one. Though it's a colour print, the night makes it grainy, all slate greys, dirty whites and deepest blacks. A lamppost in the background scatters butternut orange at its feet. It doesn't reach the two people in the centre of the picture.

The two people that could be anyone.

One of them wears what looks like a long hooded coat, and has their back to the camera. The other is slightly smaller in height, and the coat in their hand is a dirty red in the darkness. Even though I can't see the face, I know it's Victoria. Her pregnancy is barely apparent; just a small rounding in her shape.

I look at the next picture. It's almost exactly the same, except that the taller figure has moved closer to Victoria. In the third, this figure has a hand at Victoria's neck.

On Gilly Morgan's prerecorded show, the haunting melody of A-ha's 'Hunting High and Low' fills the studio. *And within the reach of my hands, she's sound asleep, and she's sweeter now than the wildest dream...*

I don't think these pictures give anything away. They are as blurred as the one my mum took of me as a child during that precious mother/daughter moment. They don't change anything.

He might be The Man Who Knows, but he has no proof.

'Is this all you have?' I ask him.

'These were the best of them,' says The Man Who Reckons He Knows. 'I wasn't prepared, remember. It was dark. It all happened so fast.'

'You can't see anything at all,' I say.

'You can,' he insists. 'Two people. Arguing.'

'You can't even see who they are.'

'Maybe.' He studies me. 'But they have technology these days, don't they? They can enhance pictures in ways we couldn't years ago. They can find details like eye colour, exact height, a fingerprint.'

'They can't change an angle though. The face of her killer is hidden by the hood, and the hands are the wrong way to get a fingerprint.'

He frowns, looks more closely. 'The face is only partly concealed.'

'And anyone would look tall next to Victoria,' I say. 'Even you.'

'What do you mean?'

'They say she was small.'

'They could work out the killer's height from his relation to more than just Victoria.'

'You're wrong,' I say. 'This is too far away. You can't enhance what doesn't exist. I remember reading this article about the ridiculous techniques used in that *CSI* TV show that just couldn't happen in real life. One was the enhancement of pictures. Experts said in a low pixel image it simply wouldn't be possible to use it as evidence. You already zoomed in quite a lot and lost the quality.'

He seems miffed. 'I always take great pictures,' he says. 'I know it's not my best work, but I just wasn't as near as I could have been. I couldn't focus because I wasn't able to see my subject.' He sighs and explains. 'I was passing the end of the alley and I heard something. An argument. I could just make out two people. They were shrieking at each other. I hid behind the bushes at the opening. Then the voices grew quieter. That seemed worse somehow. I used my camera – stretched my arm out – it could see what I couldn't.'

'You never thought to go and see if anyone needed help?'

'Not my place to,' he says, 'and I didn't know that *that* was going to happen. How could I know that poor woman would end up with her throat cut open like that? I've seen loads of arguments in the street, but no one ever ended up dead.'

'So *you* never really saw it,' I say. 'Your camera did while you hid. You're not even a witness.'

'But I *heard* it.'

'That's not reliable, really, is it?'

'With these pictures and my testimony, it could help.'

'What did you hear?'

He pauses. The song does too. We both look towards the speaker. It starts up again.

'Well?' I prompt him.

'I heard enough. Bits. Words. I heard her yelling, *my baby.*'

My baby.

How long would a baby live once its pregnant mother had died? A minute? Three? Five? I feel sick again. The studio swims before my eyes. I have to fall into the chair I thought I'd never again sit in.

'Are you okay?' he asks me, moving closer.

'What do *you* think?' I snap.

There is nothing left inside me to throw up. My father's name brought it all out earlier. Am I destined, as the daughter of a killer, to be surrounded by darkness? Does it seek me out? Or am I the one who goes looking?

'How soon did you know it was Victoria Valbon?' I ask him when the nausea passes.

'As soon as everyone else did. I heard on the news. The next day they said a girl had been found in the alley, and I felt as sick as a pig. Rang in sick at work. Just couldn't face it.'

'I still don't understand why you didn't step in to help, since you were there?'

He ignores the question.

'Are you going to the police with all this info now?' I try.

'Yes,' he says gently.

He's only a few feet from me. He leans against the desk like Stephen Sainty has so many times in the past, critiquing my show.

'They're not going to be happy that you waited so long, are they? I think it's classed as hindering an investigation. Why the hell did you *wait*?'

'I wanted to come to you first with it.' His eyes penetrate mine.

'You mean first you wanted to *play* with me,' I say. 'Ring up and tease me with about what you *think* you know. Play a game and string it out and then finally come here with your crappy pictures!'

He edges a little closer along the desk. 'But we both know, don't we?'

'Do we?'

'Stella, I *know.*'

The Man Who Knows, I think.

'What do you know? *Really*? You did not bear witness as you called it earlier. You were hidden behind a bush. You heard tiny bits of an argument.'

'You're still going to play a game?'

'You started it!' I cry.

'Even with the pictures,' he says.

'They don't show shit.' I throw them on the desk.

'They could.' He gathers them up.

'A man behind a fucking bush saw *nothing*!'

'I hung around for a while after,' he says softly. 'I didn't dare move from my hiding place. I was pretty shaken up. And then ... eventually ... I saw...'

He looks at me.

'I saw *you.*'

35

ELIZABETH

THEN

When I set off for Vicky's house that night, I wasn't sure what it would achieve. Whether I could stop her from seeing Tom. I only knew that I had to do something.

What if Stella ever found out I'd known Vicky was on her way to destroy her world, but I'd just done nothing? I'd be letting her down all over again. This time I was going be a good mother. The kind of mother who puts her child first and moves mountains to keep her happy.

I walked there. I needed time to think. It was a mild night for mid-September and I began to wish I'd not worn my heavy coat. As sweat trickled down my back, I was tempted to take it off and carry it, but it would have been cumbersome. Stella had told me about an app that lets you listen to the radio wherever you are, so I'd put one on my phone. I listened to WLCR radio as I walked. Sang along to the songs I knew. Later, if I was still out, I would be able to hear Stella's show.

I wasn't often out in the evening. I'd still not made many friends since coming back to the area. I always had plenty when I lived here years before with Stella. In some ways Vicky was the only one I'd made since I'd returned.

A sudden sadness made me briefly stand still in the street. Why did the father of her baby have to be Stella's Tom? Of all the men it could be, why *him*? I couldn't help but compare the twist of fate to the moment I met Harland. I'd been in the right place at the right time, and so had he. Now it felt to me as if Vicky and Tom had somehow been in the wrong place at the wrong time. He belonged with Stella. That was his right place.

I started walking again, full of determination.

It was a good two miles to Vicky's home, but I'd allowed plenty of time, and the music in my ears kept me company. She had said earlier, in the café, that she was going to sneak out while her family were watching the soaps, which I guessed meant at around seven o'clock. I didn't want to take any chances, so I'd set off at five-thirty. As I walked, I tried to plan. To think of what I might say.

What the heck *could* I say that would actually stop her wanting Tom? What if I made something up? Something impossible to dismiss? What would have stopped me wanting Harland?

It was better I didn't answer that.

But, yes, that could be it. *Make something up*. What could I have read? Been told? Something terrible about Tom? That he'd been involved in some unsavoury activity? Something criminal? A little voice reminded me that even murder hadn't changed my feelings for Harland, but Vicky wasn't me.

Then I realised that she would check it out, look online and see nothing, and I'd be proved a liar.

Should I admit that Tom's current girlfriend Stella was my own daughter? Could I appeal to Vicky's sensitive side? She was a sweet girl who told me she cried at NSPCC adverts and romantic films. I could use that against her. I'd been worried all this time that if I revealed that her Tom was my daughter's Tom, too, Vicky would think my efforts to stop her getting him back were selfish. But, hell, I could admit that *yes*, I was being selfish. I was behaving how a mother should. And I could say that, if she had any sort of heart, she would respect that and stay well away from Tom. From my Stella.

And if she didn't…

If she didn't, *what*?

What could I do?

By the time I reached Vicky's house, I still wasn't sure what I was going to say to her. I sat on the wall at the end of the street, knowing

I'd be out of sight, but that she couldn't go anywhere without passing me. Now that I wasn't moving, I shivered, and was glad of my big coat. I took my headphones out, afraid I'd miss the sound of Vicky's footsteps. Even though she'd become bigger, she always wore heels. She often said that she refused to give them up just because she was pregnant, though she went for a lower one now.

As it approached seven o'clock, and the sun was going down fast, I decided I would detain Vicky by getting upset about something. I was sure I could summon tears and pretend to sob over some family drama. Say she was the only one I could talk to. Then I'd suggest we go for a drink and a chat. And then I'd think on my feet.

I had to have faith that *something* would come to me.

I'd always found a way to do what I wanted in the past. And the thing that I wanted now fired me more because there was goodness in it. It wasn't purely selfish. I was doing it for my daughter.

And when she found out I had, she would love me again.

36

STELLA

NOW

The Man Who Knows edges closer.

'I saw *you*,' he repeats.

I hold his gaze but don't say a word.

'At first, I didn't know it was you,' he says. 'You walked under a lamp as you crossed over the road. You turned for a second and I saw your face. That was the first time in the flesh. You were just like your picture on the WLCR website.' He pauses. '*Glorious*,' he whispers. 'I wanted to get a picture of you then, but I couldn't take my eyes off you. You were distraught. Your eyes were wild. I wasn't sure if it was with fear ... or with adrenaline ... or with anger.'

He is inches away from me. I can smell him. Like me, he doesn't appear to use any sort of cologne. He smells clean. Of fresh clothes and soap. His odour is not what I expect, just as his appearance was a surprise having only heard his voice.

He saw me.

He smells sweet and he says he saw me.

'I saw you leaving that alley,' he finishes.

'That's all you saw?'

'Isn't that enough?' he asks.

'You didn't see the actual murder?'

'No.'

'Just me leaving.'

'Yes.'

CALL ME STAR GIRL **197**

'Then you saw *nothing*.'

'What did you ... *do*?' he asks me.

'I thought you were the man with the answers, not the questions.'

'If I went to the police with all this info, it would help them. I don't care what you say, those pictures could be enhanced and expose the killer.' The Man Who Said That He Knew looks me in the eye. 'You and I know that the person who did it should go to prison.'

'Do we?' I whisper.

'What do you mean?'

'Nothing.'

'What are you going to do?' He looks nervous.

'I don't quite know.' I stand up. He does too, moving away from me again, wary now. 'I never do what people expect from me, and tonight is no different. I think you should go now. We're done here.'

'I won't see you again, will I?' He sounds sad. 'You're leaving the radio tonight.'

'I hope the photographs bring you some recognition,' I say.

I mean it. He's just a harmless young man with a camera. He captured a moment in time that is a mystery to the world right now. His other pictures – the planned ones he takes at night – might be really good. This could help him make it into a career if he wants that.

I head into the foyer, and he follows me.

'You're the one who knows everything,' he says. 'What on earth happened that night in that alley? Why won't you talk to me? *Tell* me. You have the story and I have the pictures. Together we'd be a sensation.'

I shake my head. 'Goodnight.'

'Miles,' he says, even though I haven't asked.

I open the door. 'Goodnight, Miles.'

He steps into the night. The world is dead quiet. No traffic beyond the trees. No clubbers rolling home. Halfway down the path, Miles turns and raises his camera. I could argue. I could shut the door on him. But I let him fiddle with his focus. I let him take a photo of me. The flash blinds me. I wonder what my face says to him. I wonder if I am blurred. If it tells the truth.

If I am glorious.

'Photograph *vérité*,' I call to him.

'What?'

'You must have heard of *cinéma vérité*?'

He shakes his head.

'Look it up,' I say. 'And Miles...'

'Yes?' He looks hopeful.

'Keep the radio on, won't you?'

'Why?'

I'm not even sure why, I only know that, just as I asked my mum to stay tuned all night, I feel compelled to tell him too.

'Just keep it on,' I say, and close the door.

When I turn, I see Victoria Valbon again.

No.

Not Victoria, says the voice in my head. *Remember, she liked to be called Vicky.*

She stands by the door to the studio, her bloodied baby in her arms, as though she isn't going to let me pass. As though I'll have to give a password – like we're kids, and she's playing a game of blocking a doorway. That eternally golden hair flies away from her head. The blood at her throat is now sticky and congealed. She is drying out. She has not just been killed. She has had time to think. To get angry. She is here for me.

I close my eyes.

I whisper again, *No, no, no, my mind is playing tricks on me.*

When I open them, she has gone.

She knows, I think. She *knows*.

I have the password that she wants.

Because I know too.

And it knocks me out.

37

STELLA

NOW

I open my eyes. Bright lights above. Is it the star stopper to my beloved perfume? Can it be? I smile and reach for it. No, the lights are too harsh; too painful. Music washes over me. A discordant piano tinkles and soft lyrics rise and fall. Someone, somewhere, whispers my name. *Stella, wake up, wake up.* The voice is familiar; the one I've been hearing for weeks. But it's clearer now. Nearer.

Am I dreaming?

No. I realise I'm very awake and on the floor in the radio foyer. How the hell did I get down here? And how long have I been here? Did I pass out?

Another song filters through from the studio – a soaring ballad now – and then Gilly Morgan's deep voice follows. Was it hers I heard earlier? No, her prerecorded show is in full swing, so she could not have called to me. The clock says 3:55am. How long since The Man Who Knows left? I sit up with great difficulty. My stomach hurts. My head hurts. My *heart* hurts. I must have passed out. Never in my life have I fainted before.

What's wrong with me?

Stella, you know what it is; it's what you're carrying around with you. It's so heavy, and it's been weeks now.

Who the hell said that? Who's here with me? Did they break in while I was unconscious? The main door is shut, though. I strain to look up the stairs and then into the studio. I open my mouth to shout, 'Who's there?' but I know instantly that it's pointless.

Stella, if you just told someone.

The words come from everywhere – from around me, above me, inside me.

Stella, it's too much for anyone to keep inside.

Stop, I think. Stop, I don't want to hear it.

Stella, tell them.

Then I realise I know the voice. I heard it once before. It was sweet, lyrical, desperate. Now it's sweet, lyrical, *encouraging*. It's Victoria Valbon. No, Vicky, remember. My mum said she liked to be called Vicky. But she can't be *here*. She's gone. I *know* she's gone.

I must be losing my mind.

I get to my feet and stagger into the studio, tempted to close and lock the door after me. But how can I keep out what is already inside? I go to my window. Stars, where *are* you? The sky is the black of eternity, and devoid of a single twinkle. I stare into the darkness, afraid that, if I turn around, she'll be there – Vicky, bloody baby in her arms. I long to smash the window and feel the cold that used to freeze my feelings.

I don't want to know what I know.

I don't, I *don't*.

'You're the one who knows everything,' The Man Who Knows said earlier. Is that the definition of irony?

I squeeze my head between my hands as though to push all of the infection out. I have been able to go about my daily life until now. I have functioned. I have woken each day for the last three weeks and vomited the buried infection into the toilet while letting the taps run. Then I have eaten breakfast with Tom. I have played dead with him. I have given him a cat, who ended up preferring me. I have fought with Tom despite his recent lack of response. I have loved him, hard. I have vomited the infection again before I climbed into bed at night.

I don't want to know what I know.

I don't want to have…

But I am the daughter of a murderer. I am the daughter of a woman who left me at the first opportunity she had. I am the ward of a woman who kindly took me in. I am the lover of a man who fucked me while

I was unconscious and was the fiancé of a murdered girl. I am all of these things, but I am me, too. I am honest, I am a fighter, and I am in control.

Or am I?

I come back to the desk and sit in the chair. My bag is where I left it. I open it and take out one of the pictures of Harland Grey. I look into his dark eyes as though what I should do will be written there. He is no role model, but he is my blood. He was all about bare reality. Absolute truth. Why smash a fake glass when you can smash a real one? Why pour on red paint when you can really bleed? If only the picture was clearer. If only I could see the colours in his irises; the sparks of life. Snaps taken in those days were often blurred and out of focus. He is still as distant to me as he has always been. He might as well be a distant star in some far-away galaxy.

I frown.

What if the photographs The Man Who Knows has *can* be enhanced?

Damn.

What if he was right and there *are* techniques that can show who the killer is? What if the police put everything together using the images and what The Man Who Knows tells them? What if they already have tiny pieces of evidence that haven't been mentioned in the media because, on their own, they don't prove anything? What if these new photos and The Man Who Knows' testimony is the key to solving the case? What if in a few days they call a press conference because of this new evidence? What if everyone finds out the truth?

It will tear my life apart.

I can't let it happen.

I must protect those I love from it.

But what the hell can I do?

I know I can't leave the radio station yet. This is where I have learned who I am. I have things I want to say. Words that must come out of me. That have been simmering all evening. Now they hurt so much.

Stella, say them. Say them.

I don't know if I can.

I scroll through the Twitter feed for more secrets, for ones that might distract from mine, but all is quiet on our account. The same on Facebook. The world has finally gone to sleep. It's just me. Me and what I know. Me and Victoria Valbon's ghost.

How long do I have until someone turns up here?

Gilly Morgan's show goes on until 5am. Then between five and six we always air a collection of the best bits of the day, something Maeve usually puts together during the Love Affair. I realise that I should have done that. Shit. *Shit.* Stephen Sainty will be doing the breakfast show at 6am, and he usually comes in an hour before to prep. I glance at the clock. Ten past four. Damn, Stephen will be here in just fifty minutes. I can't have him here. I haven't put any highlights together. And I'm not done. I want to…

What do I want to do?

Stella, you want to tell them.

I shiver. Shake my head. It's her again. Why is she talking to me now? Why tonight?

Stella, I've been talking to you for weeks, but you just weren't listening. You didn't even hear me. I was that whisper in the movement of bedsheets. I was that rustle in the trees outside. I was that voice in the tap water. Now I think you're ready.

It was her when I thought I'd heard something earlier. Does she hate me? Why would she come to me like this? For revenge? Will she forgive me if I tell the truth? Can *I* forgive me?

Oh God.

Speak now, Stella.

'If I speak now, who should I tell?' I whisper.

Jesus, I'm talking to myself. To the voice of a dead girl. To an empty studio.

Tell them all, Stella. Then you'll stop vomiting every morning and every night. Then you'll be able to look at yourself in the mirror.

Them all? Who all? My mum? The Man Who Thought He Knew? Tom? Oh, Tom. I wish … What *do* I wish? I need to speak to him.

That's it. If I talk to Tom, I'll know exactly what to do. I find his name on my phone, and press it, praying he'll answer. It rings and rings and rings. I hang up and try again. After a while, he picks up.

'Stella?'

'You fell asleep.' I sound accusatory.

'No,' he says sleepily.

'You said you'd wait up.' I feel sad.

'I did. I am. I was just resting my eyes. Couldn't find my phone.' He pauses. 'You okay?'

'I'm just calling to tell you I'm not coming home yet,' I say, and I'm surprised. I didn't even know I was going to say it. I know I don't want to leave, but I didn't want to tell Tom.

'Oh.' Silence. I imagine him looking at the time. If I close my eyes, I can smell him; but this isn't a time to ache for him. This isn't a time to be soft. 'God, it's four-fifteen. What time did the show you were covering finish?'

'Over an hour ago.'

'I don't get it. Why the hell haven't you left yet? I'd have been as worried as hell if I'd woken and you weren't here.'

'Tom,' I say softly.

'Yes?'

'Do you love me?'

'Of *course* I love you. What kind of question is that?'

'But how much?'

'What do you mean, how much? What's wrong?' He sounds fully awake now. 'Is this the Vicky stuff? I knew I shouldn't have told you. Look, I didn't love her like I love you. Nothing about her compares to you.'

'I believe you,' I say. 'I do. I just want you to tell me how far you would go to show that you love me. Tell me what you'd do. I want to hear you say it. You see, I'd do anything for you. Do you know that? I don't like that I would.' I pause, touch the picture of my parents. My parents. Two of them. 'I don't like that it makes me so like my mum. I've always said I would never desert a child for some man, but what if I would?'

'You wouldn't,' says Tom.

'But what if I would? Because I'd do *anything* else for you.'

'What are you talking about?'

'It's been such a strange night.'

On the radio, Gilly Morgan is speaking in hushed tones about an upcoming charity event, and I remember the one where Tom shaved his head and I touched his naked skull beneath. The moment we met. I know that I will never love anyone the way I love Tom. I know it absolutely. The studio lights up blue; the phone. I won't answer. Probably Stephen checking if I'm still here. Or maybe The Man Who Knows again? I don't care.

'Why, what's happened tonight?' Tom asks.

'Did you and Vicky ever see each other after we got together?'

'What? *No.*'

'Did you ever call her?'

'No. Are you okay, Stella? Should I come there? Wait, is it that strange guy loitering around there again? Is that what's unnerved you?'

I laugh. 'No. Nothing like that.' The blue flashing of the studio phone dies. 'I know who my father is now,' I say. I had wanted to tell him in person, but I can't wait for that. I need him to know now but I'm not sure why.

'She told you?' he says gently.

'Yes. My mum came here earlier.' I wonder again if she ever found out Tom was Victoria's boyfriend and the father of her child. Surely if she'd known she would have told me? And does Tom know my mum was her doula? Surely he can't. I shake my head. It's all too much to process at once.

'She finally told you,' says Tom, 'after twenty-six years of keeping it from you?'

'Yes.'

'So?' he asks.

'What?'

'Who *is* he then?'

'You won't believe it.' I take a breath. 'You know that book I've been reading?'

'The Beverley Alli—' He realises halfway through his words.

'The one with the note on. The Harland Grey one.'

Silence. A song starts. 'Father Figure' by George Michael.

'*No*,' he says. 'She left you the book? It's ... Harland Grey? How the hell? But he's a...'

'I know. Go on, say it.'

'...a murderer.' The word is so quiet I wonder for a moment if I imagined Tom saying it.

'Louder,' I say.

'No,' snaps Tom. 'What's *wrong* with you?'

'You know, you look like him. And you're *like* him...'

'What the fuck? I'm not!'

'Our film,' I say. 'Playing dead. He would have loved it. Except he'd have wanted the death to be real and not pretend.'

'Don't compare us to that sick fuck,' snaps Tom. Then, more kindly, 'Sorry. He's your father, I guess. But, Jesus, what a father to have. You must be shocked.'

'Forgiveness,' I say.

'What?'

'Should people forgive something like that?'

'Stella, come home,' he cries. 'Stop arsing about and come to bed. We can talk here. I get that you've had a hell of a shock, but I'm worried about you.'

'Don't be,' I say.

'Of course I am.'

'I just want you to know I love you,' I say.

'I *know* that.'

'There's only one thing left to do to show you *how* much.'

'What do you mean?' Tom cries. 'I *know* you do. You've done so much for me. You got me Perry! You had our initials carved on a key—'

'One that you *lost*!'

'I'm sorry.'

'I thought I'd lost *you*.'

'But you haven't!' He must be out of his mind at my words. 'Never!'

'You've been different recently. Not arguing with me. It was like you'd given in somehow. I thought I had finally bored you.'

'I've had a lot on my mind,' he admits. 'The police interviews. It was scary stuff. But I always loved you. Please, Stella, come home now. I can show you how much I do.'

'I need to tell everyone,' I say.

'Tell everyone *what*?'

I look up and she is there. Victoria. *Vicky*. No surname needed now. We are closer than that. She stands in the studio doorway with her halo of golden hair – like a goddess. No baby this time. Instead she holds her bloody coat around her body. The one that was put over her after she died. It's red. I know because I have seen it before. I close my eyes. When I open them, she has disappeared, but I can smell something. Something familiar. Something gone now.

The star perfume.

The room pulsates with its scent.

How I miss it.

'Stella?' cries Tom. 'Are you still there? Answer me! If you don't come home now, I'm coming there!'

'Don't come here,' I say.

'I am if you're not here in twenty minutes.'

'Tom, I'm going.' My throat hurts. 'Just remember, I did it because I love you. I don't really mind about the key ... we all lose things ... I've lost things I love...'

'Did what? Did *what*?'

I hang up.

What time is it now? Four-thirty. Stephen Sainty will be here anytime. He can't come in. He *can't*. I rush into the foyer, open the main door and step outside. I know how to change the door code, but so does everyone else who works here. I need to disable it. This is the only entrance to the building. The fire exit on the first floor can't be reached because the metal fire-escape stairs are broken and the windows are either barred or too small or too high.

I run upstairs to the junk cupboard where everyone chucks old computers and grab a hammer from the box of tools at the back. Keeping my foot in the main door so it stays open, it doesn't take much effort to smash the small box. Once it's hanging by two wires, I rip them out. Then I come inside and let the main door slam shut. I try the handle. It won't open. With the door code disabled, I can't get out, but no one can get in either.

It's just me

Me and Victoria Valbon.

I can smell blood and perfume and night air.

Tell them. Tell them, Stella. Let me rest in peace. Only you can do that. Tell them and I might forgive you.

I sit at the desk. Gilly Morgan is talking about the charity event again. She will be there, she says, auctioning wedding dresses, raising money for cancer. I get my mobile phone and turn it off. Then I hover one finger over the fader, ready to silence Gilly, and another over the mic button. I have done my last show. I have played my last song. But I'm not done.

I have not said my last words.

What will I say though? How to tell this story? No – I will not think about it until I say it. I will not plan it. I will let the words come as they may. Let them find their own way. And then Victoria might forgive me. But will anyone else? Are they listening? Are they all asleep?

'Vicky,' I whisper to the room. 'Now you can leave me alone.'

Then I push down the fader and slide up the mic.

I am The Woman Who Knows.

And now they all will too.

I speak.

38

ELIZABETH

THEN

While I waited for Vicky to come out of her house, I thought about Harland. I couldn't help it. Thinking of him always made me emotional beyond words, but I needed to be upset when Vicky came, anyway, to create some drama and detain her. I thought of a moment in a court room. A moment I thought might be last time I ever saw him. I hadn't thought of it in a long time.

As I sat on the wall on the end of Vicky's street, I closed my eyes and remembered it. Him. The wood-panelled room. All I could see at first were the green shoes I'd been wearing. I shouldn't have been in them, not really, not being five months pregnant. But just like Vicky in her kitten heels, I had refused to give up my fashion. Refused to be frumpy. I was only twenty and the man I had loved for barely a year, who the fortune-teller had called my twin flame, was receiving his sentence. I had wanted his last sight of me to be something he would never forget, so I wore the shoes he loved me in.

Because Harland had admitted his guilt as soon as he was arrested, there had been no trial, no jury. There had been a few hearings that were to do with sentencing, when Harland had had the chance to justify why he'd killed Rebecca March, and answer questions. But I didn't go to those. I couldn't bear to hear him talking about another woman. He had committed the murder before we met, so it wasn't about any sort of disloyalty. I was just afraid of how much it would hurt if I saw his eyes glow with passion when he spoke about *her*.

I only went to the sentencing.

I looked across the small room at him, in his grey suit, no expression on his usually powerful face. Rebecca March's family were there too but didn't know who I was. I hadn't even been mentioned in the newspapers because Harland wanted to protect me. No one knew I was his girl.

I wore my green heels that day. Harland once told me that green made me look all the more wicked. I saw his eyes follow them when I took my seat. Then he looked me full on. Eye to eye. Beseeched me with those dark, deep pools of ink. I saw everything there. The passion we had shared. The pain at my last visit, when I'd told him I would not be coming to see him in prison.

I was still able to hide my pregnancy. I had found out about it while he was inside, awaiting the sentence. It had been too late to do anything but have the baby. I had been so wrapped up in Harland's arrest, the shock truth about what he had done, that I'd missed the signs.

The day before I had told him that I would always love him, but I could not forgive what he had done to that girl. I lied. How bitter the irony that if I'd not been pregnant I'd have stayed with him, gone to visit him as much I could. I'd have waited for him forever. It was my own jealousy that made me end it. My need to be number one in his life or not in it at all.

Harland was given fifteen years. I did not know then that he would be out in just twelve. In my head, I wondered if I could bring up my child until he or she was sixteen, and then go back to Harland once he was released. I would have done my duty. I would be free.

I watched Harland being taken down. The pain was exquisite. For a moment, I wondered if such pain could kill a foetus. I'm not proud to say that I almost wished it would, so I could scream out that I would visit him as much as I could. Every part of me wanted to run and grab him, to kiss him, to cling to him.

But I could not get Harland's words out of my head. The ones he had said just months earlier, as we lay in bed. I'd been so utterly happy. Then he asked if I ever wanted children. I don't think he saw my repulsed expression in the blackness, because he went on to tell me how he wanted just one child. Hopefully a girl. He said girls were more fun. He said he liked the idea of having just one, because then she could be the absolute centre of his world.

I decided then never to get pregnant with his child.

But it was too late. I would have been a month gone already. When I found out, his words about a daughter screamed at me. What if I had a girl? His love for her would eclipse his love for me.

I let my twin flame go.

And I didn't see him again until he wrote to me more than twelve years later.

I am what I am. I know I'm no good. I'm not nice. I've always been driven by my own needs. I went straight back to Harland on his release, leaving my own child. But because I know love – obsessive, desperate, selfish love – I finally know what I can do for my daughter. My Harland is gone now, dead at only sixty-one, but everything I've ever done wrong – and oh, I know there is so much – I can put right tonight.

Footsteps sounded behind me then.

They sounded like Vicky's low heels.

With tears already on my cheeks, I turned around, ready to face her, and do whatever I must.

39

STELLA

NOW

'This is Stella McKeever.

I know, I know – you're surprised to hear me again. Sick of me after I did lovely Maeve's show too. I imagine you think I've pulled poor Gilly Morgan out of her seat. But no, she isn't here. She's hopefully having an amazing time in Vietnam right now. You were listening to a prerecorded show. Like the reheated news on the hour. But this is live now. This is really me, in the flesh, right here, right now. No music, no adverts, no local news. Just me, for as long as it takes.

You see ... I have something to share with you all.

God. I don't exactly know how I'm going to do it. I haven't thought further than what I'm saying now. I ... well, I ... Let's just see.

This isn't like my usual show, where I've planned it in advance, chosen my songs and my stories and everything. Actually, you know what, in a way I *have* been planning it. For three weeks. I just didn't know it.

I didn't know it until now.

I had this caller earlier, Chloe – hi, Chloe if you're listening still; she said we should keep our secrets to ourselves. She said people unburden themselves, but they're only doing it to relieve their own guilt. *Keep it to yourself*, she said. *We don't want to know*. But what I'm going to share is something that won't serve me well at all.

It will ruin my life, but I'm ready for that.

I think...

I...

I don't know how many other listeners are still with me. It's four-forty-five so unless you're on the nightshift, or you start very early, I won't have many of you at all. It doesn't matter. Just one listener is an audience.

I'd like to think my mum is listening. If she is – hi, Mum. I'm glad you are. I bet you're confused right now. *What the hell is she doing?* you're thinking. Me being on here is how we met again after fourteen years, you see.

So, what *am* I doing, Mum?

The answer is ... I'm not entirely sure yet. I mean, I *am* sure. I'm just not sure I *can*. I want to. I do. I have to. You're going to be shocked. I know that much. But I think you might understand. You of all people will understand the most. And that makes me really happy. It *does*. You are the one who has hurt me more than anyone, but you're also the one who, I guess, I understand the most. You can be proud of me, Mum, because I don't think anyone is going to call me boring after tonight.

Wait. The phone's ringing. Shit. Sorry – I shouldn't swear on air.

But I guess this isn't my usual kind of show...

You guys won't hear the phone. We have it on silent in the studio. Should I answer it? No, I don't think so. I bet it's Stephen Sainty. He'll be on his way here for the early show and he won't be happy, but this *is* pretty irregular stuff.

Stephen, if you're listening in the car, don't rush here. There's no point. You won't be able to get in. I've disabled the door code. I'm sorry, but I had to. I can't do this any other way. I'll pay for it to be fixed, I promise. So, you'll understand that I can't answer the phone right now. Don't bother trying my mobile either, because I've turned it off. You might be mad right now, Stephen, but this won't do our ratings any harm, trust me. This is definitely going to be what they call an exclusive, and it's only at WLCR. You'll thank me tomorrow.

I don't know if *you* will, Tom.

My beloved Tom. I'm not doing it for thanks, though. I'm doing this because I love you. I'm doing this so that the police leave you alone.

And you too, Mum. So they know they questioned the wrong person ... the wrong people. I hope you're listening, Tom. You're the one I'm speaking to really.

Just you.

But if you *have* fallen asleep again, I'm recording this, so you'll hear it somewhere when you wake up. This is me shaving my head so you can see the skull underneath. The rest of the listeners won't have a clue what I'm talking about. But *you* know. Your head was the first part of you that I saw naked. And your head is what I love most. That wonderful brain. The way you think. The things you say. Really, that's where the heart is, isn't it? Our emotions are up there, not in our chest, like some cliché.

There goes the phone again.

I'm not going to answer, so you may as well stop. I suppose it could be someone else. Maybe Miles. You know who you are, Miles. I called you The Man Who Knows when you rang me, but you're not. Not really. By the time it's light you'll be able to take your pictures to the police. You'll get all the recognition you deserve. I hope that's what you want?

So, this is it.

What am I doing, you must all be wondering? Why lock myself in here and take over the airwaves? Have I got something interesting to say?

I have.

I'm going to tell you about Vicky.

Well, I'm going to try...

That's how I know her now. Vicky. I know she liked that name rather than Victoria. But I didn't know it back then. I'm talking about Victoria Valbon, of course. There can't be a single listener out there who doesn't know that name. Though I know a lot of you call her The Girl in the Alley. I get that. Everyone likes a good hashtag. She's been trending on Twitter for weeks thanks to that name. That and *#BabyKiller*. If you don't believe me, go and look. You'll see people for what they really are there. Some of you tweeted lovely things and wished her family well. Some of you were just hoping to help catch who did it. Others ... well, those people are worse than...

Worse than the killer in a way.

Because she's a real person. I mean, she *was* a real person. We all forget that when someone becomes a headline. Victoria Valbon was a girl, the same age as I am, a girl who was getting ready to be a mum. I'm sorry, you'll have to excuse me a moment. This is very ... difficult. I'm sorry.

Give me a minute.

So, yes, Vicky was an everyday, local girl. She was a nobody until ... until *that* night. She was about to be a single mum, but she still lived at home. She had a doula because her baby's father wasn't in the picture anymore. She wanted him to be. She wanted Tom. Her ex. Yes, that's *my* Tom. We share Toms, Vicky and me.

This much is all true.

But what's the rest of the story?

Where do I start?

I'll start when she turned up here. At this radio station. Back then I had no idea who she was. No one did. She was still nobody. I'd just finished my show and when I opened the door to leave, she was waiting there. I've had drunks loitering out there a few times, but you don't expect to see a heavily pregnant girl at one-fifteen in the morning. She was tiny apart from her swollen stomach. That was my first thought; she was petite and pretty with soft golden hair. Had on this big coat as though to hide her pregnancy from the world.

I asked if she was okay, thinking she'd gone into labour or something, and needed a lift to the hospital.

She said she was fine, it wasn't anything like that.

Then she said she was here to see me.

Obviously, I was taken aback. I probably said something about not knowing who she was.

She asked if she could come inside and talk to me; she said that she'd waited until my show was done to see me. Then she told me she was called Victoria. I understand why she gave me her full name. I wasn't someone she liked. I wasn't someone she thought she'd become friends with. That wasn't what she had come for.

I told her we couldn't go inside as Maeve Lynch was in there doing her show, and anyway, I wanted to get home. I'm always tired after work.

She said I could drive her home, and we could talk. She didn't ask; she *told* me. Her voice was sweet, but determined. I looked at her and said – quite bluntly to be honest – that I didn't have my car, I rarely drove here. I like the half-hour walk. It's my only exercise. She looked aghast. Asked if I wasn't worried, walking home alone at this time of night? I laughed and said no. I'm not. Never have been. What the hell would I be scared of?

She asked if she could walk with me.

I shrugged and said that she'd have to keep up.

And off we went.

That's when she told me we had something in common. I think she wanted me to ask what, but I didn't. I suppose I played the game I often play with my boyfriend Tom. He'll vouch for this. When I'm most interested in something is when I'm the least likely to ask about it. It's like a dance we do. One where we both want to lead. Victoria didn't know about the dance. She told me that my Tom used to be her Tom.

I stopped in my tracks then.

She stopped too, just a step after me.

But still I didn't ask anything. Still I danced, you could say.

She said that my Tom had been her fiancé. She held out her slender fingers and showed me the ring. I can't recall exactly what it was like. It was hard to see in the darkness. I suppose I didn't want to see, if I'm honest.

I told her she could be lying.

So she described Tom. Brought him to life for both of us, so vividly that he could have been standing next to us. I hated that she could do that. I thought, *He's mine, don't think that you conjuring him up so easily changes that*. And then she patted her tummy and said he was this baby's father.

No, I said.

It just came out of my mouth. No, no, *no*.

Yes, she said.

I started walking again, and she followed, just a little behind me. She must have been hot, I guess – it was a mild September night – because I think it was then that she took off her coat and carried it. I could be wrong. It's hard to know what order it all happened. But I demanded to know why she felt the need to tell me about Tom. She said that she thought it only fair because she intended to get him back. To give him the chance to be a dad. To tell him they should be a family.

No, I said again.

I told her that, if he'd wanted to be with her, he'd have stayed with her. She said he might not even know about the baby as she'd found out she was pregnant after they split and had never told him. And now it was time he had the full facts.

I'm not a callous person. I know better than most about not having a father. I only found out tonight who mine is. I'm not sharing that with you, though. That's another story. That's private. But that night, I was the same as Victoria's baby. In that moment, we both had absent dads. She only wanted what was right for her child. I could see that while at the same time wanting to…

I told her she couldn't have Tom.

Said he belonged to me now.

Victoria said that might be true, but she was going to find out for herself. She was going to visit him the next day and let him see her in all her glory. Pregnant with his child. Then see who he decided to be with. She said he was an honourable man. He'd want to do the right thing.

I laughed then. Spat the word "honourable" back at her. Said it wasn't my first choice of word for him. Not after the things we'd done together. The sex games we'd played. I said, no, you won't be going to see him tomorrow.

Try and stop me, she said.

We had reached the alley then. You all know which alley. Even I, who am not afraid, usually avoid this quick way home. There's something eerie about the poorly lit passage. Since I was small, I've always felt like something bad once happened there.

Or now I think of it ... did I just foresee that something bad *would* happen there?

Maybe.

Anyway, Victoria set off down the alley. Perhaps indignation made her brave. I followed her. My determination made me brave too. Halfway along, she stopped and said that I could leave her alone now. She had said her piece and she was going home.

I grabbed her. Not roughly. Enough to startle her. And I told her she was *not* going to see Tom.

She pulled free and pushed me away. I pushed her. Then...

Jesus, I can't say it. I can't. I can't.

I *must*...

What was it?

It was the star perfume bottle.

That's what it was. Victoria smashed it. She didn't mean to – it was because we were tussling. I said Tom would never take her back, and she said he would and pulled on my bag, like a child. My perfume bottle is always in the pocket. Anyone will tell you that – Tom, my mum. I take it wherever I go. Took it everywhere as a child. When we got back together. Remember, Mum?

And Victoria ruined it.

When she wrenched my bag from my shoulder, some of my things fell out. I watched the star perfume fall, as though in slow motion. Like I knew. Knew it would hit the path and smash. I screamed out as it did. My whole world imploded in that moment. The sweet smell filled the air. The scent of my childhood washed over me.

But I was not clean.

And all I felt was rage.

Rage that I'd buried when my mum deserted me.

Rage that I'd felt when these girls at school threatened to pour away the perfume.

Rage, rage, *rage*.

Victoria looked nervous then. She backed up into the tangle of bramble bush, pushing some thorns away from her cheek.

I picked up what was left of the bottle – the base was intact, but its broken edge was like a row of jagged and dangerous teeth. The star stopper was totally destroyed; that was my favourite part. I miss it so much now. You have no idea. I'm so … *sad*. I'd had it since I was a child. It was my mum's, you see, and before that, it was my father's. It was the only thing I owned that had belonged to him. But I didn't know that then. The whole time I had it, I never knew it had been his. I only knew that Victoria had destroyed my childhood treasure, and that she was not going to take the only other thing I loved.

Listen, Tom, I know you will want to protect me. But don't. *Don't.* Let this be it. Let me tell them. Love me. Forgive me. But let this be it.

The phone. Shit. Again.

I can't answer. Stop ringing, whoever you are, for God's sake. And whoever's banging on the door, *fuck off.* You're wasting your time. I'm not coming out until I'm done.

Have I even started?

You want to know, don't you? What happened? Maybe I don't remember it all. Maybe I blacked out, saw red as they say. Maybe I can't tell you after all. Bet you'd be pissed off, wouldn't you?

But no...

It was this...

Victoria said she just wanted to go home.

I said she wasn't going to get Tom.

She said *he* would be the one to decide that.

Did I think he would choose her? I did. In that horrible moment I doubted his loyalty. I was afraid that he would see her, with her golden hair and her green eyes, heavy with his child, and he'd fall for her all over again.

No, *I'll* decide, I told her.

She told me I was fucking crazy.

Maybe I was. Maybe I am.

I held up the broken bottle. I think it glinted in the streetlamp, though I could be wrong. I could have imagined that. I could have imagined a lot.

She tried to grab it, and that's when I did it.

I wasn't thinking. I didn't mean to. I *didn't*. I don't know my own strength sometimes. And it was all so fast. A blur. I can't even say how.

Just the rage.

Just a swipe of my hand.

Then her eyes like saucers. And her hands at her throat. And the blood. God, the blood. Spilling over them. Between them.

I gasped. Stepped back.

I'd done what I had threatened to do to my childhood bullies long ago.

I think I wondered how it had happened.

Who had done it?

Me, I realised.

Me.

I wanted to help her, but I was scared. Scared to touch her, to be involved. But I was. I had done this.

It was quick. It really was. Victoria was gurgling and gasping and coughing. But not for long, I don't think. Maybe minutes. And the blood. Yes, that. God, the blood. I've never seen so much. It was gushing from her neck. Horrible. Such a mess. Yes, a mess.

She slumped a bit, and kept grabbing her tummy, and I thought, *Oh, the baby*.

I wanted to undo it. To save that baby. To save her. I *did*. God, I did. But I panicked. I stepped back, didn't want to touch her, or all that blood. She fell onto her knees, I think. Stopped gasping. Her hand was on her belly the whole time.

And then she was still.

I might have waited for minutes, I don't know. I didn't want to just leave Victoria, all vulnerable like that. Or her poor baby. I cried for that baby. I did. But I couldn't stay there.

I put the coat over her.

Over *them*.

Then I left the alley with the broken perfume bottle in my pocket, and no star stopper.

God, I feel sick.

Oh, God … I hope you can … I don't know… I hope you can understand. Mum, you should understand more than anyone. You *should*. Tom … Oh, Tom … it was all for you. That is no excuse at all, but it *is* the reason. Please don't try and make this better for me. *Don't*. I know you will try to, but don't. Let me take the punishment I must. Let me take the storm I deserve.

God.

I don't quite know what to do now. The phone hasn't stopped ringing, and someone is trying to break down the door.

Shit. What have I done? What have I *done*?

I think I should leave. Yes. I'm going off air now. I'm going to … I don't know. This really is my final show now. These are my last words to you. I've been playing your lives for five years. Tonight, it was mine.

So … I guess this is goodbye.

I'm going to have to face the music now.'

40

STELLA

THEN

The last night I slept on Sandra's thin bed with the purple-and-pink crocheted blanket atop, I was afraid. I would never have admitted it to anyone; I could barely admit it to myself. But now, when I look back at that girl curled up on her bed with a perfume bottle next to her – its star stopper glinting in the weak light of the bedside lamp – I know that she was terrified.

I was leaving home the following morning. I was nineteen and about to begin my training with Stephen Sainty at WLCR. I'd beaten sixteen other girls in the interview, and still couldn't believe it. They had been vivacious creatures with overly styled hair and crisp suits. I'd worn my favourite jeans and pink shirt and tripped up over the step on the way in, dropping the pages of my CV all over the floor. I'd tried to scoop them up while ignoring rows of judgemental eyes appraising my windswept locks.

'You have that certain something,' Sandra had insisted when I excitedly told her about my success. 'The French call it *je ne sais quoi*.' She studied me intently. 'Stella, you do. Your mother was a beauty, and though you don't look much like her, you've got that ... that life to you. I can't lie and tell you you're pretty. But you *are* different.'

She hadn't mentioned my mum in a long time, and we both instantly realised this; we both changed the subject.

'When do you—' she said at the same time as I said, 'I don't know when—'

Sandra then insisted I didn't need to leave home yet; just because I'd got the dream job didn't mean I had to go anywhere. She had turned her nose up at the studio flat I'd decided to move into, alone. She had viewed it with me a week earlier, sniffing at the damp air with disdain and running her fingers over the dusty surfaces.

'I want to leave home,' I'd insisted. 'I'm ready to do things alone.'

But I wondered if she could see through my brave façade.

How easy it would have been to stay with Sandra. To continue letting her feed me and fuss over me. To sleep in the safety of her back room, sheltered from the real world, depending on her to run my life, pay the bills and remind me when I had to do anything. But I no longer wanted easy. I was restless for more, even if it was going to be difficult.

On my last night there, I hardly slept at all.

I heard Sandra make her Horlicks and take it up to bed. I eventually heard her gentle snoring. I got up and opened my window. It was early April and the cool air kissed my skin, raising goose bumps. How many times over the years had I stood there at midnight, letting the frost freeze my feelings and wondering what it would be like if I climbed over the ledge and let go? Wondering whether I would fall and smash into pieces on the ground below or would somehow fly, float up to the stars that I had reached out to touch so often?

Now I sat on the ledge, a hand on either side of the window frame, my back to the outside world. I tested how far back I dared lean. I was surprised at myself. Then I let go with my right hand. How easy it would have been to let go with the left.

But I was excited about my new job and my new flat, even if it was tiny and stank of garlic.

I had one of my curious gut feelings then.

It hit me so hard I had to grab onto the window frame again, with both hands.

It left me gasping for air.

Not yet, it said. *Don't let go yet. You have so much coming. There are things coming that you don't want to miss. Your life is only just starting.*

You don't know everything there is to know yet. Just take the star perfume with you wherever you go...

I went back to my bed. By the time the sun's rays were lazily climbing the walls, I had already packed the few things I owned into four boxes. Some of Sandra's friends had donated an old sofa and an armchair, and she had been buying me pots and pans and tea towels, so I had enough to make do for now.

Sandra had made a pot of tea and was sitting at the kitchen table waiting for me. She looked like she had been crying. I was the fairytale child left by a wicked mother. She had kept me like Rapunzel in a tower, protected from the world. She had done more for me than any blood parent could, and I would never forget it.

I poured myself a cup.

'I'm going to be coming over all the time,' I said. 'It's only a twenty-minute walk away. You're going to get sick of me, I promise.'

'I won't,' Sandra said. 'Be safe, won't you, Stella. Be *happy*.'

It was like she could sense that my new job would in fact keep me from her. That the training and the events involved would mean I only got to visit once a week.

She died three years after I left home. A sudden stroke. All I could think of then was her in the kitchen that day, saying *be happy*. I think I destroyed her happiness when I left and then became too wrapped up in my new life to see her much. I think that killed her. She is the one person in this world who never hurt me. Not once. Without her, I have no idea what would have become of me aged twelve.

I hugged her when I left that day.

I thanked her for all she had done.

Of course, the star perfume came with me.

It never left my side until a dark night seven years later.

41

STELLA

NOW

When I finish speaking, I'm silent.

For what feels like minutes, but could well be just seconds, I'm as mute as the phones. I wonder if my eyes flash blue like they do. The airwaves are quiet, too, and will be until someone goes live; until Stephen comes in.

The studio phone sparks its lightning, blinking over and over and over. Then – like the bassline to its repetitive song – someone starts pounding on the main door again. The peace is over; I sense that it will never again be so still.

I look at the clock; ten past five. God, I was on air for half an hour. It passed by in an instant, and now I can hardly recall what I said. It has been recorded though. It exists forever. But I don't want to hear it. Just like when I played dead with Tom. I watched it once, with him, because I was unconscious and hadn't been able to see it when it happened live. Then I never wanted to see it again. I have played dead, and I have spoken about the dead, and now I won't look back. Now I must go where I'm supposed to, but I have no idea where that is.

Where do I belong?

Who do I belong to?

The pounding continues. Stephen will be trying to get in. Now I'm not speaking, I can hear him calling my name on the other side of the door. There is another voice out there too, one I don't recognise, male. What if they get in? They *can't*. I need to get out, escape, get away from

here, but that's the only door. I stand, sending the chair toppling over.
I put my head in my hands. Then I scream; at the ceiling; at the door;
at the foyer beyond.

At the world.

What have I done? What have I *done*?

Now I'm afraid. Sorry, sad, and desperately afraid.

I can't undo any of it, though, I can only plan what I do next. But
there's no escaping this building until whoever is out there leaves, and
they're not likely to go anywhere if they heard my final words. God,
the police. Will they be here too? Some listener may well have called
them. Would there have been sirens, or would the early hour mean they
would come quietly, stealing through the night, flashing radio-phone-
blue lights?

I really am alone now.

It's just me and what I have done.

I turn on my phone, thinking I want to reach out, but regret it.
Notifications ping and vibrate. I don't want to read or listen to any of
them. I don't want to know what they think of me. Maeve Lynch has
sent a text, and I can't help seeing some of the message in a snippet at
the top of my screen:

I've been listening. Stella, please tell me it's not true?

I can't bear that she is disappointed in me. I want to call her and say
… Say what? I want her sweet, Irish voice to talk about songs to me, not
ask why I have done such a terrible thing.

There are seven voice messages. Three are from Tom. I want to listen
but I'm afraid. My finger hovers over one of them. Will he be angry?
Shocked? Will he love me still? *More*? I'm afraid he won't love me at
all. That I cannot face. I don't listen to what he has to say.

There are fifty-seven Twitter symbols indicating that I've been
tagged in numerous tweets. Frowning, I look at the first one.

*@StellaMcKeever is live on #WLCR right NOW!! She says she DID
IT!! #VickyValbon #girlinthealley #BabyKiller*

I can't help it – I don't want to, but I look at another. And another.
And another. Until they blur into one mass of words.

Oh. My. God. #StellaMcKeever Anyone listening to this????
#girlinthealley
  Is it April Fool's Day early??? #StellaMcKeever #StarGirl
  She did it with a star perfume bottle!!! #StarGirl #GirlInTheAlley
#StarGirl #StarGirl #StarGirl

I look at my slither of window, at the narrow slit that has given me
a limited view of the sky for the last five years. I want to see the bigger
picture. I go closer to it. I remember reading once that the glow from
the nearest star is four years old by the time we see it. That's how far
away they are and how long it takes for the light to travel. There's just
one shining there in the absolute centre of the glass. How soon will it
be morning, and will that final star be gone?

I turn my phone off, throw it in my bag, grab my coat and head into
the foyer. I scream again.

Victoria stands in front of the main door. I close my eyes and open
them. She is still there. She's not bloody now. Her face is angelic; pain-
free, glowing, serene. But she shakes her head, takes off her red coat
and holds it out to me. I know that she is part of my imagination. My
breakdown. My conscience. She always has been.

The pounding on the door continues.

'You're not real,' I say aloud. 'But I listened to you…'

Stella, why did you do it?

I won't listen to her now. What's done is done. Go forwards, not
back. Go up, not down. I hear her voice all around me, a whispery
whirlwind.

Stella, why did you do it like that? That's not how I wanted it…

I cover my ears and close my eyes.

Come with me, then. I think you want to. Come with me.

I open my eyes. Victoria moves towards the stairs, beckoning me.
I'm sure I feel a breeze on my cheeks as she does. She heads up the steps.

Still, the pounding on the door continues. Stephen's voice on the
other side. 'I heard you scream, Stella! Heard you talking to someone.
Who's in there? Are you okay? Open the door, won't you? If someone
made you say all that stuff on air, it'll all be okay, just let me in!'

Victoria has disappeared. The foyer smells of the star perfume. I ignore him and head up the stairs. On the first floor, I pause. Listen. I go to the fire door behind one of the sofas and open it. With the metal stairs from here to the ground broken, no one can reach me this way either. I can hear voices. They must all be at the front of the building.

Not that way, Stella.

Victoria's words come from above me. I close the fire door and follow them up the stairs. To Stephen's office on the second floor. To his immaculately tidy space, where I was once interviewed, where I once tripped, spilling my belongings everywhere. To the room where my life changed, and I started playing people's lives.

Victoria waits by the stairs to the next floor. She beckons me and begins to ascend the steps.

'Where are we going?' I call.

She turns and puts a pale finger to her rose-pink lips. I remind myself that it's *my* mind creating this. That I'm just talking to my own guilt. My conscience. Because it still isn't eased; I still feel guilty.

I follow Victoria – this figment of my pain – because I have nowhere else to go. It's just me and her now. Who else will have me? By the time I reach the next floor – the third, where we have all abandoned broken chairs and old laptops over the years – she has already disappeared up the final flight of steps. The ones to the roof.

I follow her.

Outside it is dark. The chill October air bites at my thin blouse, numbs my nose, and stirs me. Despite the long hours, I feel more awake than I ever have before. I know the dawn light is less than an hour from birth, but the soft hum of traffic on the nearby motorway tells me the morning is under way. The new day will start whether I want it to or not.

I let the door slam shut and lock it from this side, so even if anyone gets in downstairs they won't be able to reach me.

I've never been up here before. I scan the flat area slowly, the chimney, the skylight. And my heart sinks; at the opposite side of the roof, Victoria stands with her back to the carpark and her eyes on me, shimmering like one of those fake candles. The flicker is as regular as a heartbeat. The grainy world behind her is suffocated by the intense light she emanates. She is all I can see. All that exists. She holds the baby to her chest again, wrapped snugly in her red coat. Its face is concealed by the collar.

This is not what I wanted, Stella, she says. *This is not how it was supposed to happen.*

'I told them,' I whisper. 'I *told* them.'

Victoria shakes her head sadly at me. Despite the sorrow, she looks stronger than she did that night. Taller. Brighter. Bigger. I am the one who is small. She will eternally be a somebody. I will forever be known as a killer.

This need never have happened, she says.

Then she closes those green eyes and she falls. Backwards. Hair wild. Arms out, like she's a child making snow angels, her baby tucked under her chin. Both gone in a flash.

'No!' I scream and run to the edge. 'I'm *sorry*!'

Below, nothing. No Victoria. No coat. No baby. My heart hammers so fast I think I'll choke. Then people stream into sight. They emerge from around the corner where the main door is. They must have heard my screams. A man I don't recognise points up towards me, so I back away, into the shadows again. Others gasp.

'Stella!' This voice I know: Tom. My Tom. 'Stella! What the hell are you doing up there?' I peer over the edge. He's at the front of the crowd. He has his coat on over the T-shirt and shorts he wears in bed.

'Stella! Please go back inside.' Another voice I know: my mum. 'Go inside and come down and let us in!' She is at Tom's side. I realise this is only the third time they've ever met. What a night to be a family.

'Stella, the police are here, and they want to make sure you're okay.' This time it's Stephen Sainty. 'We just want you to come out. If someone is with you, we want to speak to them too. Stella, can you answer us, *please*?'

I feel sick, but I can't throw up now. I inhale deeply and take a tentative step towards the edge of the roof. When I'm a foot away from it,

I peer down at the tiny crowd. At my mum, Tom, Stephen, two police officers and all the other faces I don't recognise. I frown, look harder: Miles – The Man Who Knows – is with them too. His camera swings from his neck like a pendulum. He stands behind the rest of them, wringing his hands. Was he listening to WLCR earlier? He must have been. Were my words what he expected?

'Stella, please,' cries Tom. 'Move away from the edge.'

'I like it here,' I call. 'I can see everything.'

'Stella, you're scaring me!' He cups his hands around his mouth. 'Why did you say all that on the radio, for God's sake? That isn't you! What are you playing at? Tell them you didn't really kill Victoria. Tell them!'

'But I did,' I cry.

'I don't believe you.'

'I love you,' I say.

'Then come down, Stella, and we can sort this out.'

'You win,' I cry.

'*What*?'

'The chopping board. In the kitchen. Our dance!'

'Our what? Stella, what the *hell* are you talking about? Just come down!'

'I'll let you leave it all wild and diagonal now!' I cry. 'You can leave crumbs wherever you want! You can put it right near the edge if you want to!'

Tom looks distraught. Even from up here I see the colour drain from his face. It makes me want to reach out and touch him in his fearful moment. To comfort him. To tell him I did all this for him. He must know that.

'I don't want the bloody chopping board near the edge,' he yells. 'And I don't want *you* there either!'

I laugh; I can't help it. He's right. I should be further back, the way I put the chopping board. But, in this, I'd rather lose. I move a little closer to the edge.

'I've never been up here before,' I yell. 'I've opened the door and looked out, but I've never walked onto the roof. Not in five years. It's really quite wonderful. The city looks so different.'

'Come down, *please*, and admit you didn't kill anyone!' cries Tom.

'But I *did*.'

'I don't believe you!'

'He knows what happened.' I point to Miles, The Man Who Knows. 'He *saw* me.' They all turn to him. He shrinks back. 'He was there! He saw me leaving the alley! Tell them, Miles.'

One of the police officers approaches him.

The other one calls, 'Stella, we can deal with all of this at the station. Please come down and talk to us. Whatever did or didn't happen, this isn't the way to do it. Someone might get hurt.'

'Miles will tell you everything he knows,' I cry.

'Stella, please come down.' It's my mum now. 'I'll come with you to the station and we can straighten it all out. I think you're not feeling like yourself. This is some sort of breakdown. You've had a lot going on recently.'

'You mean like trying to look myself in the mirror each day?' I yell. 'Yes, it's been difficult. You must know about that, though?'

She nods and says something I can't hear.

'You'll have to shout,' I cry.

'I've made many mistakes,' she yells, and then covers her mouth as though embarrassed.

'You once told me I began wrong,' I call. 'Remember that? You said when my feet emerged before my head, all bloody and stuff, you knew I'd be an awkward girl. Well, you were right, weren't you? I began wrong because I *am* wrong! Maybe it's because my father is a murderer, eh? Maybe because you didn't even want me! I think babies can sense that, even before they are born.'

'No,' she cries, holding an arm out pleadingly. '*You're* not wrong! I'm the one who has been wrong. The one who *did* wrong. Come down; let me say it to you. I don't care what you said on the radio, I love you.'

'You do now,' I yell.

'Maybe,' she admits. 'But isn't that better than never? Come down and we can put right everything between us. I'll do whatever it takes, I promise you. Just come down and let me explain.'

'I used to think you were with the stars,' I say. 'Not when you left me. I was old enough to know better then. But when you went out at night when I was small and weren't back in the morning. I thought, that's where she's gone.'

'I'm so sorry I left you,' she cries. 'We're all here now, like this, because of me, not because of you.' She pauses. 'Show us the star perfume bottle.'

'I can't,' I say. 'You heard what happened to it.'

'No,' cries my mum. 'I don't think you're capable! Show me the perfume!'

'I can't,' I scream. 'It's gone!'

'Stella,' yells Tom. 'Stop this and just come down now!'

I shake my head. I have to make them believe me and there's only one way to do that.

'I wish I could come down,' I tell Tom. 'You have no idea how I wish that you and I could just disappear together.'

'Maybe we can!'

'No. We can't. You know that, and I know that. The minute I open that door, they won't be all nice and, *Oh, it's going to be okay, we'll sort this out*. They'll arrest me. They'll interrogate me. I'll be all over the news. I'll be hated.'

'Retract what you've said then,' he says.

'I can't.'

'Stella!' It's Stephen. A police officer is whispering in his ear. 'I know you. Your family does. And if you *did* do this, the way you—'

'She *didn't*!' cries my mum, urgent.

'The way you described,' continues Stephen, 'then we know they were circumstances beyond your control. You're not a cold-blooded killer. You were driven to it. So please come down and let us help you.'

'Stephen,' I yell. 'Just think how this will send the WLCR ratings through the roof! You'll be the hottest station around. Promise me you'll go all the way with it. Tell them everything about tonight.

About this. Just don't reheat it, will you? Give them something new every time.' I pause to control my voice as the emotion builds. 'And tell Maeve she was the best thing about working here. Tell her I hope she will understand one day.'

'You tell her,' cries Stephen. 'Come down and we can take you to her, right now, at the hospital.'

The stars are fading. The four-year-old light will die until tomorrow night, when it emerges again. There's a hint of sun in the lower realms of the inky sky. Soon the night will be gone altogether. And I'm not sure if I want to be here either. I belong to this night. I have belonged to it since I handed in my notice, since that night in the alley, since I met Tom, since my mum left me and then came back, since I found out who my father is.

The Man Who Knows – no, *Miles* – moves away from the crowd, from the policeman at his side, and he slowly lifts the camera. I imagine I hear a magnified click as he takes a picture. No flash. Perhaps it isn't needed. He knows what he's doing. Will I be clear, or blurred like the ones in the alley, like the one of me as a child? Will it be a truth photograph? Will he share it on social media and use the Star Girl hashtag? Will it go viral?

'Come down, Stella!' screams my mum.

I smile and blow her a kiss.

'Listen to her!' yells Stephen.

I ignore him.

'Please, Stella!' cries Tom. 'I love you! It's only ever been you!'

'It's only ever been *you*,' I shout back. 'This is what love is.'

There are still a few stars, dim but present. I want to cry, but my tears are as frozen as they often were in Sandra's back room, when I tested to see how far I dared lean back from the window.

What would happen if I leaned back now?

What would happen if I fell?

What would happen if I *fell*?

What would happen if…

I turn around, close my eyes, and I fall. It is slow. I fly. Somehow, I join the sky. Where do I belong? The stars. Who do I belong to? The sky. And I hear them all screaming my name; my mum, Tom, Stephen, The Man Who Knows. I hear, almost lost in the chorus, Victoria calling me too. And then there's another voice; one I don't recognise. Yet it's one I know. My father. Yes, I think it's my father. Harland Grey.

Stella, Stella, Stella, they all chant. *Stella, Stella, Stella*.

But they've got it wrong.

Don't call me Stella.

Call me Star Girl.

42

ELIZABETH

THEN

There is a moment I had forgotten.

No, I don't really think I forgot it. We can choose what we look back at, can't we? I'm a coward so I never could bear to see it. But I do now. Now she's gone. All the time. Can't get it out of my head.

The memory hit me as Stella fell that terrible night. As we all lurched forwards, and I knew we could not save her. As we screamed her name and heard that horrible, horrible sound as the back of her head hit the concrete near my feet.

I was the first to reach her. To hold her bloody and disfigured head to my chest. To know there was no chance she had survived the impact. But I could not let go of her, not when the ambulance arrived, not when they tried to prise her from my grip. I had barely wanted to hold her when she was born, but now I *had* to be the one to.

When they carried her into the ambulance, her left foot fell from the stretcher. She had socks on. Pink ones, the same as her pastel work blouse. The one on that foot was wrinkled and had fallen right down. It brought back a memory I'd ignored all these years. I sobbed desperately. How could I have left her when she was just a kid? That abandonment had led to this, to her suicide.

It was all my fault.

Long ago, on the day I would leave her, I had watched my twelve-year-old Stella flounce down the path to school. So young and vibrant. So unlike me, tired at thirty-two by then, smoking thirty a day, still clubbing when I had the energy, trying to hide tired lines with make-up, and working my way through men who rarely bought me perfume anymore.

Frumpy Sandra was pulling her wheelie bin out that day and made time, as she always did, to chat to Stella for a moment. Stella's face broke into a natural smile. A pang of jealousy gripped me, despite my wish to escape being a mother. I hadn't known then that it was the penultimate time I'd see my daughter for fourteen years. If I had, I might have gone after her. Hugged her, even though that was not our way. Pushed her hair off her face. Said sorry.

When the letter arrived from Harland saying he was free, and I got everything together to escape, I'd felt terrible about deserting Stella so suddenly and absolutely. I *did*. I'm not just saying it now, after all that has happened.

When the taxi I'd called arrived, I wondered if fate would bring that driver with the memorable name: Bob Fracklehurst. It didn't. Fate was frowning on my decision to go. But still, I got in the car and ignored the young, chatty driver. As we passed Stella's school, I shot forwards in my seat and asked him to stop a moment. Asked him to wait.

I got out and approached the metal fencing. It was break time. Some of the kids were huddled close to the fence, gossiping and giggling as young teens do. I looked for Stella. I made a deal with myself; if I saw her I'd stay. I'd do the decent thing. I scanned the yard. She was sitting on a bench not far from me, facing the other way. If she had turned she would have seen me. But she didn't, and I was glad because I knew she would have come over to me and asked a million questions.

I had challenged myself to stay if I saw her.

But Harland. Oh, *Harland*.

I turned to leave.

I looked back just once. It was then I noticed that one of Stella's socks – a bright pink one, rebellious against her school uniform grey – had fallen down. It was wrinkled about her ankle. Such a thin ankle. I recalled how she had been born feet first. Awkward from the start, I'd often told her. She looked so young sitting there; so vulnerable. Lost in her own world. I knew I would have to erase the image of that sock from my head. Have to *never* think about it again if I wanted Harland.

I pretended to myself that I had not seen her and got back in the taxi.

I managed to bury that true last sight of Stella, and her errant sock, until I was with her in the ambulance, heading for the hospital. When I saw that pink sock loose around her still-slender adult ankle, I broke down. Tom was there, too. He looked stunned rather than grief-stricken. He patted my back as I sobbed, one of my hands gripping her ankle. The paramedics said they had to get her into the ambulance, so I followed, still holding it. As we travelled through the dawn streets, they were doing things to Stella, and I wanted to scream at them to stop because I knew she was long gone.

She had left me.

And I deserved it.

I *deserved* it.

Much later that day I took home that one pink sock. To remind myself that the girl who had arrived feet first had left the world as she should have been born – head first. She had lived her whole life with only those two feet to stand on. No decent mother, no father.

I could forgive anything that Stella might have done.

Anything at all.

I just couldn't forgive myself.

43

ELIZABETH

NOW

I didn't go to Stella's home while she was alive. As much as I wished to, she never invited me. I used to try and imagine what it might be like. Tidy. Organised. Perfect. Everything in its place.

I was right. The front is immaculate. The little patch of grass is short, and the windows are clean, the curtains neatly tied back. She has only been gone a week and I wonder for a moment if Tom has kept it this way in her honour. To remember her. But it's late October now, so the grass wouldn't have needed cutting again, and he may not have touched the curtains since she died.

I love the small house. I only wish Stella was inside it.

I suddenly remember a pretty key she showed me once; a sterling silver one that didn't actually open the door. It was large and had the initials S and T delicately inscribed into it. Stella and Tom. A strange thing, quite sharp. Stella had said it nicked her finger occasionally when she rummaged through her bag. Tom had an identical one. She gave him it as a moving-in gift.

The thought of her being so kind, so happy to live with her love, brings a painful lump to my throat. But I can't cry now. I'm here to be strong, not weak.

I open the gate and go up the path, then compose myself before knocking on the door. For a moment, I think I smell the star perfume, fleeting, on the cool breeze. Is Stella with me? I have sensed her these past few nights; I've imagined her shadow in a window or mirror behind me, and then turned around to nothing. I might not have treated Stella how I was supposed to. I might not have been a true and good mother. I certainly didn't see right by her in life, but I can make sure I do now she's not here anymore. I will be her voice. I will say what she can't.

Because she didn't kill Vicky.

I know this.

I knock on the door.

After what seems like forever, just as I almost turn and leave, Tom opens the door. He looks dishevelled. His cheeks are sunken, as though they are pulled down by grief. For a moment, I want to reach out and stroke his face, but I resist. I've always found it far easier to touch and show affection for men. I'm not sure if it is because of the promise of sex, of attention, of love. But that now doesn't come into it. Tom is not mine and I don't want him to be.

He says, *oh*, like he is confused.

I ask if I can come in for a moment.

We haven't seen one another since that terrible night. Not since we went in the ambulance together, since we hovered over Stella's broken body at the hospital and got the horrible news we already knew. The funeral won't be for a while yet. Due to the nature of her death, her body hasn't been fully released yet. As next of kin, it's my responsibility to claim it, though I will run all decisions by Tom. It's only fair. I think she would want him to be involved.

Tom opens the door wider and I follow him inside. It is just as tidy as the outside. In the living room there's a huge, blood-red sofa. The cushions are neat and opposite each other. It's too neat, in fact. Too perfect. Like it's calculated and not someone's natural way. I want to mess it all up.

I realise he has the radio on. It's not a presenter that I recognise, but then I rarely listen during the day. Maeve Lynch has been doing Stella's evening slot the last few nights. She has the most beautiful voice. I almost feel guilty for enjoying her. She sounds sad, though. Like she misses Stella too.

Coffee, Tom asks me, as though this visit is all normal, as though we know each other well and I've been here many times before.

I suppose grief does strange things to people. It has certainly taken me unaware. It wakes me in the night – a pain that shoots right through me. The pain is mixed with horrific guilt – and self-pity I suppose – which makes it all the more wretched.

I tell Tom that coffee would be good.

Then I follow him into the kitchen and watch him put the kettle on. The radio is on in here too, like he needs it wherever he goes. Maybe he's hoping to hear Stella, just as I do when I tune in. I sometimes hope it is all a nightmare and I'll wake up and there she is, all elegant and confident on the airwaves. I remember knowing it was Stella that first night I came back to live here, before she said her name.

They have been playing snippets of Stella's final show – the confession, as they call it. But I turn that off. I can't bear to hear it. It just doesn't sound like her. Not the her I got to know.

Sugar? asks Tom, and I shake my head.

I notice the chopping board. It is placed straight, about four inches from the edge of the work surface, and it's so clean it reflects the light above it.

I remember, I say to him, *that Stella shouted that you could leave it all wild and diagonal now. On the roof... that night.*

He nods; says that she always liked it dead straight. That he was messier, and they always tried to outdo each other with where they put the chopping board. It was just a thing they did. He looks at it. He doesn't need to say that he has put it how she would want it to be. We both know it.

I like to think... he begins, but doesn't finish.

As the kettle bubbles, he fiddles with the two cups.

Now I'm here, where should I start? How on earth do I *tell* him? The room sways. I am wracked with guilt and sadness and knowledge. What will he do if I do tell him?

Tom, I say eventually, *I came because there are some things you don't know.*

He frowns. *About Stella?* he asks.

Yes. But about Vicky too.

About Vicky?

The kettle clicks off, but he doesn't move. Doesn't make our drinks. He doesn't turn around either. Just remains immobile. I continue speaking to his back.

I was Vicky's doula, I tell him.

Her what? Tom turns, confusion on his face.

It's a trained woman who helps another woman through her pregnancy and labour when she has no one else. I used to be one. Until ... well, Vicky was my last.

So that's what it's called, he says.

What do you mean?

Tom ignores me. He turns back to make the drinks, so I can't read his face.

I got quite close to Vicky. I liked her. I pause. *So I know.*

Tom turns. *What do you know?*

I know she wanted you back.

Maybe. Tom stirs the drinks. *But she would never have got me back. I loved Stella. Is that what this is all about? You think I was cheating on your daughter? You couldn't be more wrong. I loved her.*

I know you did, I say gently.

Tom hands me my coffee. Close up, his eyes flash with intensity. I can see again why Stella was drawn to him. He has the simmering presence Harland had. An electricity that fills the air. When he goes into the living room I follow him. A white cat is curled up on a red sofa. She – it looks like a she to me – looks up at us and then scurries away, brushing past my leg on her way out.

She's Perry, says Tom quietly. *Never really liked me. Loved Stella though.*

He motions for me to sit on the sofa, so I do. He remains standing. I wonder briefly if he wants to appear bigger, stronger – in charge somehow.

Should I be scared of him? Maybe. But I'm not. Just as I never was of Harland. But I'm afraid to tell him the rest.

Tom, I say, *one night I went to Vicky's house.*

He studies me but doesn't speak.

She had told me earlier on that day that she was coming to visit you, to tell you she still loved you and she was going to get you back.

I sip my coffee and watch for Tom's reaction.

Nothing.

I couldn't let that happen, I say. *I knew how much it would hurt Stella. How much she loved you. So I decided I was going to intervene. Stop her. Whatever it took. I went and sat outside her house all evening. Until midnight...*

And? asks Tom.

There is no going back.

I tell him.

44

BOB FRACKLEHURST

NOW

It takes three attempts for Bob Fracklehurst to open the police station door and go inside.

He almost wishes that no one will be sitting behind the desk; that way he can sneak back out and return home. But a young man in a uniform is there, and when he looks up with enquiring eyebrows, Bob knows there is no going back.

He has been thinking about coming here for days. Four times he has even set off in the car and then turned back. But this morning he knew absolutely that it was the right thing to do. He got up early – trying not to disturb Trish, because he didn't want her embroiled in anything too emotional, not after her recent hysterectomy. He put on his smart slacks and the shoes with the tassels that Trish got him, and then he drove around in his brand-new, not-a-taxi car until it was light. It took Bob a further half-hour to make himself go inside.

'Can I help you, sir?' The officer looks too young to be in the job, as though he has tried on his father's uniform and wandered in here by mistake.

'Um, yes, I hope so.' Bob goes to the desk. 'I have something to report.'

'A crime, sir?'

'Not exactly.' Bob clears his throat. 'I mean, it involves a crime, but one that's already been committed. It's about the Victoria Valbon murder.'

'Yes?'

'It's just that ... well, I ... I don't know where to start really.'

'If you think you have some new information, I'll go and get someone to take your details.' The young man disappears. After a while, he returns with a much older, female officer. Her smile is brisk, her manner even brisker, and her ash hair so tightly pulled back that her eyes are catlike.

'We'll go in here,' she says, leading Bob into a private room. 'Cup of tea?'

'No, thank you.'

In the small space, they sit opposite one another at a wooden table. It's too warm and Bob wonders briefly if this is intentional, so criminals sweat and make full confessions. No, that's ridiculous; he's been watching too many crime shows with Trish.

'Okay, sir,' she says, opening a folder. 'I'm PC Greatfield and I'll get some info from you here, and then if I deem it necessary, the officer in charge of the case will question you himself. He's away until tomorrow so you'll have to come back. Is that okay?'

'Yes, whatever you need to do.'

'Can I take your name?' Her pen is poised.

'Bob Fracklehurst.'

'And your—'

'It's all official then, is it? You've decided Stella McKeever did it?'

'I can't comment on that.' She frowns at him. 'But I can say that the case isn't closed yet, so any info you have could still be immensely helpful. Can you give me your date of birth, address and phone number please?'

Bob does so.

'And what do you—?'

'I don't think she did it.' Bob spills the words. They have been going around in his head for two days. It's good to get them out. He was afraid to come, afraid he would be in trouble for not coming weeks ago. 'I don't think she murdered Victoria Valbon.'

'Okay, sir.' PC Greatfield studies him, as though to assess his mental capacity. Is he a lunatic? An attention-seeker?

'I listened to her all the time on the radio,' he says then. 'Stella McKeever, I mean. I drive you see; taxis. Or I did. I retired a few weeks ago. I miss it, you know. It's a long time to be doing a thing and then *not* to be. I got to meet all sorts of folks, from all walks of life. I always had me radio on, listened to music, sang along. Sometimes now I get in the car and drive around, just to feel like I'm doing it again. My Trish thinks me quite bloody barmy. She said—'

'Sir, if you could just tell me about Stella McKeever.'

'I'm sorry. I ramble when I'm nervous.'

Bob scratches his cheek. Though he gave up smoking three years ago, he suddenly longs for one. In the crime dramas he and Trish watch, suspects are allowed to smoke. But he isn't a suspect. And this isn't TV. A young woman's innocence could be in his hands though.

'It's so terrible what happened. I just couldn't believe it when I saw it on the news. I cried, I tell you. Cried like a baby.' Tears fill his eyes now. 'My Trish said she'd never seen me that way. But a young woman, doing *that*. Saying those things and then jumping from a roof. What a waste.'

'Sir, you said you don't think Stella McKeever did it. Can you please just tell me why that is?'

'Yes, yes, I will. I just ... I just get emotional.' Bob pauses. 'You don't realise...'

'What don't I realise?'

'She said all that stuff on the radio that night, but it just *can't* be true.' Bob leans forward, impassioned. 'She wasn't in her right bloody mind. You could tell by the way she said it all. Nothing like the calm and warm way she usually speaks.'

PC Greatfield doesn't look convinced. 'Sir, reading the weather and confessing to a crime are two entirely different things.'

'But I don't think it was a confession!'

'What *do* you think it was?'

'A *false* confession.' Bob sits back and exhales hard. He crosses his legs and notices the tassel on his left shoe is missing. *No*. These are Trish's favourites. He suddenly feels desperately sad. Trish is quite spiritual and always sees signs in everything. Is this a good one or a bad one?

'Sir, why do you think someone would confess to a murder they hadn't committed?'

'I think she was protecting someone.'

'I suppose it's possible.' Other than Bob's name and address, PC Greatfield hasn't written anything down yet. 'What makes you think that's the case?'

'She was in my taxi the night it happened.'

'The night she fell you mean?'

'No,' says Bob. 'The night Victoria Valbon was murdered.'

'In *your* taxi?'

'Yes.'

'You're sure?'

'One hundred percent. It was my last-ever shift. I retired that very night. She was the last passenger I ever had.'

'Why didn't you come and report this sooner?' asks the PC, frowning.

Bob runs his fingers through his greying hair and shakes his head. 'I thought about it. I *did*. But that was before this stupid confession. I didn't think Stella had done anything, so there was nothing to tell until now. I thought if I came in cos I'd had her in my taxi, all upset, that I might incriminate her somehow. Ruin a young lass's life. But now ... well, now everybody thinks she killed that poor pregnant girl. And I don't think she did, so I *have* to speak.'

'Sir, just tell me exactly what happened.'

'I will. I *will*.' Bob braces himself; he touches the remaining shoe tassel. 'I might get emotional. This has been going around in my head for weeks now. I never had a daughter, you know. Me and Trish just have one son. I thought Stella could be my daughter. She was the right age. Kind of gets you teary.' He pauses. 'Sorry, I'll tell you, I will. So that night ... it was very late. I was about to finish. Then this girl flagged me down. Now, we're not supposed to do that – pick up customers who haven't booked. But she looked distraught. She was waving to me, desperately. I couldn't leave her.'

'She got into your car?'

'Yes. It was about three streets away from the alley. You know, the one where ... Of course, I didn't think that at the time, only afterwards, when the news broke.'

'Sir, please go on.' Bob can tell PC Greatfield is trying to stay patient.

'At first she couldn't seem to say much. I couldn't even get out of her where she lived, so we hadn't pulled away yet. I didn't recognise her right away, you see. I've picked her up a few times before and I'd recognised her voice then, even though she didn't speak how she does on the show. Much faster. Less clearly. But that night she was so upset I didn't realise straight away it was her. She was just shaking like a leaf. I asked if she was okay. She nodded her head, and then changed her mind and shook it. I said we could wait a moment and I would turn off the meter. I don't how long we sat there. But eventually she looked at me and said, "I can't go home yet." I told her, okay, no rush, I would wait. And then she told me something really terrible had happened. Of course, I was thinking all sorts. Wondering what had happened to the poor lass.'

'Go on, sir.' PC Greatfield taps the pen on the form even though she still hasn't recorded a word of his story.

'She said then that she usually walked home, even at this hour. That her job kept her out until past one. That she didn't usually take that alley – the one where they found ... But that night, she said, she had been walking past there and something had happened, and now her legs were like jelly and she didn't think she could make it back home.'

'And what *had* happened, sir?'

'She didn't exactly tell me that.' Bob looks apologetic.

'So how can you be sure that her confession was false and that she wasn't the murderer?'

'She said that she had *seen* something terrible happen. She didn't say that she had *done* something terrible. Can you see the difference?' Bob pauses as though to allow the PC to answer, but she doesn't. 'The wording is very important I think.'

'Maybe,' says PC Greatfield. 'But if Stella was distraught, as you say she was, she might not have been making much sense. How can you be sure what she meant at all?'

'I can't.' Bob's brow is damp. He wishes they would turn the heating down. He takes off his jacket and hangs it over the back of the chair. 'But it isn't just what she *said*...'

'What do you mean, sir?'

'Cases like this are all about the evidence in the end, aren't they?'

'Yes.' PC Greatfield frowns.

'And do you have all the evidence?'

'Sir, I cannot discuss with you the ins and outs of the case. Please just stick to telling me what you know. The facts. What you witnessed. What Stella told you.'

'But it isn't just about what she told me.' Bob knows he is starting to sound a little hysterical now and rolls the remaining shoe tassel between his fingers to stay focused. He just wants to do right by that poor girl. By both of them. Stella *and* Victoria. 'As I said, Stella was hardly coherent. She said she had *seen* something terrible. Said she'd been walking home and had heard something and she should have just kept walking, but something made her investigate. She broke down again then and screamed that she should never have done that. She was inconsolable. She didn't tell me any more details. She asked me to take her home. We drove off and she was sobbing. I asked if she wanted to go to a police station, because I reckoned she must have seen something awful. But she got hysterical again and said, *No, no, they can never know.*'

'Why do you think she said that?' PC Greatfield is the one leaning forwards now, her mouth slightly agape.

'I'm not sure.'

'You look like you are,' says the PC.

'I think her confession was false.'

'Why would she lie? Why on earth would she share such a detailed story – and it was very detailed, as I'm sure you heard – and then throw herself off a building?'

'I agree that it was detailed,' says Bob. 'But she seems a very bright girl. She has wonderful oratory skills. I have every faith that she could weave a tale if she wanted to and make it sound like the truth.'

'But why, sir? *Why* would she do that?'

'If your mother or sister or friend had committed a crime, what would you do?'

'I beg your pardon?' PC Greatfield looks suitably outraged. 'Can we stick to this case, sir?'

'If it was my Trish,' says Bob, 'I would do anything to protect her.'

'That would be a crime in itself.'

'But if I knew she had acted in haste or in passion, done something because she wasn't herself, I'd do anything to stop her being caught. I'd lie, and I'd lie well.'

'What are you saying?' demands the PC.

'That Stella McKeever was lying to protect someone.'

'Who?'

'Well, *that* I don't know. Isn't that your job? I'd say it was someone she loved. Aren't those the people we want to protect?'

PC Greatfield closes her folder. 'Sir, I really appreciate you coming in, and this might be helpful in building an overall picture, but it really won't make much of a difference. You're assuming a lot based on the ramblings of a woman in great distress. A woman who was capable of suicide, and perhaps a lot more.'

Bob shakes his head, frustrated. 'It isn't what she said or didn't say the night of the murder that made me come here. No, it's what she said *on air* the night she jumped.'

'With all due respect, sir, I'm sure that has been fully analysed in the last few days.' PC Greatfield starts to get up. 'If there's something there, it will have been picked up. Thank you for—'

'When we got to her house that night,' Bob says, quickly, to keep her in the room, 'Stella fumbled in her bag to get her purse. I insisted I didn't want paying, that the meter hadn't been on. This made her cry for some reason. She tried to insist but I wouldn't hear of it. As she got her bag, it got caught on the handle, and she wrenched it to get free. I watched her go into her house and pulled away.'

The PC is standing but she doesn't move. 'What does this have to do with what she said on air?'

'Two days ago, I gave up my taxi. Not only cos I retired, but because of all the miles on it. I'd have used her myself otherwise. Taxis have very short lives. And she – I called her Jean – was worn out after five years. When I dropped her off to be scrapped, and to pick up my new car, someone from the scrap place called later and said they had found something under the passenger seat. I knew exactly what it was as soon as they handed it to me.'

'And what was it?' PC Greatfield drops back into her seat.

Bob slides a hand inside his jacket pocket and takes something out. He holds it to his chest a moment, fist wrapped protectively around it. Then he places it carefully on the table in front of PC Greatfield.

She looks at it. Frowns. Moves closer. Even in this dim room, it catches the light of the fluorescent strip above them, scattering mini stars on the table surface.

It is a delicate glass bottle with a star stopper, half full of perfume.

And it is perfectly and beautifully intact.

45

ELIZABETH

NOW

My voice falters. I sip my coffee again, needing the sharp heat to keep me focused. To keep me from trembling as I try and tell Tom what I know. I wish he would sit on the sofa with me. I don't like the feeling of him towering over me. When the words don't come he speaks.

What happened with you and Vicky that night? he asks.

She never came out, I say eventually.

What do you mean? Tom narrows his eyes, but it doesn't lessen the intensity.

It got to half-past twelve and she hadn't appeared. I shrug. *So I presumed she'd changed her mind.*

Tom looks intrigued.

I just hoped she'd seen sense and decided not to bother, I continue. *And I went home. If I had only managed to talk to her. If only she had come out, I might have been able to stop all this. She would still be alive – and so would Stella.*

I look directly at Tom again.

I planned to go back the next night...

And did you? he asks.

I study Tom. *I was going to, but I fell asleep in my chair, woke at one-thirty and thought it was too late. And it was, wasn't it? She was murdered.*

Tom says that I'm right about one thing – that Vicky must have seen sense and decided not to bother because she never came here.

I think she was still intending to come to you, I say. *Something stopped her coming the night I waited. But she must have gone the next night. If we believe what Stella said in her confession.*

Tom frowns. *What do you mean 'if we believe'. You think Stella lied?*

Yes, I say. *I do.*

And why the hell would she do that? he demands.

Because—

At that moment, Stephen Sainty's voice fills the room. We turn to look at the radio. It's the news on the hour, and Stella is still the hot topic. He talks about her first; his usually smooth voice is more ragged, and I sense something big coming. He says that someone has come forward with further evidence on the Victoria Valbon murder enquiry. Evidence that suggests Stella McKeever may not have disclosed the full truth in her live radio confession a week ago.

Evidence?

I look at Tom, but he turns away.

Then Stella's voice comes out of the speakers, so clear and full of life that it's as though she is in the room with us.

This really is my final show now. These are my last words to you. I've been playing your lives for five years. Tonight, it was mine. So ... I guess this is goodbye.

Tom looks distraught. He now drops onto the arm of the sofa, wraps his arms about his body, and shivers.

It's just hearing her voice, he says.

I understand, I say softly. Then after a moment I ask, *Are you sure that's all it is?*

Yes. His voice is a croak. *I miss her.*

What do you think the new evidence is? I watch for his reaction.

How would I know? Could be anything. Probably some crank! Everyone wants a piece of the action. To be famous. To get in the papers. They'll do and say anything. Do you know how many calls I've had?

Me, too, I admit.

It's been endless. I've had journalists at the door, some pretending to deliver flowers just to speak to me. I've changed my home phone number and I rarely look at my mobile any more. This is the region's biggest story in decades. In a headline in one of the national newspapers they said there was a *Star Girl* film in the pipeline because of the trending hashtag and the newsworthy drama of the story. Already. They say such tasteless things just a week after a young woman died by suicide. A month after another was killed in an alley.

And I hate that they call Stella 'Star Girl'.

It seems cruel somehow. I meant it affectionately when I said it the day we were reunited, but now it's used as a taunt.

Stephen Sainty doesn't strike me as a sensationalist, I say to Tom. *Stella respected him. She said all news is usually old anyway, so they must have really checked out this evidence before releasing the info.*

He just reports what he's given. Tom sounds exhausted now. *He won't know if what he's told is true.*

I sip my coffee. It has gone cold. Stephen Sainty moves on to other, lesser news. His voice is not as intense. I suggest again to Tom that I think Stella lied that night; he wearily asks me why she would do that.

To protect someone, I say.

He glares at me.

I tell Tom how her voice changed when she talked about him. How her face flushed. How her eyes lit up. His eyes mist at these words, and he quickly looks away to hide it. I tell him that I know that feeling. I know the things we will do when someone affects us that way. I tell him I left Stella because someone made me feel like that. That now I have to live with the guilt of abandoning a child because I loved a man that much.

Stella wasn't you, says Tom. *She would never have left a child.*

No, I cry. *And she would never have killed one either.*

Tom stands again as though regaining his power and demands that I say what I came here to say and then leave. I stand too. I'm not afraid now. There might be evidence on my side.

I think Stella was protecting the person who really killed Vicky, I say. *Maybe it was you she was protecting.*

Tom moves a little closer to me, but I don't back down.

Me? What? I didn't commit that crime!

No, I mean protecting you from the truth.

Tom is right in front of me, his eyes bright now. *Maybe she was trying to make you think it was me as a double bluff, just so you didn't have to think your own daughter was a killer.*

I'm briefly thrown. My mind works overtime.

She didn't say anything that night to suggest that it was you, I say, without taking my eyes off Tom. *She did her absolute best to make us think it was her. But it's like she tried too hard or something. Bad liars always overstate a story.*

Tom says that Stella wasn't a liar.

I say that she wasn't a killer.

Have I even said I think it's you? I ask him.

You haven't spelled it out, he says. *But we both know you mean me. Who else did she love enough to protect? Aside from you.*

I realise that it might only be me who *really* thinks it wasn't Stella. The world seems so happy to take her words as absolute truth and then sensationalise the story. Or at least it *was* that way. Stephen Sainty said someone has come forward with new evidence to suggest the confession wasn't all it seemed. Will this witness shed new light on things? People like to see the worst in others. It will take a lot for them to think it wasn't Stella after all the media attention.

I can't prove anything right now. I only have a mother's instinct – belated, I know – and the need to be Stella's voice now she can't.

I guess I was hoping you...

What? asks Tom.

...might be honest with me.

I am being.

He doesn't sound it.

I wouldn't judge you, I say.

You did live with a murderer, I suppose, he says.

I ignore the comment, though it is a fair one. Who am I to judge? The thing is, I'm not judging anyone. I just don't want the wrong person to be blamed for a crime.

And I think my daughter did, too, for the last three weeks of her life, I say.

Tom shakes his head slowly.

On the radio, they play 'Starboy' by The Weeknd, and I realise that's who Tom could be. Should he be the one in all the headlines? Did *he* kill Vicky with the star perfume, so it would look like Stella had done it? No, I don't think he wanted anyone to think it was her. I only think *she* wanted us to think it was her.

What are you going to do? asks Tom, calmly.

Nothing, I say. *If you did it, I can't prove it, can I? I know that I didn't do it, and I don't believe Stella did. Who else has a motive? There isn't anyone. Shall I tell you what I think happened?*

Tom tells me I have a hell of an imagination.

Then he sits back down on the sofa and tells me to go ahead.

Tell me what you think happened, he says.

46

BOB FRACKLEHURST

NOW

PC Greatfield's finger hovers near the star-shaped stopper of the perfume bottle, as though to make sure isn't an apparition. She looks at Bob, both confusion and understanding apparent in her eyes.

He nods. 'If Stella was telling the truth, and she killed Victoria Valbon with the broken perfume bottle the way she described, how could that very bottle have been in my car and now here in one piece?'

PC Greatfield looks like a fish blowing bubbles.

'It must have fallen out of her bag that night,' says Bob. 'After she was in the alley, clearly *witnessing* something but not committing the crime she confessed to. I imagine she was heartbroken to have lost it.'

'I'll have to take this from you,' says the PC, resuming her brisk professional mask. 'This is evidence. You'll have to be fingerprinted, too, and you'll have to come back in tomorrow to speak to the officer in charge of the case.'

Bob nods. 'That's fine. I can do that.'

'You'll have to tell them your full story again.'

'I understand. Anything to help Stella. I can't bear to read all the awful things being said about her, especially when it probably isn't true. All those hashtag thingies they do these days. Those awful, blurry pictures of the alley that got released to the press. And that heartbreaking one of her final moment on the roof. She looks so ... *desperate*. She only died a week ago. They should have some respect. My Trish even saw some pathetic article about her father being that murderer Harland

Grey. The things the media will latch onto! Her poor family – they must be going through hell.' Bob stands and puts his coat back on. 'The weird thing is, the day before the murder I had Stella's *mum* in my taxi.'

'Did you?' PC Greatfield stands too. 'How do you know it was her?'

'It was during the day. I picked her up from a café in town. She said that Stella McKeever was her daughter. And I thought, wow, what a small world. Turns out it was even smaller. Then Stella got in my cab the very next night.'

PC Greatfield heads to the door and Bob follows. He looks back.

'When she talked about her daughter,' he says, 'she sounded so proud. She must be so sad that all this has happened. I hope my bringing the perfume bottle in will give her some peace. And reveal the truth.'

'I'm sure it will, sir.'

Bob looks back as they leave the room. The cut-glass bottle still sits on the table, surrounded by tiny reflected stars. He hasn't heard Stella's full radio confession that night, only the edited version played in bits since, here and there. He's heard a snippet in which she says the perfume had belonged to her mother, and also to her father, and he realises that to lie and say she had used it as a murder weapon in a brutal attack must have been traumatic. Whoever she had wanted to protect with her lie, she must have loved more than anything in the world.

'Are you leaving that there?' Bob asks the PC.

'It'll need to be bagged as evidence,' she explains. 'I don't want to touch it without my gloves.'

Bob nods, feeling sad that Stella's cherished treasure will be scrutinised by cold hands and eyes. But if it cleared her name, then it would be worth it.

'Will you give it back to her mum, do you think?' he asks.

'I'm sure it will go back to her family eventually.'

They arrive back at the desk, where the impossibly young officer is speaking on the phone.

'The officer in charge of the Valbon case will contact you to arrange a further interview.' PC Greatfield holds to her chest the folder with only the facts of his name, date of birth and address recorded in it. 'We really appreciate you coming forward, Mr Fracklehurst.'

Bob leaves the police station. Outside, the October day is bright, the edges of the crisp leaves as sharp as cut glass. As he kicks his way through them on the walk to his new car, he notices the tassel on his right shoe is missing now. He bends down and touches the place where it once was. What would Trish think of it? What sign would she say the universe was giving him?

Everything is equal now, thinks Bob.

Maybe *that's* it. Two tassels missing, and two young women found. Maybe now the truth will give both Victoria and Stella the peace they deserve. He remembers the 'Star Girl' headline in one of the big papers yesterday, a name they had stolen from one of those hashtag things. Trish has said she hoped both girls were up there, with the stars, where they belonged.

Bob hopes so too.

47

ELIZABETH

NOW

I tell Tom what I think happened; how I think Vicky went to his house the night she died.

I tell him I think he went for a walk with her because he didn't want Stella to come home and catch them together. I insist that I know he loved Stella and that I think he didn't want her to know that an ex-fiancée was pregnant with his child. He didn't want anything to hurt her.

I say that I don't know *how* it happened, but I think Vicky said she wanted him back. I think they argued, and she begged him. In desperation, said she would tell Stella and ruin what they had. And Tom couldn't let that happen. I said I didn't know how, but Tom killed her. In passion. To shut her up. To keep Stella.

For love.

I tell Tom I think Stella was in that alley and saw it all. That that's how she knew so many details. She just changed the story. Made herself the murderer. She didn't want Tom to go to prison. I can understand this. I *know* this pain. I remind Tom that we know now, from the papers, that the man who took those grainy photos that night had gone to Stella with them. I tell Tom I think she panicked when she saw them. Wanted to stop Tom being arrested.

She did the ultimate thing anyone in love would do – she took the blame for it.

My loving Stella.

I end by saying softly that I think that's what *really* happened.

Tom says nothing. He won't look at me, and hunches forwards on the red sofa.

I'm not going to do anything, I say.

What could you do? he asks, holding my gaze.

I think it's up to you to do something.

Tom says nothing.

We all do crazy things for love. I pause. *And then I think we have to pay for that. I'll pay forever. The night Stella jumped from that roof began the day I left her almost fifteen years ago. My actions started this whole thing. Made her what she is. I have to live with that. But you have to live with what you have done. You killed a baby, Tom. Your own child. I have been a terrible mother, but you are a terrible father too. So, let's put it right. Let's do right by my daughter and your baby.*

And I realise.

I realise as I study Tom what I am prepared to do. Perhaps I knew when I set off to come here. Perhaps I knew yesterday. I did wonder when I arrived earlier whether to tell Tom what I know first, or what I *think* first, and if I then should ask what *he* knows.

But I hadn't realised what I want to *do*.

On the radio, there is a song I can't remember the title of, one I know Stella loved, because she played it all the time.

Tom, I say gently. *I think Stella wanted to protect you. I feel in my heart that she did not kill Vicky. And I don't want the world to think the wrong thing about my daughter. It isn't right. She was a good person. Strong, wilful, and good. Maybe this new evidence will help prove her innocence. If Stella loved you enough to cover for you, I can honour that. I'm prepared to do as she wished.*

Tom very slowly says that he did *not* kill Vicky.

I tell him just as slowly that he needs to tell me the truth.

He says nothing.

I need to know every detail, I say. *Then I'll go to the police and say it was me.*

Don't be ridiculous. Tom attempts a laugh, but it is more of a cough.

I will, I insist.

The police won't simply take your word for it. Tom shakes his head, serious now. *They won't just listen to every crank who comes forward. They'll be looking for more than that – actual proof. Blood. Fingerprints. A weapon.*

What if that's the new evidence? I say.

Stella's confession is still the main evidence.

False confession, I hiss. *Listen, they have more or less said in the papers that those grainy pictures taken in the alley prove nothing – they can't tell who the killer is in them. Stella's confession is all they've been able to use so far. But now they say that someone has evidence to suggest she didn't do it. What if they really do? They'll come to you, Tom.*

Tom still says nothing.

I failed Stella miserably in life, I say. *Now I'll honour her. If she wanted to cover for you, then fine. I'll do it too.*

I move closer to Tom and scream that I simply won't have her going down in history as a killer when she isn't. I beg him to give me the details of what happened that night.

I need to know! How did you do it? How can I do right by Stella if you don't tell me? Where is the star perfume?

What? Tom is caught off guard.

That perfume must be somewhere in this house. She must have lied about it being smashed. So where is it?

Not here! yells Tom.

You did it. Tell me you did it.

Tom stands and says in a slow voice that he did *not* kill Vicky.

What did you use? How did you do it?

Tom shakes his head.

I don't believe you, I say. *You even said that night that you didn't believe Stella. You yelled it up to her on that damned roof! You screamed at her to retract what she was saying! You said she was lying. Because you knew she couldn't have done it! You knew as well as I did!*

You should go, Tom says.

I stand, try to slow my breathing, calm my heart.

How can I help you if you won't tell me? I plead. *Do you really want Stella to be remembered for something she didn't do?*

Tom walks to the front door. I have no choice but to follow him. He opens it and stands aside, without catching my eye. Some golden leaves have fallen onto the very tidy grass. I want to sweep them up. Keep Stella neat. Keep her world how she would want it to be.

I step outside.

I'll go anyway, I say to Tom. *To the police, I mean.* I pause. *Tom, did you really and truly love Stella?*

He has begun closing the door after me, but he stops. I can only see half of his face. Then he says that he did, more than anyone he ever has or ever will again.

And that, he adds, *is why I want to let Stella have the final word.*

He shuts the door. I stare at it, speechless.

After a moment, I walk back down the path and close the gate after me, still not happy about the leaves messing up Stella's patch of grass. I look back, expecting Tom to be watching me from the window. But he isn't there. I glance at the upstairs one and for a moment I think Stella is there. But the clouds move – it was just the sky I saw reflected.

I realise that's where she is now.

I look up at the sky.

I have finally done my best by Stella. Can she see that I have? Does she see me here, leaving Tom's home? Can she see what I am prepared to do for her? Does she know that I am sorry about everything? That I love her now and it's just too late.

Let me make it right, I whisper.

I head towards the police station.

Elizabeth.

I turn. Tom has opened the door again. I go back along their path. I stand in front of him. He crumbles. Collapses against me. I catch him. Hold him. He sobs.

Should I come back inside? I ask him.

I do.

48

BOB FRACKLEHURST

NOW

Three days after his visit to the police station, Bob Fracklehurst drives around the town centre. He often does this. He tells Trish that he is going to his pal Eddie's house or to see the guys in the taxi office again, but he's sure she knows the truth. That he misses the job. Misses the journey. He has arrived where most of us want to be: a lovely home, a family, a good pension, retirement. But his hands miss the wheel, his eyes miss the road, and his heart misses the passengers.

After circling the centre and taking the roads often travelled – those lined with pubs – Bob finds himself in the layby near the alley where Victoria Valbon died. He leaves the engine running and the radio low, ready for the news on the hour. Then he glances at the now less leafy entrance to that dark passage. Bunches of flowers, large and small, have been placed there. Some have long since died while others look to have been left more recently, their colours still proud in the autumn sun. Like flags in the hedge, fading notes of condolence flutter in the breeze.

Bob hasn't stopped thinking about Stella McKeever. About the star perfume. He told Trish about his initial trip to the station the day after he went; about the night Stella was in his taxi; about how he had *had* to make sure the police had the bottle because he was sure the poor girl was totally innocent.

Bob had to go back and tell the whole story again to the officer in charge of the case, and this time Trish went with him. Since then they have both been following the news.

It's noon. Bob turns up the volume on the radio. After a moment, Stephen Sainty's rich voice fills the car. He lists the upcoming headlines, the first of which is that there is more news on the Victoria Valbon murder inquiry. It's always the first item; always the story people want. Bob holds his breath.

'Police have further reason to believe that Stella McKeever might *not* have been responsible for the murder of Victoria Valbon more than a month ago. The WLCR presenter admitted live on air to killing the local pregnant woman, before committing suicide by jumping from the radio-station roof. Last week a witness supplied evidence that suggested Stella might have a made false confession. This was revealed to be an intact perfume bottle, the very one that Stella claimed to have used – broken – to kill Valbon.'

Relief saturates Stephen's words. Bob can only imagine how hard it must be to have to report the news when it's about former colleague, and when it's so tragic. Stephen was interviewed in one of the local papers yesterday; he said he didn't think Stella was capable of hurting, let alone killing, anyone.

'At a press conference this morning,' Stephen continues, 'police announced that another witness has handed in key evidence that was found just half a mile from the Valbon crime scene, which police are now analysing. When asked if this item belonged to someone other than Stella McKeever, police declined to answer, saying further tests were needed.'

Bob wonders what the item is, where it was found. He hopes it can clear Stella's name once and for all. He hasn't slept properly for weeks and can't imagine what her family must be going through. Victoria's poor family, too.

Stephen continues: 'Police also told members of the press that someone has come forward saying they are responsible for Victoria's death. Police cannot reveal any names until they investigate further. All they can tell us is that this person was very close to Stella, and they have said that Stella was protecting them when she lied on the roof.'

Bob speaks aloud to himself. 'Well, *thank* God.'

Stephen moves on to another story, his voice audibly less intense when revealing that the fire in a local nightclub was caused by faulty wiring. Bob glances back at the flowers by the alley. Now the truth can emerge fully. Peace for poor Victoria, and peace for Stella.

Bob's mobile phone lights up. It's a message from Trish, asking if he's heard the news about the Valbon/McKeever story.

Bob messages back that yes, he has.

Trish asks if he has seen the stuff on Twitter.

He shakes his head. She should know better. He doesn't go on any social-media sites. What they post on there is all scandal and lies and nonsense to him. Anyone can say anything. No filter, no care for who they hurt. With what he has often heard in his taxi over the years, Bob has never needed to seek gossip online.

Trish messages him again. *It was a key.*

What was? he types.

That got handed in. Photos all over Twitter. Has a T and an S on it. Found in a skip not far away from the alley. They reckon S for Stella and T for Tom – her boyfriend.

Bob frowns.

Could be any key, he types.

The phone flashes after a moment. *Someone from local police has shared it too.*

If so, it must be Tom's key, Bob types slowly.

There is a pause. Then his phone flashes again.

Or Stella's, says Trish.

Bob shakes his head.

Stella didn't do it, he types firmly. *It must be Tom's. Talk when I get in.*

So, it's a key. A key might be the key. But what harm could a key do to anyone? They said they still have to analyse it. Could be nothing. Those initials could be mere coincidence. Trish, of course, always argues that there's no such thing. Coincidence, she says again and again, is the universe telling you something. Whatever the universe, the evidence or Twitter might be saying, Bob's gut tells him – and has all along – that Stella did not kill Victoria.

He turns off the radio. Drinks in the silence. Wonders who has come forward. Stephen didn't say whether it was a man or woman. Only that they are close to Stella. In the many crime shows he and Trish watch, the detectives always say look close to home before you look anywhere else.

Home is where it all starts.

Bob starts up the car. He might go home and see if Trish wants to go out for lunch. He might just drive around one more time. He looks back at the alley. A young girl is reading the notes in the hedge, a small bunch of pink carnations clutched in one hand. When she's finished reading, she places the flowers carefully next to the many others. Then she walks up the street without looking back.

Bob drives home.

49

ELIZABETH

NOW

Inside the house, I lead Tom back into their living room and make him sit him on the sofa, where he hunches over, head in hands, sobs still wracking his body. I sit next to him. I feel such a conflict of emotions. Sadness for him. Relief that he might tell me everything. Fear of what that means.

Do you have any alcohol in the house? I ask.

He looks at me, eyes red. *You need some?*

For you.

Kitchen cupboard. Under the hob.

I find a bottle of rum – the kind likely to have been a Christmas gift – and pour generous portions into two tumblers. Tom takes his from me with a shaking hand. He swigs heartily. I sip mine. And wait. The song on the radio seems too loud, intrusive. Without asking Tom, I turn it down so that it's less distracting and resume my seat next to him.

Eventually he says, *Vicky did come and see me that night.*

I nod.

Perry returns to the room and leaps into my lap. Surprised, I spill some of my rum. I stroke her head and she purrs. Does she sense my link to Stella? Is she here to comfort me while I hear the truth about that terrible night? Is that what I'm about to finally learn?

Tom ignores her. He shakes his head, puts it back in his hands.

I can't, he whispers.

You can, I say.

I wait.

It was late, he says. *I was about to go to bed. There was this soft tapping on the door. I was dead surprised when I saw Vicky on the doorstep. We hadn't seen each other in, oh, at least nine months. It ended amicably, it really did.* He looks at me, pained. *No one believes that, but it did.*

I believe you, I say encouragingly.

When we broke up she said she found me ... challenging. Anyway, I saw she was pregnant. That's another thing I'd never known until she turned up. I asked why she was here so late, and she said she'd been walking around, building up the courage to come. She asked if she could come in – said we needed to talk ... about our baby ... us. Our baby? I asked her. Ours? Tom shakes his head. *God, I should've just invited her in. If I had...*

He drinks some more. I wait for him to go on. Perry purrs under my stroking hand.

I guess I was nervous about Stella coming home in another half an hour, he says, *so I got my coat and said we should walk a little, as it might be a bit of a shock for my girlfriend to come home and find my ex here, and pregnant too. Hell, I could hardly take it in myself.*

Tom pauses again. I imagine he's afraid of getting there; to that moment. Of revisiting it. What if he hasn't until now? God, the effort that must have taken. The pain of carrying it around, squashing it down. I want to touch his arm and offer comfort, but I don't.

We walked around the block a few times, and I let her talk. I guess I was too stunned to say much. I was adding up the months, thinking, is this really my kid? And knowing if it was I'd step up, I would. But I didn't want Vicky.

Tom looks intensely at me.

You have to know that. I loved Stella. I love Stella. I wanted to spend the rest of my life with her. Now ... I sleep in her spot in the bed ... and I ... I try and fill it ... and I can't ... she ... she gave her life for me! To cover what ... and I have to live with that...

Tom starts to sob again. I take the glass from him. I wait. After a while he calms down a little. I give him the glass back and he swigs more rum.

Vicky said we should be a family. She said she'd had this helper woman – it was you. I know that now. You were her ... what was the word you said?

Doula.

Yes. Tom nods. *Vicky said her helper had been great, but it wasn't the same as having the real father with her. The man she loved. Me. She stopped me then and put her arms around me, squashing her belly to me, and said she had never stopped loving me. I wanted to pull away but thought it would be cruel, you know, to someone pregnant. But she must have thought I loved her too ... and she tried to kiss me. So then I had to pull away. And she took my hand ... and she led me into the alley...*

Tom puts his empty glass down. He shakes his head as though to get rid of the memory, free himself from it.

She kept whispering that I was her twin flame. I don't know what she meant but she kept saying it, over and over. She said we were special because we'd made a child; she said she'd do anything, anything, anything to have me.

These were my words, coming back at me. I had said these things to Vicky. God, *I* had done this. This was my fault. I wanted to turn up the song on the radio and drown them out. But at the same time I wanted to hear Tom. He continued.

I told Vicky I didn't love her anymore, that I loved Stella; but it didn't stop her. She kept kissing me, so I shook her off. Her hands were all over me. Up my back, in my pockets, you know. I tried to pull her off, but I was scared of being too rough with her. I just wanted to calm her down and get her home, but there was no appeasing her. She cried out suddenly then and I thought I had hurt her. But she'd cut herself. It was that bloody key Stella got me...

Tom looks at me.

I loved it, I did, the meaning behind it, but that key had cut me so many times. Vicky pulled it from my pocket. The blood from her finger was on it, smeared over the S. I think it incensed her, seeing our two initials there. She looked at it and then at me. And ... she...

She what? I ask gently.

He shakes his head.

What? I push.

She put the sharp point of the key against her...

Her what? I ask.

Her wrist.

You mean?

Tom nods. He is trembling again. Perry looks at him, wary.

She held it there and she was yelling, 'My baby, my baby, don't you love my baby?' I yelled that I did, I would, and I'd be there for it, I just didn't love her, but please give me the key. I don't know if it was hormones, but she was wild. She said she'd rather not be here if we couldn't be a family. I tried to approach her to hold her, to calm her down, but she pressed the key harder to her wrist. I said I'd walk her home ... that we could talk more calmly tomorrow...

What happened, Tom? I ask.

His eyes beseech mine.

It was Vicky. The words rip from him. *She did it.*

What do you mean?

It was Vicky. It was her ... she did it ... but I can't ... who would believe me?

Tell me, I say firmly. *I'll believe you.*

Oh God, oh God, oh God.

Just tell me exactly what happened.

As he tells me I see it vividly. See it as though I'm there. As though I'm Stella, passing by on her way home from work, watching in horror from the shadows and seeing what must have looked like murder from afar. My poor girl. Poor Tom. Poor Vicky.

She moved it, says Tom. *The key. She backed away from me, into the hedge and she put the sharp corner ... Jesus ... she put it to her neck. I reached to stop her, I did, but she yelled that she'd do it, she'd really do it, so I backed off a bit. I just wanted to calm her down and get us both home safely. That's all. She said ... she said, 'Tell me you'll be with me.' But I couldn't. I should have. I should have just lied. And she pressed it harder to her neck and this little bit of blood trickled down her hand. Jesus, I panicked then.* Tom's voice is wild now. *I leapt at her, to stop her, and she did it! She did it! I must have scared her! It was my fault!*

No, no, I say softly. *It wasn't. You were trying to save her.*

Tom looks at me like he has forgotten I'm there. *The blood,* he cries. *The fucking blood! It was everywhere! Spilling over her hands! Down her neck! And she was making these awful gurgling sounds. Jesus!*

Perry jumps out of my lap and escapes the room as though it's too much for her.

I tried, Tom cries. *I put my hands over her neck to stop the blood, but it was … Jesus … I've never seen anything like it. Her eyes were wild and she couldn't talk and she was clawing at me. Then she went white and she fell. I went with her. Tried to stop her falling too hard. And … oh God … she … it was so fast. She wasn't breathing and the light in her eyes died. She died. Right in front of me…*

Oh Tom.

Finally, I touch him, gently on the arm. He leans into me and I put my arm around him while he sobs.

So much for you to have carried around all this time, I say gently. *Why didn't you tell anyone? You didn't do anything wrong.*

Who'd believe me? he cries, looking up. *Her blood was all over me and my fingerprints are all over that key! I had my hands over hers on her neck! Even Stella thought I'd done it. I know how it must have looked in the dark! Me leaping at Vicky, my hands over hers!*

What did you do afterwards? I ask calmly.

Tom sits up, away from me, closes his eyes. *Vicky had taken her coat off when we were walking, and it had fallen when she … when she … so I picked it up.* He opens his eyes and looks at me. *I put it over our baby. Over her stomach.*

I nod. I realise that I put the coat over Stella too late as well. I loved her most when she was gone.

And then? I ask.

God, it's a blur. I must have left her. I would have looked a state. I had blood all over my top and hands. I walked home. I can't even remember it. I threw the key away. Stupid, I know, and I can't even remember exactly where. Some wasteland on the way home. I went back the next day, when I was thinking straight but I couldn't find it.

What about when you got home? To Stella?

With his head in his hands again, muffled so I can hardly hear, Tom tells me how he got home first, showered away all the blood and hid his top at the bottom of the bin, under a rotten chicken carcass and potato peelings. He says that when Stella got home he pretended to be asleep. That he didn't know then what she thought she had witnessed. In his own horror he would have been blind to hers.

Didn't you see Stella in the alley? I ask.

No. I didn't see anyone. But it's long and it bends. She could easily have hidden once she ... once she saw us...

She never said anything?

Tom says no, she never said anything, and he didn't either.

We just played the game, he adds, looking at me. *I had to bury what had happened. And I did. Somehow, I did.*

Tom is trembling, his face a picture of pain.

Stella and me ... we did things ... intense things ... things I suggested because I needed to distract myself from what had happened. Things to make her think we were the same as we always had been ... to let her know my love was as intense as it always had been. Tom wrings his hands. *But she had seen what she thought was ... She had been going through all that ... and she ... God, she died for me. She died to cover for me. If I'd only had the courage to confide in her! She'd still be here!*

Suddenly we hear Stella's voice, soft and ghostly from somewhere.

So ... I guess this is goodbye. I'm going to have to face the music now.

Is she here? My heart stops. Tom looks towards the radio, his eyes haunted. The news again. Why must they keep playing her final words?

I miss her, he says desperately.

Me, too.

I take his hands and say, *None of this is your fault.* I mean every word. *It's mine. I was the one who encouraged Vicky to get you back when I was her doula. I was the one who left Stella and made her what she was. Made her think she had to do such a thing to prove how much she loved you.*

Tom stands and goes and turns the radio off. Perry comes back into the room, perhaps sensing the worst is over, and leaps into my lap again.

We could go to the police, I suggest. *Tell them what really happened. I believe you and they will. Surely* – I pause, not wanting to be insensitive – *they'd be able to prove that it was Vicky's own hand that cut her neck?*

Wouldn't they have determined that already? Wouldn't they have said?

I don't know, I admit. *But the case isn't officially closed, is it? Maybe that's why? And what about this new evidence Stephen mentioned earlier?*

What if it's the key? Tom says.

He doesn't sit down again. He seems calmer, as though, now he has shared the truth, he's free to think straight.

That key will incriminate me. But I can live with it. I just don't want...

What?

Imagine what it will do to Vicky's family, says Tom, sadly.

What do you mean?

If they find out it was ... suicide. Wouldn't that hurt more than thinking it was someone else? Jesus.

Do you have anywhere you can go? I ask suddenly.

What do you mean?

Somewhere ... not here.

My mum and dad live in northern Spain. They retired there five years ago. Tom looks at me, frowning. *Why?*

Leave. I stand and join him in the middle of the room. *Go now, before they come for you again. If they've found that key, they will. I'll go to the police now and say it was me. They already questioned me because I was her doula. I'll tell them I lied then, and I did see Vicky that night.*

Tom looks afraid, doubtful.

I take his hands in mine, say firmly, *Stella wanted to protect you. Now I'll do it for her. She'll want you to be free. She'll be watching us from wherever she is now, knowing you didn't kill Vicky, and she'll want you to be free. This is the only way. Let me do right by my daughter. Let's both make her happy.*

Perry leaves the sofa and curls her body around my legs. *I'll take her*, I say to Tom, and pick her up. *You need to go.* I have to put the last coat over Stella.

50

ELIZABETH

NOW

My Darling Stella,
The only other letter I've ever written you was that terrible one I left on the table when I abandoned you. It's long gone now, but I remember I wrote that I did love you, I just didn't think it was enough, and that one day I'd tell you why. Now you know why. Because I put my love for someone else first.

I've finally put my love for you first, but far too late.

I wrote that letter because I was leaving. I'm writing this one because you're the one gone. I finally got you back, but today I have to let you go for the very last time. It took so long to get your body, what with all the procedures they had to follow and the things they had to do. Then once I had you, I didn't know what you would have liked me to do. I decided on cremation.

I couldn't talk to Tom about it, though I knew he should have a say. I know that's what you would have wanted, but he isn't here now. I tried to continue the thing you began. I tried to make sure Tom was okay.

You wanted everyone to believe you'd killed Vicky, but I didn't, and I just couldn't have the world thinking you were guilty of a brutal crime when I knew absolutely in my heart that you weren't. Wherever you are now, you probably know that Tom told me what really happened. The sad truth is that you gave your life for him, but he hadn't done it. My beautiful girl, to love like that.

I went to the police station after I'd been to see Tom. They questioned me for hours. I could tell they weren't convinced by my story and were just humouring me. Stella, I don't have your wonderful way with words.

While I was there they told me a new piece of evidence had been found – one that suggested it wasn't me; that contradicted my story. They showed me it and asked me what I knew about it. I said nothing, even though I knew exactly what it was. Tom's key. The one identical to yours. I knew they would test it, and that Tom would be all over it.

They have done. It was covered in Vicky's blood, and Tom's fingerprints and DNA were on it too. They have released that info to the public now. They are still calling it murder. I have to hope that the fact that the case isn't closed means they're not one hundred percent sure. That they are exploring other possibilities. That they might still get to the truth.

It's still all over the radio every day. I try to avoid it, but I listen to WLCR because, now you've been cleared, they sometimes play the best bits from your shows. I never get tired of your voice. You could be here in the room with me. Oh, Stella, I wish you were, and I could say all the things I never did. Make right all the things I did wrong.

I was released and cautioned that day at the police station for wasting their time. I'd been given one of those free solicitors; she told them I was in emotional turmoil, that I'd lost my mind. I suppose it's true. I did. I have.

But at least they know it wasn't you.

They think it's Tom now, which breaks my heart.

And they are looking for him.

He left England the day I went to see him. I gave him full permission to do it. I know it's what you would have wanted. As he closed the door that final time, he thanked me for listening to him. For believing him. I'm glad he had the courage to unburden himself. I think he wanted to protect you from the truth, just as you were trying to protect him. I told him all I'd wanted was for the world to know that you were no killer, Stella.

And now they do.

Someone who is wrong for the world can be perfectly right for you.

I felt that about Harland. But Tom isn't wrong for the world. Neither were you. The world was just wrong for you.

I don't know if Tom went to his parents in Spain. Stephen Sainty said on the news yesterday that someone reported a sighting of him there, but I can't imagine he would want his mum or dad in the headlines. I can't imagine he stayed with them for long. You never mentioned his family, but I wonder if Tom ever talked about them to you. I suppose with the parents you have it might not have been a topic you wanted to broach.

I don't know if anyone can run forever, but whatever happens, I'll look after him for you in any way I can. I know he can't contact me, so I can't tell him that. But I think he knows.

You told me when you were on the roof that when I wasn't around you used to think I was with the stars. You've always liked them.

I think of you when I look at the star perfume. I finally have it back now. It's a bit more battered than it was, but when the light hits it there are still stars everywhere. It sits next to me on my bedside cabinet now, and it reminds me of your father, and of you.

I miss him. But I miss you more.

I have to say goodbye, though.

Tonight I'm going to scatter your ashes from the bridge.

Set you free. Give you to the stars. Let you fly.

51

STAR GIRL

THEN, NOW, ALWAYS

Mum, I'm happy you're back. I've wished for this. Every day. But you don't need to stay. I talk to you at night. See you in the stars. And that's enough. You're better up there where the light never goes. If I let you back into my daytime world you might leave again. So I'll be with you in the sky.

Portobello, Eva at Novel Delights, Linda Green, Victoria Colotta, Celeste McCreesh, Karen Mace, Katie Jones, Susan Hampson, Mart or Mr Gravy, Kate at Bantam Bookworm, Adrian Murphy, Ellen Devonport, and the northern bird at Bookish Chat.

Thanks to all the amazing book and literary groups who invited me to be with them this year – the Walkington Wordies, Newbald Book Group, Tower Hill Book Group, Willerby Library Group, the Osprey Ladies Who Lunch, the East Riding Festival of Words, and Hessle Library. The journey would NOT be the same without you.

Thanks to all the other people who continue to support and champion me, many talented writers themselves – Anne Cater, the Women of Words girls (Vicky, Cass, Julie, Lynda, Jodie and Michelle), the Prime Writers (too, too many to mention), Nick Quantrill, Sue Wilsea, Fiona Mills, Mel Hewitt, Claire Allan, Dean Wilson, Louisa Treger, Melissa Bailey, Carrie Martin, Liz Robinson, and Fionnuala Kearney.

Thanks to the online groups – Book Connectors and The Book Club (TBC) – who are my go-to place for tips, laughs, and help.

Most of all, thanks to my publisher Karen Sullivan for continuing to believe in and publish me. For trusting my work enough to sign me based on a book title and scrappy blurb. Love you loads. And to West Camel and Karen for the eternally perceptive edits and patience. And of course super-talented Mark Swan for the endlessly stunning covers.

ACKNOWLEDGEMENTS

Thank you to my daughter Katy for being my saviour during this book and letting me bounce ideas back and forth so much, hiding well her annoyance when I burst into her bedroom to declare yet another light-bulb plot idea. I have her to thank for the doula idea, which was a key part of the book.

Thank you, as always, to my early readers who helped shape what the novel became: John Marrs for the insightful suggestions and for making me see it how it was supposed to be, Tracy Fenton for her always honest and uncompromising words, and my sisters Claire and Grace, the latter of whom was with me the moment we realised Bob Fracklehurst would be BACK.

Thank you to Mary Picken, Claire Thinking, Donna Maguire, Sharon Bairden, Vicki Goldman, Lisa Adamson, Joy Kluver, Karen Cole, Leah Moyse, Amanda Duncan, Gemma Wiles, Claire Knight, If Only I Could Read Faster, Alex at Paperback Piano, Vonni Bee, Clair B, Joanna Park, Sandra at Beauty Balm, Hayley at rather Too Fond of Books, Adele at Krafti Reader, Beverley at Beverley Has Read, Anne Williams, Cheryl at CherylMM's Book Blog, Tamzin at Cramlington Book Club, Nicola at Short Book & Scribes, The Book Whisperer, Jo Robertson, Steph Warren, Silvia at Book after Book, Emma Mitchell, Sonya at A Lover of Books, David at Blue Book Balloon, Melisa at The Book Collective, Beth M of BiblioBeth, Carol Lovekin, Jo at Jaffa Reads Too, Kate at The Quiet Knitterer, Caryl Williams, Marianne at Books Life Things, Maria at Varietats, Jen Lucas, Nicki Murphy, Book-Mark That UK, Stephanie Rothwell, Audio Killer The Bookmark, Zoe at Zooloo's Book Diary, Karen Cocking, Candi Colbourn, Joanne at